W9-CES-375

ANGEL FACE

A Selection of Recent Titles by Stephen Solomita

DAMAGED GOODS
A GOOD DAY TO DIE
NO CONTROL
A PIECE OF THE ACTION
POSTER BOY
TRICK ME TWICE

MONKEY IN THE MIDDLE *
CRACKER BLING *
MERCY KILLING *

* available from Severn House

ANGEL FACE

Stephen Solomita

NEW HANOVER COUNTY
PUBLIC LIBRARY
201 CHESTNUT STREET
WILMINGTON, NC 28401

This first world edition published 2011
in Great Britain and in the USA by
SEVERN HOUSE PUBLISHERS LTD of
9–15 High Street, Sutton, Surrey, England, SM1 1DF.

Copyright © 2011 by Stephen Solomita.

All rights reserved.
The moral right of the author has been asserted.

British Library Cataloguing in Publication Data

Solomita, Stephen.
Angel face.
1. Prostitutes – New York (State) – New York – Fiction.
2. Gangsters – Crimes against – Fiction. 3. Organized
Crime – New York (State) – New York – Fiction. 4. Suspense
fiction.
I. Title
813.5'4-dc22

ISBN-13: 978-0-7278-8076-5 (cased)

Except where actual historical events and characters are being
described for the storyline of this novel, all situations in this
publication are fictitious and any resemblance to living persons
is purely coincidental.

All Severn House titles are printed on acid-free paper.

Severn House Publishers support The Forest Stewardship Council [FSC],
the leading international forest certification organisation. All our titles that
are printed on Greenpeace-approved FSC-certified paper carry the FSC logo.

FSC
www.fsc.org
MIX
Paper from
responsible sources
FSC® C018575

Typeset by Palimpsest Book Production Ltd.,
Falkirk, Stirlingshire, Scotland.
Printed and bound in Great Britain by
MPG Books Ltd., Bodmin, Cornwall.

ONE

Carter exits the M14A bus at Fourteenth Street and Ninth Avenue, stepping into a light, but steady, May rain. He stops for a moment on the sidewalk to adjust his leather hat's six-inch brim, turning it down at the back to deflect the rainwater on to the sidewalk. Beneath his arm, he carries a small cardboard box wrapped in a plastic shopping bag. He wants to protect the box from the rain, even knowing that its contents, the ashes of his sister, Janie, will soon be consigned to the waters of the Hudson River.

Death is nothing new to Leonard Carter. Carter's been to war in Afghanistan, a Delta Force spook operating far from the main force, and far from any concept as irrelevant as rules of engagement. From Afghanistan, he'd moved to Iraq, working as a mercenary for Coldstream Military Options, a private contractor with a penchant for summary executions. The west coast of Africa followed, where he spilled enough blood to color the waters of the mighty Hudson. Searching for diamonds soaked with that same blood.

Carter walks two blocks to the West Side Highway, his eyes sweeping the ground for enemies, a reflex cultivated in war and never surrendered, though he doesn't think himself pursued. He waits several minutes for the light to change in his favor, watching the cars zoom along, the whine of their tires and the growl of their engines rising and falling as they cross his path. He finds little release from the din when he finally reaches Hudson River Park, a narrow pathway running north and south along the banks of the river. The traffic sounds continue to dominate, as they dominate all of Manhattan, as much a part of the city's character as the trash on the sidewalks.

Carter turns south, toward Wall Street and the financial district. Normally, the bike and pedestrian pathways are crowded, even on a Wednesday afternoon, but today, what with the mist and the rain, he has the park pretty much to himself.

As he walks along a wrought-iron fence separating him from the river, Carter's thinking – and not for the first time – that he's supposed to reflect, to measure out the ways Janie anchored his life, the protections she offered, the justifications. But he can't permit himself to grant death any great importance, death being only a bit less common than birth. Which is not to say that Carter isn't affected by his sister's passing, only that her death was not just expected, it was a blessing as well. And truth be told, Lou Gehrig's disease had taken her life months before a doctor placed a stethoscope against her chest and failed to detect a heartbeat.

Janie had begun the long descent into paralysis six years before that day, the progress of the disease as unrelenting as it was slow. Her feet first, then her hands, then her legs, her arms, her mouth, her lungs, until she was unable even to blink her eyes.

When her heart finally stopped, everyone at the Cabrini Center for Nursing and Rehabilitation – the aides, the nurses, the administrative staff, the doctors, the nuns – used the same word.

Blessing, blessing, blessing, blessing.

Carter had nodded agreement. Stirring controversy wasn't his game. But he couldn't help wondering what the fucker assigned to bestow blessings was doing when Janie originally contracted the disease.

Carter turns a corner to find himself confronted by a series of rose beds fronting a Department of Sanitation garage that extends out into the Hudson. These are shrub roses, rising waist high and growing tight enough to form a hedge. Their intricate petals drift between a soft pink and the red of a baby's blush, the blossoms clustered together at the end of narrow, fragile stems. Taken off-guard, Carter stops to stare. Drops of water on the leaves and the blossoms sparkle despite a mist that blends form and color into a seamless whole. Behind him, the traffic rolls by.

Carter's impressed, but he moves on after a moment,

wondering, as he goes, if the roses were planted here to soften the featureless brick façade of the Sanitation garage, this being, after all, a city park. If so, the landscapers weren't entirely successful. The fragrance of the roses and the fertile odor of the Hudson are overlaid by the smell of garbage emanating from a dozen trucks parked in a fenced yard.

The park widens a bit as Carter passes an elaborate wrought-iron gateway set before a concrete pier. Faded letters reveal the pier's original function: CUNARD LINES. Back in the day, between the two World Wars, Cunard's many ocean liners ferried passengers between Europe and New York in luxury. No more. Though cruise ships still dock at piers to the north, the liners disappeared, the luxury too, with the advent of the airplane. Carter equates coach with steerage.

Further on, Carter approaches a freshly mowed lawn. On clear days, when he'd happened to pass by, he'd found sun worshippers, their blankets spread across the lawn, the better to encourage future melanomas. As many of these were young, attractive women, Carter's attention was naturally drawn to them. He'd failed to notice a low granite wall that curved around the back of the lawn, but now he reads the legend inscribed on the polished gray stone in bold white letters:

I can sail without wind, I can row without oars, but I cannot part from my friend without tears.

How long has it been since Carter cried? In fact, Carter can't recall ever crying, though he assumes he must have.

The rain picks up now, spattering on the pathway hard enough to mute the traffic sounds. Carter barely notices. Ahead, Pier 45, the Christopher Street Pier, extends into the Hudson, its far end obscured by the closing weather. This is Carter's destination, and, as before, where there would ordinarily be dozens of strollers, Carter sees only a pair of fishermen packing their gear about halfway down. He walks by them without speaking, to a railing at the very end of the pier.

Carter's been to the Christopher Street Pier many times before. He knows that a skyline of high-rise apartment buildings crowds the waterfront on the Jersey side of the river just a bit to the south. But he can't see them. Nor can he see the Statue of Liberty a mile away in the harbor. Water and rain and mist recede into a blank curtain that might be vertical or horizontal or any combination thereof.

Now that he's made it this far, Carter hesitates. He's remembering the day Janie came to him after the years in foster care. That was back home in Indiana. She'd rescued him, no doubt about it, from a family that treated him as they would a crop on their farm. Carter's presence was intended to produce a return on investment, the less invested, of course, the greater the return.

Carter first reaction to his sister's appearance – he'd been told nothing beforehand – was fear, pure and simple. He'd adjusted to life without, to a paucity of food and clothing, to a world without even the pretense of affection. The Abernathys didn't beat him, as long as he did his chores, and they didn't try to guide his thoughts. Nor did they ask him to attend the Assemblies of God church they visited on Sundays for the service, and on Wednesdays for the prayer meeting. They didn't take the pigs or the chickens, either.

Safety first. The Abernathy's were safe, their demands simple and clear. They protected him and they wanted him, if only for the cash payments sent to them every month by the State of Indiana. When his mother died, when his sister was taken away, after months in a group foster home, the youngest of the young, Carter had wanted refuge. Not love, not kindness, not concern, not even food. Carter's dreams were of safety.

Carter leans out over the railing to look down at a ledge running over the outer pilings supporting the pier. About ten inches wide, the ledge is three feet down and wet with rainwater. But Carter doesn't hesitate. He vaults the rail one-handed and drops into a crouch before sitting down. The soles of his feet are within a foot of the gray waters now, and he can see individual raindrops pock the surface, unleashing small eruptions that hang in the air.

For a time, Carter loses himself in the heaving river, but then the waters suddenly part and a large black bird emerges from the depths, a cormorant. The cormorant throws its head back and swallows the fish caught in its sharp bill, then bobs on the swells for a few seconds, its head turning and tilting. Is the bird looking up, scanning the sky for predators? Or down into the depths, scanning the waters for prey? By way of answer, the cormorant slides beneath the surface, graceful as an eel, and vanishes. Back to work.

Janie had provided refuge, along with love, kindness and concern. She'd saved her brother, though she couldn't make him whole. But at least he knew that children didn't have to be treated like machines, that it wasn't some kind of rule. That has to count for something, although Carter can't say exactly what.

Carter unwraps the cardboard box and shoves the plastic wrapping into the pocket of his microsuede jacket. He opens the cover of a white box and discovers another box, this one black. Inside the black box, a clear plastic bag filled with gray powder is held closed at the end by a simple green twist-tie. Carter finds himself wishing for some more elaborate device, but it's too late. He might have buried Janie in a polished coffin and erected a marble headstone – he has the money – but he couldn't deal with the thought of his sister lying in a grave that nobody visited. Too much guilt. When Janie first contracted Lou Gehrig's disease, he was rampaging through West Africa, killing when he might have consoled. By the time he returned to the United States, Janie was bedridden, her movements limited, the end written plain.

So, now what? Carter has no religious beliefs. Beyond the occasional blasphemous epithet, religion plays no part in his life. Though his sister was religious, though he read to her from the Bible whenever he visited, even after Janie was unable to respond, he can't bring himself to pray, or even to recite the few verses he's memorized.

'I guess it's just goodbye,' Carter says, the words lost in the mist before he closes his mouth. He removes the twist-tie and leans forward until he's looking down at the water. As he tilts the bag, as the powdery gray ashes slide into the Hudson, Carter thinks, as he often does, of the boy soldiers, of their drug-fueled courage, their unthinking cruelty, of how easily they were killed. He remembers their scattered bodies in the ruins of an African village, remembers the smell of their blood and an unrelenting sun that beat down on the living and the dead alike. He and his companions, thieves all, had briefly considered burying the children. But there was no time and they'd left the bodies to the vultures circling overhead.

'Goodbye, sister,' he whispers.

Carter shakes the bag to release the last flakes of ash. He places the bag inside the black box and the black box inside the white box. Then he sits for a time, until the dark gray water is again marked only by the falling rain, until there's nothing more to see, until what remains of his sister is gone. Only then does he rise to his feet and vault over the rail to drop on to the pier. A short distance away, a man wearing a yellow raincoat stands with his mouth agape. And not without reason. Carter is thoroughly drenched. His chino pants cling to him like a second skin. Did he emerge from the depths only a moment before, a monster come to feed? Judging from the expression on the man's face, he's not sure.

Despite the soaking, Carter's not uncomfortable. After years of special forces training, after a winter in the mountains of Afghanistan where the cold burrowed into you like an invading virus, May afternoons in New York don't intimidate him, rain or shine. He turns on his heel and marches off toward the beckoning skyline of Manhattan.

Back to work.

TWO

On one level, Angela Tamanaka, called 'Angel' by friend and client alike, is pleased by the steady rain. At least she's not being hit on by every jerk who passes by. She's still pissed, though, because the client's late and she's been walking up and down Broadway between 108th and 109th Streets for twenty minutes. Huddled under a baby-blue umbrella speckled with pink rosebuds.

Stay positive, she tells herself. Use the time, don't let the time use you. Angel has culled her rules of success from a dozen websites, and she might have perused thousands more. A Google search for 'rules of success' had turned up ninety-seven million hits in 0.22 seconds. On the first three pages, she discovered success rules for the mail order business, the music business, the trucking business and the business of politics. Nothing specific about the business of whoring, though. No good advice for sex workers.

Focus on the outcome, Angel tells herself. Success breeds success. The happier the client, the more jobs Pierre will send your way. At this stage of her working life, Angel's about the business of accumulating capital. And that's another maxim: Poverty leads to dependence, which leads to more poverty.

An articulated city bus pulls to the stop at the corner of 108th Street, its accordion pleat flexing and folding as the driver works in close to the curb. The bus rocks on its springs when it finally comes to halt and the front door opens to reveal an elderly woman in a lavender pants suit. The woman comes down the steps slowly, leading with her right leg. Her left hand grips the railing, her right the curved handle of a long black umbrella. Safe on the sidewalk, she presses the umbrella's release button and it pops open, spraying the man poised on the step behind her with rainwater. He closes his eyes for a moment, too exhausted, apparently, even to become annoyed.

Angel watches the drama unfold, thinking this is what I don't want, this is my big motivator. Not to come home every single night of my life, utterly spent, with nothing to show for it at the end of the week. But, no, not *nothing*. Enough to provide the bare necessities, enough to get me out the door on the next day, and the day after that and the day after that. Until I'm used up and nobody wants to employ me and I get to retire on Social Security and food stamps.

Call her a communist, but this is the way Angel sees it. This is a fate she's determined to avoid. Better to lose everything.

As she rehearses the scenario she's worked out over the

past couple of days, Angel paces up and down, accompanied by the spatter of rain on her umbrella. If the client doesn't show by the time she finishes, she decides, she'll call it a night and head back to her apartment. She'll call her agent, too. She'll call Pierre to demand payment for time she might otherwise have spent profitably. She knows the client has paid in advance, and with a credit card.

There's a simple rule of thumb operating here. The client specifies the fantasy, but the provider brings the fantasy to life. In this case, the client, a mob guy named Enrico Benedetti, a real jerk, was predictably vague. A demure young woman, a drudge, visits the office of her therapist, as she has many times before. Only this time she finally divulges the terrible secret she's been hiding all these years: she was molested by her stepfather. Her therapist listens sympathetically for a while, then informs her that she can escape her pain by reliving the original experience. She's reluctant at first, but finally agrees, only to discover that her therapist was right. Before morning, she finds herself transformed, from a sexless drudge to a sex-crazed nymphomaniac.

Three other girls turned the job down. Angel said yes. Not because she wasn't repulsed. Angel was disgusted, too, but she wasn't about to be distracted by her feelings.

Be the one who's there for the team when everybody else quits. Be the last woman standing. Be the go-to girl. Tomorrow morning, her agent will direct-deposit $800 into her account at Citibank. She'll put aside four hundred of those dollars to pay for general living expenses and her taxes. The rest will go into a second account at Chase, her capital accumulation account. Angel has forty grand in that account and she's proud of every damned penny. Most of her schoolmates at Brooklyn College, even the ones who work part-time, have already accumulated enough debt to keep them broke for the next decade.

Be Prepared – you don't have to be a boy or a scout to accept that piece of advice. She's supposed to remain in character from the minute she slides into the car until she's dropped off tomorrow morning at seven o'clock, three hours before the client's wife and kids return from a visit with the grandparents. That's why she's wearing a brown corduroy dress a size too big, a dress that hangs all the way to mid-calf. That's why she didn't put on make-up, why she's wearing a plain white bra and cotton panties thick enough to pass for a diaper.

So, all right, remember to stare down at the floor when you get into the car. Answer in monosyllables and don't forget to mumble. You've made up your mind. This time you'll tell Dr Rick the whole truth, which he suspects anyway. You'll do it, but you're scared out of your mind and . . .

Angel's thoughts are interrupted by the honking of a horn. She stares for just a moment at the Lincoln Towncar parked in the bus stop while she slips into the part. Then she walks forward, slowly, as if approaching a gallows, to peer through the window. The client is sitting at the wheel. Marked by acne scars on both cheeks, his meaty flesh, the color of ground beef, drapes his jawbones like a shroud. But his little black eyes are on full alert. They're balls of desire. Most likely, he's been jerking off all week in anticipation.

The client reaches across the seat to open the door and Angel, after only a brief hesitation, closes her umbrella and slips inside. Without looking up, she fumbles in her worn brown purse, pulls out an aerosol breath freshener and squirts it into her mouth, a good touch.

'Hi, Dr Rick,' she mumbles.

Angel takes a certain amount of pride in her theatrical talents. Creative by nature, she can improvise with the best of them. Still, she needs cooperation. She needs the client to participate, to work the game. But Dr Rick's imagination is as thick and meaty as his complexion. He keeps reverting to Ricky Ditto, which is what his gangster friends call him, and he can't stop bragging about the bars he owns in Queens and Staten Island, or his string of Manhattan laundromats, or the house he owns in Riverdale, or the house in Flushing he bought for his mom.

Maybe he wants me to admire him, she thinks. Or maybe he thinks the game doesn't start until he gets into the house. Whatever, Angel decides to stay in character.

'I feel little, Dr Rick,' she says. 'Like I can't do anything.'

'Yeah?' Ricky Ditto chuckles. 'Well I could show you a few good moves.'

And what's she supposed to say to that? Except that she's not going to work with any more gangster jerks. Most of her clients are wealthy and successful businessmen. They're sharp and quick and they know how to play the game. Sometimes, they're even fun. But this guy? He's a CFA, born and bred, a Complete Fucking Asshole.

'Please, Dr Rick, you're making me very nervous.'

Ricky Ditto has the seat pushed all the way back to accommodate his belly. His arms are stretched out, both hands on the wheel, and he stares fixedly through the wiper-streaked windshield. They're driving north on Broadway, headed over the Broadway Bridge connecting Manhattan to the Bronx, running four blocks at a time between the red lights. Ricky finally turns left on 234th Street and pushes the Lincoln toward the steep hill leading into the neighborhood of Riverdale, an upper middle-class enclave tucked between the Hudson River and the slums on the other side of Broadway. On Riverdale's far western edge, the views over the Hudson River are spectacular.

'Hey, check this out,' Ricky says when they're about halfway up the hill. 'See that apartment building?'

'It's very nice,' Angel replies, although she's looking at a six-storey, red-brick, plain-as-mud structure with a sagging cornice.

'There's an apartment in that building, right now it's got three hundred grand sittin' under the fuckin' floorboards. You wouldn't believe just lookin', right? Me, I could put my hands on the cash right now. And that's just one place. We got others.'

Angel's trying to decide where to go with the bragging. How can she work it into the scenario? Make a reference to his exalted credentials? Make him a Harvard graduate? Or maybe he's won the Nobel Prize. Yeah, that's good. She'll look directly into his eyes when she congratulates him. She'll project trust and awe and deep, deep respect. He'll come around.

They drive the rest of the way in silence, finally turning

into a cul-de-sac lined with single-family homes on generous lots. At the far end, a garage door opens and Ricky guides the Lincoln into the space, inching forward until his bumper touches a wooden rail on the far wall. Then he presses a button and the door rumbles down.

Show time, Angel tells herself, as she always does. She gets out of the car and half-drags herself to a door leading into a kitchen. Ricky Ditto walks ahead of her. He flips on the overhead light and crosses the kitchen floor.

'Lemme show ya where the office is gonna be. I got a couch in there, ya know, like in a shrink's—'

A loud crack brings Rick's broad body to an abrupt halt, a crack Angel knows to be a gunshot, though she can't bring herself to think the word. But then Ricky falls backward, his body tipping over, his spine straight. His head bounces when he crashes on to the linoleum, just once before he lies inert, eyes wide open, staring up at the ceiling. Blood runs in three directions from a hole in his head, to the right and the left and into his stiff black hair.

Angel's only beginning to process the data when Carter steps into the kitchen. He's holding a small caliber revolver in his right hand and he's looking directly into her eyes.

'Did you touch anything?' he asks.

THREE

Not that it makes any difference, but Carter's stunned for just a moment. He's looking at one of the most beautiful women he's ever seen. Eurasian, no doubt, with big dark eyes that taper sharply at the corners, an assertive little nose and a luscious mouth. Her face is heart-shaped, her chin rounded, her complexion is the color of newly carved ivory. Carter's eyes rake her face in search of a flaw, a pimple, a blackhead, a mole, but her skin might have been painted by an artist working from his personal fantasy of the ideal woman. And not a sexual fantasy, either.

Only at the very last minute, before he gets back to business, does Carter realize that she's not wearing any make-up.

'Did you touch anything?' he repeats.

'Huh . . . I . . . Oh, God, don't kill me.'

Carter's virtually devoid of sadistic impulses. Good thing for this woman. If he did harbor a well of sadism, if he liked to cause pain, her fear would only turn him on.

'Stop for a minute and think. Did you touch anything?'

Angel finally does stop, long enough at least to draw a breath. He's hasn't killed her yet. That has to be good news, right? Assuming he doesn't plan to drag her into the basement and take his time about it.

'I don't think so,' she says.

'What about inside the car?'

'The handles? Maybe the door?'

Carter pulls a navy-blue handkerchief from the back pocket of his trousers. 'We're going to go into the garage and I'm going to wipe down the car on your side. You're going to walk ahead of me and you're going to stay between the front door of the car and the wall of the garage. Do you understand what I just said?'

'Yes.'

'Repeat it.'

Gradually calming, Angel does as she's told, careful to focus on the task at hand, and not on Ricky Ditto, whose head rests in a swelling pool of blood.

'OK, move.'

Angel walks into the garage, around the Lincoln's trunk, to the far wall. Her legs wobble slightly, but they get her there. She's about to lean back when Carter shakes his head.

'That wall is rough brick. If you touch it, you'll leave fibers behind. Just stay upright. We'll be out of here in a few minutes.'

Carter begins on the outside of the car, but instead of wiping the door handle, he dabs at the chrome, only giving a little twist at the end. His painstaking approach catches Angel's attention. Then she realizes that he's wearing gloves, silk gloves by the look of them. She didn't notice them earlier because they're almost the same shade of tan as the skin on his forearms.

'How did you do that?' she asks.

'Do what?'

'Find a pair of gloves that color.'

'I didn't.' In fact, Carter dyed a pair of white gloves with tea, a trick learned when he was still a soldier proudly serving in the armed forces of the United States. He leans into the car's interior and dabs at the dashboard. 'Any more questions?'

'Yeah, why are you dabbing like that? You look like you're cleaning a spill off your suit.'

The answer is simple enough. If the cops fingerprint the car, they'll notice any wiped surfaces and draw the appropriate conclusion. 'I'm not wearing a suit. And something else you might want to consider: if it wasn't for you, I'd already be gone. So I'm probably not in the best of moods.'

There's a door leading into the backyard on the other side of the Lincoln. For just an instant, Angel indulges herself. She imagines vaulting over the hood, tearing through the door, fleeing across the lawn. But then Carter backs out of the car. He nudges the door closed with his knee and turns to face her.

'Tell me what you're doing here?'

Carter knows that he's best served by killing this woman. Avoid collateral damage? Minimize civilian casualties? Sure, by all means. There are innocents on many battlefields. But minimize doesn't mean eliminate. Neither does avoid. Besides, Carter doesn't know whether or not she's an innocent bystander. Maybe she's a warrior, like Ricky Ditto, in which case she has no rights at all. In which case her beauty won't save her. She'll never leave the garage.

'I'm, like, on a date,' Angel finally says.

'What's your name?'

'Angel.'

'Show me some ID.'

'What?'

'You're a whore, isn't that right? When you say "date", you mean he's paying you to fuck him.'

Ordinarily, Angel lies about her profession. Not this time. 'I'm a sex worker,' she says.

'Congratulations, it's a lot better than being his girlfriend.' Carter has trafficked with whores in the past, as a uniformed soldier, a mercenary and as a soldier of fortune. He harbors them no ill will. Mostly – though probably not in this case – their working lives were about survival under harsh circumstances. 'So, what's with the outfit? And I meant what I said. Show me some ID. In fact, just toss me your purse.'

Angel complies eagerly. She watches him extract her driver's license, her Social Security card and her Brooklyn College ID card. That he's memorizing her address and Social Security number is a given. That he wouldn't bother if he intended to kill her is also a given.

When the door opens, don't hesitate, walk on through. Seize the day. Angel opts for submission. She's thinking that she doesn't have to cringe. This weird-looking man, with his green jacket and his plaid sport shirt and his khaki chinos, doesn't care what she's feeling. He wants her to obey.

Carter tosses the purse to Angel. At least she didn't lie when he asked her name. Angela is close enough to Angel. And her last name, Tamanaka, confirms his guess about her ancestry.

'Your mother's Caucasian, right?'

'My mother's a drunk.'

The answer takes Carter by surprise, though his expression doesn't change. He's thinking it's time to get out of Dodge. Past time, actually. 'Here's what happens next, Angel. You and me, we're going through that door at the back of the garage. Then we're gonna walk around the house, down the driveway and make a right turn. There's a van parked near the end of the block. We'll enter it through the side door, no delay, no hesitation. Understood?'

'Yeah.'

'Good. Now, I want you to open your umbrella so we can huddle beneath it when we get to the end of the driveway. I want us to be a loving couple just going about our business, no reason in the world to pay us any attention.' Carter shoves the gun into his pocket. 'Don't make a mistake here, Angel. Plan B is real simple: I kill you. Now, tell me what's up with the outfit? You look like a nun.'

Angel's mind boils with unanswered questions. What if someone, a neighbor, sees them walking away from the scene of a murder? What if someone saw her drive up with Ricky? What if someone noticed a strange van parked on the block? How can he be sure that she won't run to the cops the minute he releases her? Angel has no time to consider the answers, though she can't stop the questions. She's too busy doing what she does so well, entertaining a man. Angel tells Carter all about her work as they make their way around the house and along the driveway to the sidewalk, as they boldly march up the block. Her tone is engaged and somewhat intimate, as if she was revealing some juicy bit of gossip to a close friend.

'I mean, you look in the phone book under escort services, you find hundreds of ads. But not my agency, not Pigalle Studios. At Pigalle, you have to be personally recommended. We don't even have an address. It's all word of mouth and Pierre runs the whole thing out of his loft. Pierre says that what we do is an art form.'

Angel notes Carter's occasional smile and wonders if he's turned on. 'Far from controlling my life, I haven't seen Pierre since last August when I ran into him at a party. He collects the fee – credit card only – and deposits my commission in my bank account. At the end of the year, I get a 1099 tax form in the mail and I pay what I owe. No harm, no foul.'

Carter unlocks the van with his remote. He opens the side door, motions Angel through and follows closely behind, forcing her against the far door. Then he locks the doors and flips a child protection switch that allows him to control the door locks throughout the van. Finally satisfied, he starts the engine and drives away.

'If I was your client, what fantasy do you think I'd pick?' he asks.

Angel tilts her head to one side and peers at Carter. Talk about forgettable. Carter's neither ugly, nor handsome. He's a twenty-something in good shape, though not especially broad or tall, with medium-length, light brown hair, not quite a nerd, but definitely edging toward that side of the spectrum. That he should be a professional killer amazes her.

'OK, like you're this hard-hearted, cold-blooded, merciless assassin. You've murdered so many people you can't even remember their faces. And what you're thinkin', though you don't say it out loud, is that you have to kill me, too. I mean, keepin' me alive? It doesn't make sense. But there's something about me, so young, so innocent, that your heart is touched . . .' Angel's about to say, 'And your cock, too,' but censors herself at the last moment. Which is not to say that she wouldn't trade sex for her life.

Carter laughs for the first time in weeks, laughs at Angel's boldness. 'In the end, of course, I let you go. I let you go and everybody lives happily ever after.'

'Or words to that effect.'

'Do I get laid along the way?'

'Do you want to?'

'No, I want you to pass a little test for me, a one-question test: How can I be sure you won't run to the cops if I let you go?'

Angel's already asked herself the same question. Now, hearing it from Carter's lips, she knows there's an answer. She knows because she's looking right at him and he's not worried.

Carter takes the scenic route back to Manhattan, Broadway instead of the West Side Highway. He doesn't want to pass over the Henry Hudson Bridge with its toll plaza and surveillance cameras that photograph every license plate. He wants more time with Angel, too.

'Here's a hint,' Carter says. 'You probably won't have to go to the cops. Most likely, they'll come to you.'

Damn, Angel thinks. She must be a complete idiot. Ricky Ditto can be tied to Pigalle Studios through his credit card records. And Pierre? Pierre's a nice guy, but if the cops press him, he'll give her up in a heartbeat.

'So, what are you gonna tell them, Angel? If the cops should knock on your door? Will you claim that a mysterious hitman just happened to be waiting in the house when you showed up? How will you prove it? I didn't leave any trace evidence in that house. It's your word against nothing.'

'OK, I get the point. So tell me what you'd do, if you were in my position.'

'I'd call my pimp—'

'My agent.'

'I'd call my agent and tell him the trick didn't—'

'The client.'

'I'd tell him the client never showed up. I'm cold, I'm wet and I'm really pissed off.'

'What about the cops?'

'If you get any warning that the cops have been around, hire a lawyer and keep his business card in your pocket. If you don't get a warning – if the cops snatch you off the street – invoke your right to remain silent and ask for an attorney. They'll keep coming at you, right? They're not gonna stop the first time you ask. But if you keep your mouth shut long enough, one of two things will happen. If the cops have enough to make an arrest, they'll put you in the system. If they don't, they'll let you go. This is true whether you talk to them or not. No matter what you say, if the cops have enough evidence to make an arrest, you'll be arrested.'

They drift into silence as they pass through the valley at 125th Street, heading south, then climb a steep hill running alongside elevated subway tracks that disappear underground a third of the way up. They're in another world now, Harlem behind them, Columbia University and Barnard College to either side. Landscaped medians, carefully attended, run the length of each block. Even in the rain, even lit by the odd amber light cast by the street lamps, the contrast with the black and Latino neighborhood to the north catches Carter's attention, as it has before. Thousands of tulips rise straight from the earth, tulips of every color, proud as soldiers on a parade ground. And there's at least one cherry tree on every block. In another week, if the weather stays warm, they'll be in their full glory. For now, their tight blossoms cast a fuzzy pink haze over the rain-slicked branches.

They crest the hill and head down toward 110th Street, another borderline. No more gardens, no more tulips or daffodils or cherry trees, no more Columbia University. They're in an obscure neighborhood called Manhattan Valley. Twenty years before, Manhattan Valley was an open-air drug market that would have put a Moroccan bazaar to shame.

Now it's partially gentrified, like all of Manhattan. This is where Angel lives.

Carter double-parks in front of a fire hydrant midway between 108th and 107th Streets. He looks at Angel in the rear-view mirror as he releases the door locks, but he's thinking of his sister. Only two weeks ago, he'd be heading for the Cabrini Nursing Home on the Lower East Side to pay Janie a visit, maybe read a little from the Bible. Angel looks back at him, catching his eyes in the mirror, and again he's struck by her beauty.

'This outfit you work with . . .'

'Pigalle Studios.'

'Yeah, Pigalle Studios. Do you have some kind of stage name? So the clients know who to ask for?'

'Sure.'

'What is it?'

Angel's smile reveals porcelain-white teeth. 'Angel Face.'

'OK, Angel Face, one more piece of advice. Over the next few days, you're gonna be sorely tempted to tell somebody what happened. Don't do it. As far as you're concerned, everyone's a cop. You run your mouth, you'll go to jail. Let the cops prove you were in that house. Don't help them. Benedetti was a mob guy and there are plenty of suspects out there, so it's entirely possible the cops won't connect you to him. In which case, it's even more important that nobody else knows what happened. And get rid of the outfit, the dress and the shoes. Do it tonight.'

FOUR

Carter spends the evening, until ten o'clock, at Milton's, a sports bar off Queens Boulevard in the community of Woodhaven. Milton's is all about the American male's addiction to athletics. Twenty flat screen televisions, small and large, suspended from the ceiling or attached to the walls, are tuned to networks telecasting every sport currently in season. Priority naturally falls to New York teams, the Yankees and the Mets, and to the ongoing play-offs in hockey and basketball. Lesser attractions play in the corners, a soccer match from England, thoroughbred horse racing from a California track. On a small set to Carter's left, a mixed martial arts champion beats his hapless opponent to a bloody pulp.

Carter's chosen Milton's partly because it's close to Janie's condominium apartment, where he's spending the night. But Carter's also drawn to the bar's vibrancy, and to its varied clientele. There are as many degenerate gamblers as there are sports fans, a few bookies taking last minute wagers, and a bevy of young women out for an evening with their perpetually adolescent boyfriends. They root their favorites on, fueled by alcohol, marijuana (the bathrooms reek of weed) and the cocaine peddled by Milton's resident dealer, a small-time jerk named Sal who pretends to be connected.

Carter hangs by himself at a free-standing table near a back wall, munching on a hamburger and sipping at a mug of Bass Ale. He has no friends here, or anywhere else for that matter, but the intensely social behavior of the fans enthralls him. Carter believes that athletic contests simulate the more serious business of mortal combat, the big differences being that fans get to watch and the losers don't go home in coffins. But the ability to slap a puck into a net doesn't impress Carter, nor do the virtually subhuman fist fights between the hockey players. He doesn't feel himself diminished by loss, or enhanced by victory, only fascinated by those who are.

The fans gathered before the largest television emit a collective moan. The New York Yankees are playing the Boston Red Sox and one of the Boston players – Carter doesn't know who – has hit a home run. Carter watches him jog around the bases, then watches a series of replays, none of which alters the outcome. Two men standing at a table only a few feet away attempt to hide their satisfaction. They're gamblers, these men, and they've bet against the home team, a fact they'd just as soon keep to themselves, but which doesn't escape Carter's attention.

Carter finishes his hamburger and orders another beer from a harried waitress. Despite the charged atmosphere, his thoughts turn to his sister's ashes drifting on the gray waters of the Hudson. Janie was his anchor. Tending her gave him purpose, much as athletic contests give purpose to Milton's patrons. But there's always another game for the sports fan, another season, another chance. Janie can't be replaced, or so Carter thinks as he tips the waitress when she returns with his beer.

'Thanks, sport,' she says with a wink.

Like most males, Carter's easily distracted. He's also a master of the hook-up, the casual encounter, sex as pure sensation. An Australian merc named Arthur had explained the principle on a rooftop in Basra while they awaited the appearance of a doomed tribal sheikh.

'Friction, that's all it is, mate. Friction, friction, friction. The testicles are two organs that fill up every forty-eight hours and have to be emptied. There's nothing more to the game.'

Now Carter observes the bar maid's butt as she sashays across the room, his gaze speculative. Was she flirting? Or is flirtatiousness part of the show? Angel had flirted with him as they walked to the van, describing this fantasy and that. Not only didn't he blame her, Carter was impressed with her control, and her obvious skill at projecting unfelt desire.

The beauty of the hook-up, Carter thinks, is that you can be certain your partner is attracted to you, at least physically.

But the waitress flirts with her next customer and with the next, leaving Carter to conclude that she's just not into him. Carter isn't disappointed. He finishes his beer and heads back to Janie's apartment, walking the few blocks beneath clearing skies.

An hour later, still restless, he stands in Janie's gallery, a narrow hallway lined on both sides with photographs taken many years before. The newest, judging from the Chevrolet parked at the curb, dates back to the 1950s. On this night, Carter's eyes are drawn to one of the oldest photos, a wedding portrait. Here the groom is seated in a finely carved chair while the bride stands to his left and slightly behind him. She wears an embroidered white dress, tightly pinched at the waist, with a high collar that rises almost to her ears. Her veil drops from a spray of flowers to brush the floor.

Carter steps a bit closer. The bride's lips are thin and her eyes appear sad to him. The groom isn't smiling, either, although it's hard to be sure because he sports a Kaiser Wilhelm mustache thick enough to obscure his mouth. In any event, they don't touch each other, don't stare lovingly into each other's eyes, don't exhibit any sign of affection. They might be strangers hired for a photo shoot.

These are photographs, Carter assumes, of his relatives, his and Janie's, a family legacy. There can be no other reason why Janie went to the trouble of framing and hanging them. But Carter doesn't know who they are because Janie compiled the photos after he left for the military. He's searched the apartment for some sort of inventory and taken several of the photos out of their frames, hoping to find them labeled. Not happening. Janie has taken their identities with her. There was a time, of course, while Janie was still being cared for at home, when she might have identified the anonymous faces, might have connected them, one to the other. But Carter was in Sierra Leone, a soldier of fortune dumb enough to believe that blood can lead to anything but blood.

Soldiers learn to sleep when the opportunity presents itself and Carter nods off shortly after he gets into bed and pulls up the covers. Most nights, he sleeps soundly for about six hours and awakens refreshed. But on this night he rises just before dawn. Outside the room's single window, the spring air is filled with birdsong.

Carter lies on his back, overwhelmed by the tattered remains of a dream. He's in bed, as he is now, but there's no room surrounding him, no walls, no floor, no ceiling, no sky, no Earth, no wind, no sun, no stars. He is utterly alone.

'Goodbye, Janie,' he whispers. 'Goodbye, goodbye.'

* * *

Carter's up and out of the apartment by six thirty, heading west over the George Washington Bridge and across New Jersey, to an outdoor gun range near the Delaware River in Pennsylvania. As he proceeds inland, from the warmer coast to the Watchung Mountains of western New Jersey, the season reverses. The grass on this end of the state is still winter-brown and the leaves on the trees barely formed. The day is warm, however. Even at this early hour, the temperature approaches sixty degrees and the sun, rising in his rear-view mirror, seems playful and determined. This is especially true as Carter crosses a bridge spanning the Delaware. The river's running high and the angled sunlight dances in the spray. Fishermen stand on the banks of the river, casting out, while a flotilla of blue, red and green canoes braves the rapids in the main channel.

Carter reaches his destination, a shooting range tucked into the hardwood forest that covers most of north-eastern Pennsylvania, at eight o'clock. He's driven all this way for two reasons. First, the Liberty Shooting Range has a training facility designed for handgun combat, a skill Carter's determined to acquire. Second, Carl Maverton, the range's owner, is an NRA nutcase obsessed with the constitutional right of high school students to carry weapons.

'I'll say this,' he told Carter just two weeks before. 'If every kid in Columbine was packing heat, a lotta lives would've been saved.'

Carter's beliefs run in the opposite direction. He'd be happiest if the entire population was disarmed. Except for him, of course. He also finds Carl's lectures as tedious as they are repetitive. But there's good news, too. Carter's weapons are illegal and Carl doesn't give a shit.

Carl's sitting behind a battered metal desk when Carter walks into his office, the first customer of the day. There are two American eagles on the desk. One augments an ashtray filled with cigar butts, the other carries the flag in its talons. A Gadsden rattlesnake flag – 'DON'T TREAD ON ME' – decorates the wall to Carl's right. A framed poster of Gentleman Jerry Miculek hangs to his left.

Gentleman Jerry wears a blue and white shirt with the name

of his corporate sponsor, Smith & Wesson, emblazoned across the chest. A competition speed-shooter, he holds a world record unlikely to be broken any time soon. On September 11, 1999, Miculek fired twelve rounds, hitting a target with each shot, in 2.9 seconds. That wouldn't be impressive if he'd used an automatic with a capacious magazine, but Miculek accomplished this feat with a revolver, which meant he had to reload in the middle. Without the reload, Gentleman Jerry's able to draw and empty a revolver (a Smith & Wesson, naturally) in less than a second, the shots coming so fast they sound like rolling thunder.

Training is what Carter's life is mostly about. Contracts come to him once a month, on average, and are usually filled within a week. The rest of his time is devoted to staying sharp, an orientation developed in the military. Delta Force specialized in covert ops and was only sporadically deployed. Their assignments were invariably dangerous and filled with a tension that could only be overcome by training. The more you prepared, the greater the chance you'd survive. Carter harbors no illusions about the chance part. In the world of war, there are no certainties. At any given moment, the bullet might already be in the air. As, even now, the police might be knocking on his door.

Carter exercises three afternoons a week at a mixed martial arts gym in Manhattan, working alongside ranked cage fighters. Whenever possible, he spends his mornings and evenings at a locksmith shop, which he owns. Carter doesn't install locks, or drill out locks for citizens who've lost their keys. He has an employee for that. Carter spends the hours opening locks with various tools, including picks and drills, and memorizing the wiring schemes for home alarm systems. As an assassin, he much prefers the privacy of a target's house or apartment to the street.

'So, how's the big bad city?' Maverton leads Carter to a yard enclosed by an earthen berm lined with bales of hay. There are eight targets in the yard, stationed at distances ranging up to thirty feet.

'Still big, still bad,' Carter responds.

A large man with broad shoulders and a swelling gut, Carl

Maverton fancies himself a tough guy, a self-image Carter never challenges. New York might be the safest big city in the country, but Carl believes it to be the center of all that's evil, a cauldron of mixed-race liberalism committed to the destruction of America.

'Time to get out, old buddy.' Carl winks and grins. 'Because it's comin'.'

Carter doesn't inquire into the 'it' part. That's because he knows Carl will launch into a rant about taking back his country – by any means necessary – that won't end before sundown. The very idea seems pitiful to Carter, a bunch of jerks marching around in the forest with semi-automatic assault rifles as they prepare to battle the United States military. Carter was in Falluja, working as a merc, when the Marines stormed the city. He was at Tora Bora, watching American jets slam missiles into cave openings six feet wide. Should Maverton and his survivalist buddies ever become a serious threat, they'll be eliminated forthwith.

For the next hour, Carter devotes himself to his training. He uses a Smith & Wesson revolver and a Glock semi-automatic, working with single and multiple targets from various positions. The pinnacle of the exercise occurs halfway through, when he rolls from a squat on to his left side and notches a tight, six-round pattern into a target twenty feet away.

Carter fires off more than a hundred rounds with each weapon, until his wrist aches and he can't fight the recoil. Then he puts his weapons away, satisfied with his overall progress. The military hadn't placed much emphasis on handgun training, but his speed and accuracy have both improved since his return to the States. He's not as fast as Gentleman Jerry Miculek, of course, not even close, but he's not really competing. For one thing, Miculek's weapons are heavily customized, while Carter's, for good reason, are not. Carter discards his weapons (as he discarded the .22 used to dispatch Ricky Ditto, along with the stolen license plates on the van and the clothing he'd worn) after a single use. There doesn't seem to be much point in customizing them beforehand. No one misses from six feet away, not if he's got a hand as steady as Carter's.

As Carter hikes across the yard to the rifle range, he wonders about Miculek's heart. How would he react if bullets were coming back at him from all directions, accompanied by the occasional RPG and mortar round? Unless Miculek's been to war, he can't know.

Carter was far more skilled with a rifle than a handgun, when he left the military. In the field, he'd consistently buried his first round into living targets eight hundred yards away. But eight hundred yards is nearly a half-mile, a distance covering ten New York City blocks, and there are very few ten-block sightlines in New York, or even in the surrounding suburbs. Thus Carter practices out to a distance of three hundred yards, a bit more than three city blocks, calculating distance with a fairly low-tech rangefinder purchased second hand at a gun show.

At these distances, Carter is deadly from any position, standing to prone, and he doesn't prolong what amounts to a boring practice session designed only to maintain his skills. He's on the road by eleven o'clock, stopping for an outdoor lunch in Stroudsburg on the Pennsylvania side of the Delaware River. He attracts no attention while he eats, blending into the scenery, virtually invisible. Back in his van, he stays five miles above the speed limit, just another weary traveler heading home. But not to Janie's apartment in Woodhaven. Janie's name and address appear on Carter's service record and he's already been tracked to her apartment by a man out to kill him. Now he lives, for the most part, in a condo he sublets on the Lower East Side of Manhattan. The arrangement is private, with the utilities remaining in the name of the condo's owner. Carter's locksmith shop is down here as well, Gung-Ho Locksmiths on Avenue A near Tenth Street. He'll spend the next few hours in the shop, examining various ways to open magnetic locks. Then he'll go for a run along the East River, only a few blocks away.

Carter's thoughts turn to Angel Tamanaka as he crosses the George Washington Bridge. He'd been standing in the dining room when he first heard her voice, and he'd assumed she was Ricky's wife, returned unexpectedly. Killing a man in front of his family isn't Carter's style, but there was no going back and he'd pulled the trigger without regret the minute his target presented itself. Then he'd stepped into the kitchen to find this doll of a woman, eyes wide as saucers.

I'm horny, Carter thinks. I'm a victim of the itch that must be scratched. All those stories, the fantasies Angel described, have finally done their work.

Carter likes goals, perhaps because he has so few of them in his life. He doesn't really care about money, doesn't dream of limos or mansions or watches big enough to substitute for wrist weights, doesn't fancy ocean-going yachts or bespoke suits. That leaves only the necessities with which to fill his days: food, drink, shelter and the itch.

Carter maps out a weekend of bar hopping. His mission will be to find a woman equally determined to scratch that same itch. A woman who'll head back to her workaday life on Monday morning, a woman whose imaginings of him, should she remember him at all, will begin at his neck and work their way down.

FIVE

Bobby Ditto loses his temper for the first time that day. He slams the desktop with the side of his fist and tosses a jar of mint-flavored TUMS at the hapless tech sweeping the room for bugs. The TUMS jar bounces off the tech's shoulder and he begins to shake.

'What, you're gonna be all fuckin' day?' Bobby demands. 'I got things to do. I'm runnin' a business here and I can't do it with you in the goddamn room.'

Benedetti and the tech, Levi Kupperman, are in the Bunker, an underground room in a wholesale carpet warehouse in Red Hook, Brooklyn. Benedetti had the room built when he purchased the warehouse in 2005, the year his first big deal went down. The walls and ceilings of the windowless bunker are solid concrete, two feet thick, and proof against any remote listening device. That leaves the mismatched furniture, the alarm, the sprinklers, the ventilation system and the computer (used only for the carpet business and not connected to the Internet) as the only points of vulnerability.

'You want me to stop?'

Bobby Ditto stares at Levi for a moment, then shakes his head. When he first hired Levi, the kid was a hotshot with his own equipment and an expanding electronics company. That was before he got too strung out to think about anything but cocaine and more cocaine. Now he's a scarecrow who works for an eight-ball of coke – three and a half grams of white powder that'll be gone up his nose by tomorrow morning.

'Ya know, you're tryin' my patience.' Benedetti notes the kid's panicky look with some satisfaction. Bobby's renowned for his bad temper and his willingness to act on it. Not this morning, though. Now he's got more important things to consider. 'Just finish up and get the fuck outta here.'

Fifteen minutes later, Levi opens a door thick enough to defend a castle and disappears. Two men replace him, Marco Torrino, called 'the Blade', and a man named Samik Atwal. In the old days, the Blade would have had a formal title: *capo*. But the old days are gone, brought down by a get-the-wops mentality that allowed black, Latino and Russian gangs to freely organize. Thus, Torrino has no title. He's just the man who'll come to kill you if you fuck with Bobby Ditto, a role he'd played for Bobby's father, now deceased.

The Blade's companion, Samik 'Sammy' Atwal, has come to the Bunker as a courtesy. Atwal's a second-generation Indian-American who captains a small crew located in the Queens neighborhood of Jackson Heights. The crew deals powder and crack to Atwal's countrymen. That's fine with Bobby Ditto, who's as big on ethnic identity as he is on entrepreneurship. But he does sometimes wonder how the raghead came to be best buddies with his brother, Ricky, now deceased.

Ricky Ditto's murder is the sole cause of Bobby Ditto's foul mood. That's because Bobby has to do something about it. Revenge, retribution, an eye for an eye? That's how the system works. That's how it has to work when you can't go to the cops. You want justice, you either get it yourself or appear weak. Bobby and his crew are mid-level drug wholesalers. They purchase ecstasy, heroin and cocaine in bulk and sell it off in smaller units, untouched. Large sums of money are exchanged along the way and rip-offs are a constant hazard. It really doesn't pay to look weak, not at all.

'First thing,' Bobby Ditto says when Atwal takes a seat on the other side of his desk, 'I wanna thank you for comin' down. I appreciate the courtesy.'

'Hey, Ricky was my friend. You find out who did this, you tell me. I'll do what's necessary.'

Bobby stares at Sammy for a few seconds before he speaks, a move he knows to be disconcerting, but the man fails to react. Still, Bobby tells himself, the raghead's gotta think he's a suspect.

'You want coffee?' Bobby Ditto asks. 'I got a machine upstairs. Cappuccino, espresso, you name it.'

'Nah, I got somethin' I gotta do this morning.'

'Have a cup anyway.' Bobby nods to the Blade and says 'Do me a favor, Marco.' He waits until Marco takes the hint and disappears. Then he turns to Atwal. 'You shouldn't take this the wrong way, Sammy, but it'd be good if we had this moment to ourselves.'

'Whatever you want.'

Bobby Ditto brings his chair forward. He's a big man, much bigger than Atwal, and he leans across the desk to stare into Atwal's round eyes. Bobby's thinking that Sammy looks soft, what with his chocolate-brown skin and fat cheeks, but that appearances can be deceiving. The man's eyes reveal only patience. 'You told the Blade there was somethin' I needed to know.'

'Yeah, it's this. I'm like ninety-nine percent sure that Ricky had a date that night.'

'A date?'

'With a whore.'

Bobby sits back and stares at the ceiling for a moment. 'OK, so he wanted a little strange. What's the big deal?'

'He told me he was takin' her back to the house.' Sammy spreads his hands and smiles apologetically. 'Rose and the kids were off visitin' Rose's mother. Ricky wanted to do an all-nighter at home.'

Bobby Ditto groans. 'Sammy, this is something you really should not spread around. Rose's got problems enough without knowin' her husband was gonna party with a whore in her bed. Besides, we can't be sure it's even true.' Bobby traces a little circle with his forefinger. 'Ricky, as you know, had a way of stretchin' the facts.'

The door opens and Marco enters. He's carrying two cups of coffee and a plate of anisette-flavored biscotti on a tray. He sets the tray down and disappears.

Sammy takes a biscotto and dips it into his coffee. He bites into it and nods. Compliments on the pastry are mandatory at meetings of this kind and he plays his part. 'This ain't from the supermarket,' he observes. 'This is the real deal.'

'The Blade's grandmother,' Bobby explains. 'She was born in Sicily, like a hundred years ago. So, tell me about the whore. Do you know her? She from the neighborhood?'

'Sorry, but I never laid eyes on her. See, what happened is that Ricky hooked up with this high-end escort service about a month ago. They do some kinda fantasy thing where you get to make up a story and the girls act it out. According to Ricky, the girls are beautiful. Any color you want, any age, too. They got like a website with pictures, but you have to be a member to get on it.'

'So, what you're telling me, it's like nothin', right?' Bobby allows a trace of annoyance to creep into his voice. 'You don't know who she is, where she came from or even if she was there?'

Atwal picks up his coffee, leans back and crosses his legs. 'I was with Ricky on Wednesday afternoon, playin' pool in the Bronx. When he left around three, he said he was going straight over to pick up the girl.'

'Pick her up where?' Bobby doesn't like any of this, not at all. The way the raghead's lettin' out the information, bit by bit? There's gonna be a pay-off somewhere down the line.

'On a corner in Manhattan. I remember he told me Broadway and 106th, only I could be wrong about the street.'

'But the Broadway part is right?'

'Broadway and somewhere uptown on the West Side. That I'm sure of. Plus, I got a business card from the escort service, Pigalle Studios.'

'The card have an address on it?'

'A phone number, that's it.'

Mollified, Bobby finally takes his coffee cup from the tray. He lays it on his desk, then picks up a biscotto. He won't have any problem linking the phone number to an address. He watches Atwal take a business card from his shirt pocket and lay it on the desk, a gift.

'I never wanted the card in the first place,' he explains with a shrug. 'Plus, I couldn't use it anyway. Ricky woulda had to vouch for me first.'

Bobby Ditto picks up the card and looks at it for a moment before sliding it into a drawer. 'Don't take offense, Sammy, because I'm definitely grateful for you comin' in. But what you told me, it's gotta be what actually happened, word for word. See, I don't know you, which is why I'm worried you might be sendin' me on a wild goose chase. I don't need to be whackin' some bitch whose only crime is givin' my brother a blow job. Are you sure you got the day right, the time?'

'Swear on Krishna, Bobby. When Ricky left the pool hall on Wednesday, he was goin' straight to pick up the whore. I remember because it was rainin' pretty hard and he was worried about the traffic comin' out of Manhattan. I mean, you gotta think—'

Benedetti completes Atwal's thought. 'You gotta think, what with Ricky being killed in his own home, that the whore was with him at the time. And if the whore survived, you also gotta think that she was the one who killed him. And if she was the one who killed him, she can tell me who paid her to kill him.' Bobby Ditto cracks his knuckles. There's nothing to be gained by further discussion with an outsider. He's got the business card. The ball's in his court. 'Like I already said,

I appreciate your comin' down. So, if there's anything I can do for you . . .'

'Well, maybe there is something. Just an idea.'

Bobby smiles to himself. He doesn't begrudge Sammy Atwal. Giving up the business card before requesting a favor? That shows respect, and class, too. 'Let's hear it.'

'I don't know what Ricky told you about me and the boys . . .'

'Everything.'

Atwal laughs. 'Like you said, Ricky liked to talk. But the thing is we're movin' up. We've outgrown our suppliers. We need more product.'

'How much more?'

'Like three or four ounces every couple of weeks.'

Bobby Ditto's thrilled, though he's careful not to show more than mild interest. It could've been a lot worse. 'You understand, Sammy, there's no credit thing happening here. It's cash up front.'

'I understand.'

'And you gotta be ready to jump. I don't hold product, not for nobody. If you tell me you need a week to raise the money, I'm gonna walk away from ya. And once I walk away, I don't walk back.'

'OK, understood.'

Bobby stands up. The meeting's over. 'You did good today,' he tells Atwal as they walk to the door. 'You showed respect and respect is how we do our thing in America. You'll be hearin' from us, count on it.'

They come through the door to find the Blade talking to a warehouse worker, a woman whose name Bobby doesn't know. Par for the course with the Blade, a pussy hound if ever there was one. Bobby's about to make the Blade very happy. He's about to tell the Blade there's a hooker who needs to be taken off the street and questioned. He's about to tell the Blade he doesn't really care what happens to the hooker afterward.

SIX

Carter fires up his computer shortly after finishing breakfast on Monday morning. He's expecting confirmation of a wire transfer to his bank in Panama, payment for a job well done. Sure enough, the money's right where it's supposed to be and Carter immediately transfers the full amount to a bank in Moscow. Instructions for the Moscow bank are already in place. After deducting their commission, the bank will move the cash to a smaller bank in the South Pacific that doesn't record the money's next – and final – destination.

His business concluded, Carter turns to his email box, deleting the spam before opening a heavily encrypted email from Paul Marginella, universally called Paulie Margarine. Paulie is Carter's agent. He secures the jobs and makes the payments after deducting his commission. But not any more.

> Hey kid, I got some bad news for you. Or maybe not. It depends on how you're doin these days. But I ain't been feeling right for a long time now and I'm gonna have to shut the operation down. No hard feelins, OK? We did good while we could (hey, that rhymes – I'm a poet who don't know it) and we have to move on. Best of luck. Paulie.

Carter takes the message to Sweat & Strain, a gym on 10th Avenue in Hell's Kitchen. He focuses on three words as he rides cross-town on the L Train: *Or maybe not.* For some time now, Carter's been tempted to break off the relationship himself. In his own mind, he compares each job to a combat deployment. Maybe the odds against being killed or wounded in any given operation are great, but if you're deployed over and over again . . . Carter doesn't bother to complete the thought. He's killed twenty-three men in fourteen cities over the past two-plus years, and the cops investigated every death.

Sure, he's protected himself. The emails that pass between Carter and Paulie are the sum total of their contact, and they do not go directly from Paulie's computer to his. Paulie's emails are addressed to an email forwarder in Minsk, the capital of Belarus. From Minsk, they voyage to the websites of three forwarders on three different continents before Carter retrieves them. One of the spook agencies, the CIA or the NSA, might be able to track and decrypt the emails, but not a local cop shop.

But if Carter can't be traced through Paulie Margarine, there's still the possibility that he'll be caught at the scene of the crime, say by a police cruiser turning on to the block at just the wrong time, or be tracked down because he missed a surveillance camera or left a minuscule bit of DNA behind, despite his many precautions.

In Carter's opinion, there are no guarantees. In Carter's opinion, the most remote outcome is rendered probable by enough repetitions.

So Carter's relieved on the one hand. Paulie's absolutely correct – it's time to move on. But coming right after Janie's passing, the prospect of a career change adds fuel to an already smoldering fire.

Carter doesn't neglect his workout. He works harder than usual, in fact. S&S is run by a mixed martial artist named Jordan Boone who promotes his self-defense system, which includes a dozen manuals selling for ten dollars each on the gym's website. Boone claims to have distilled his method from 'every martial art on the planet.'

Forget about tactics that work in a ring or a cage. Self-defense is about protecting yourself from attack by incapacitating your opponent long enough to get away.

That's all bullshit, of course, at least in Carter's opinion. Half the patrons of Boone's gym are serious knuckleheads far more likely to be the attacker than the attacked. But the system, with its kicks, strikes and throws, works as well as any other. You practice the moves, over and over and over, until each and every opening draws the appropriate counter-attack, until you see and strike before you're conscious of what you're going to do next. Then, if you're Carter, you run away. Carter has no criminal record and the last thing he wants to do is draw the attention of the police.

Most of the regulars at Sweat & Strain outweigh Carter, especially the ones who juice with steroids. But Carter's not only fast, he's also fearless, and he's acquired a bit of a reputation. He's not surprised when a pro named Johnny 'The Crusher' Carpenter asks him to work out. They go at it for an hour, until Carpenter breaks it off and heads for the showers. Carter would like nothing more than to follow – he's gotten much the worse of the exchanges – but he has one additional task ahead, one he absolutely hates, skipping rope. Which is why he forces himself to do it.

Six hours later, at four o'clock in the afternoon, Carter approaches the front door of a house on a tree-lined street in Astoria, Queens. The single-story house isn't much to look at – brick walls, shingled roof, a picture window in the living room – but it rests on a generous lot surrounded by a thick hedge in the back. Carter hesitates only for a moment before ringing the bell.

The man who opens the door is about Carter's age, but that's the only resemblance between the two. He's fifty pounds heavier than Carter, with a serious gut and jowls befitting a man twice his age.

'Can I help you?' he asks.

'I'm here to see Paulie Marginella.' Carter knows this must be Paulie's son, Freddy, who was in prison the last time Carter and Paulie met. 'Does he still live here?'

'And who are you?'

'My name's Carter.'

Freddy's double take proves one thing: Paulie's got a big mouth. Carter smiles. 'I know I'm not expected, but I heard that Paulie's not feeing well . . .'

'My dad's in the backyard, catching a few rays.' Freddy steps aside to let Carter into a small foyer. 'This is about what exactly . . .'

'It's about me paying my respects to a sick friend.'

Although Freddy fixes Carter with a hard stare, he's not his father's son. Carter's not intimidated and he simply returns the stare, his eyes blank.

'All right, hang out here for a minute. I'll ask if he wants to see you.'

Freddy's back two minutes later. He nods and leads Carter through the living room to a sliding glass door. The door's open and he points through it to a man sitting in a wheelchair positioned on a small patch of sunlit grass. There's a second chair next to him, a folding lawn chair with plastic webbing stretched across a tarnished aluminum frame.

'Lemme know when you're ready to leave,' Freddy says. 'Dad wants to talk to you alone.'

Paulie Margarine's backyard is nicely sculpted. A small bed of yellow tulips, a cluster of intertwined birch trees, a Japanese maple, its spider-thin leaves barely opened, that might have been lifted from a Bonsai pot. Against the side of the house, an enormous lilac, more a tree than a bush, perfumes the warm May air.

Carter acknowledges the contrast as he crosses the lawn. Every living thing in Paulie's yard has dedicated itself to renewal, except for Paulie Margarine. Paulie's as thin as a rail and his skin is a shade of yellow that no tulip will ever reproduce. Emblazoned with the logo of the New York Mets, a thick blanket wraps his body from his neck to his feet. The hand that emerges from beneath the blanket is bony enough to be the claw of a diving raptor.

'Hey, Carter, check this out.' With great effort, Paulie manages to pull up the blanket to reveal a black boot. 'I'm ready,' he announces.

'To die with your boots on?'

'I gotta.' Paulie's grin reveals gums the color of bone. 'It's part of the culture. It's our thing, our *cosa nostra*.'

Carter's laugh is genuine. He's always liked Paulie, a man true to himself, a genuine tough guy. 'So, what's up, what do you have?'

'Hepatitis C, which is destroyin' my liver. I'm on the list for a transplant.' Paulie's hand disappears beneath the blanket. 'But it's not lookin' good. I turned down the last round of chemo. Whatever time I got, I don't wanna spend it leanin' over a toilet, which in fact I can't even do any more. I gotta throw up in a bedpan.'

Carter lets that pass and they sit quietly for a few minutes, until Paulie asks, 'So, whatta ya gonna do? Now that you're outta work?'

'I'm thinking you were right, Paulie, it's time to move on. I don't know to what exactly, but I've got money put away, so I'm not all that worried.'

'I'm not worried, either. I know exactly what I'm gonna be doin' six months from now and that's breathin' dirt. But my kid has big ideas. He's gettin' out of all the old businesses. The way it is now, with the Feds, you make a wrong move and they put you in jail for a thousand years. The money's in computer crime and that's where Freddy's goin'. We'll be done with our other businesses, including the business you and me had together, within a few months.'

Behind Paulie, a truck rattles up the block, its gears grinding when the driver shifts. 'Hey, Carter, you wanna hear somethin' funny?'

'Anything.'

Paulie chuckles. 'My hearing, it's gotten better somehow. At night, I can't sleep for the traffic on Ditmars Boulevard and that's three blocks away. The planes at LaGuardia? They hit my ears like a toothache.'

'You should try earplugs, or one of those machines that make white noise.'

'I thought about that, but these days I'm not too crazy about sleepin'.'

Again, Carter doesn't know what to say and they observe a second silence, this one prolonged. The afternoon warmth is seductive, in any event, a perfect spring evening. Carter's eyes move to the bed of late-blooming daffodils, the tips of their feathered petals a smoky orange, and to a trellis covered by a climbing rose, its buds as green as peas this early in the year.

Carter's always been comfortable with silence, a quality that served him well as a sniper. There's an art to remaining both immobile and alert that begins with resisting the allure of your own thoughts. But this time Carter's quiet because he's remembering a Nepalese merc named Lo Phet. Lo Phet practiced Tibetan Buddhism and his belief in reincarnation approached the absolute.

'Can go up or down,' he'd explained. They were on their way from Kirkuk to Baghdad, their mission to ferry a suitcase filled with American dollars from one warlord to another. 'Can have rebirth as bug. How you like that? To come back as flea on elephant's ass? Or can go to world of Gods, or go down to world of hungry ghosts. Hungry ghost have big fat belly and tiny mouth. Can never get enough food.'

'Is that the bottom?' Carter had asked as they slowed to a stop at the end of a line of vehicles awaiting inspection at a checkpoint. 'The world of hungry ghosts?'

'No, bottom is Hell World. We in Hell World now.'

Carter had thought it over for a moment, then said, 'You're claiming that we died somewhere along the way and were reborn.'

'Yes, die and go to Hell World.'

Lo Phet had moved on three weeks later when an improvised explosive device cut him in two. At the time, Carter had wondered if he'd be reborn into the Hell World, if he'd have to do it all over again. Carter now wonders the same thing about Paulie Margarine.

'Paulie,' Carter finally says, 'any chance you'd be willing to give up your computer? Or the hard drive at least?'

'Is that what you came for?'

'I came for two reasons. To have a look around and to visit my partner, who told me that he was sick. I have to tell you, though, I wasn't too happy when your boy recognized my name.'

'So whatta ya gonna do, shoot me? He's my kid. We got no secrets between us.'

In fact, Carter's not carrying a gun. But he does have a combat knife strapped to the inside of his left calf. 'You can't blame me for tying up loose ends. Freddy can talk his head off and it won't matter. With you gone, there's no proof, except for the emails in that computer.'

'I thought you said everything in the computer was encrypted?'

'And you just told me your son's going into the computer business.' Carter's voice drops. 'Do you really want me sitting around worried that my back isn't covered?'

Paulie sighs. When it really mattered, Carter had out-maneuvered him at every turn. What chance would Freddy have? Better they – meaning the Marginella family and Mr Carter – be quits forever.

'All right, take it. But I should charge you. Now I gotta replace the computer.'

'Tell you what, Paulie. I'll get a new computer delivered to the house by the middle of next week. Something faster, with a hi-def screen.'

'Don't bother. The porno I watch ain't gonna be improved by high definition.'

A robin drops on to the lawn, catching Paul Margarine's attention. He watches its head swivel, watches the bird turn its eyes this way and that. There are lots of creatures that eat robins, creatures that slither and stalk and drop down out of the sky.

'Hey, Carter, you wanna hear a funny story?'

'Another one?'

'This one's better. The guy you whacked, Ricky Ditto? He's got a brother named Bobby. What I heard, Bobby Ditto's talkin' revenge and he's talkin' it loud, which means he has to do something or look like an asshole. Anyhow, Bobby found out that Ricky had a date with a whore that afternoon and now he's goin' after the whore. Me, I wouldn't wanna be in the whore's shoes when Bobby Ditto comes callin'. The guy's a complete jerk. But it's good for you, right? There's no way to get from the whore to you. The whore's a dead end.'

SEVEN

Carter knows damn well that he's supposed to let Angel Tamanaka swing. Whatever ethical debt he owed the universe at large was amply paid when he let her go in the first place. Paulie was right. Angel can't lead Ricky Ditto's brother to him. She doesn't even know his name.

Carter's van is in the CASH lane at the toll plaza on the

Triborough Bridge connecting Queens to Manhattan and the Bronx. He's in the CASH lane, despite the heavy back-up, because the E-ZPASS system links every use of an E-ZPASS device to a specific time, place and vehicle. Carter routinely leaves as few traces of his movements as possible.

But Carter's not in a hurry. When he gets home, he'll nap until eight or nine o'clock, have dinner at a local coffee shop and then set out to find the woman, if not of his dreams, at least of his weekend. That was, and still is, Carter's only plan. Or so he tells himself as he watches a gigantic SUV, a Mercedes, try to cut into the CASH lane. A chorus of horns blends with the steady thump, thump, thump of the speakers in the SUV, a challenge to a challenge.

Carter doesn't lean on his own horn. As far as he's concerned, the man driving the Mercedes is just another knucklehead. Now he's forcing the SUV between two cars, his message clear enough. I'm going ahead of you because I'm bigger and more powerful than you are, and there's not a damn thing you can do about it. He's right, too. Aside from a few face-saving curses, and the horns, of course, nobody attempts to prevent this affront to common civility.

Carter's big on civility, as he's big on dignity and honor. He associates civility with cooperation, and cooperation with the ultimate survival of the species. This was a lesson repeated in the course of every firefight, a lesson held so close that many soldiers confuse mutual dependency with love.

When his turn comes, Carter hands the toll collector a ten dollar bill, pockets the change and heads south to the apartment he's subletting on the Lower East Side. The idea is to put Angel in his rear-view mirror, but it's not working. Paulie's words rise up, rise again, despite Carter's best efforts: *I wouldn't wanna be in the whore's shoes when Bobby Ditto comes callin'.*

So what? Carter's viewed the innocent dead stacked like firewood, and more than once. Sierra Leone, Congo, the Ivory Coast. Piles of arms and legs hacked off by the boy soldiers, women raped until they bled to death. The victims were always the most vulnerable, farmers without the means to fight back, small tribes hunting monkeys with primitive bows.

What entitles Angel Tamanaka to special consideration? Besides her beauty? Why should he take the slightest risk to protect her? Much less the very substantial risk of going to her apartment? For all he knows, Angel went to the cops first thing. For all he knows, the cops are with her right now, working on an artist's likeness. What he should do is get out of New York, maybe take a trip to Panama so he can be near his money. What he should have done, when he had the chance, was memorize her phone number. As it is, if he wants to warn her, he'll have to knock on her door.

Carter's thoughts turn to Janie as he backs the van into a parking space on Tenth Street off First Avenue. Janie's religious convictions were as unshakeable as Lo Phet's and she'd done her absolute best to guide him along the path of righteousness. Yet, somehow, and for the longest time, he'd confused virtue with obedience. He did whatever Janie asked him to do, with no complaints. If she'd told him to jump out the window, he probably would have done that, too.

If Janie were still alive, she'd tell him to warn Angel Tamanaka, the opportunity to save a life somehow becoming an obligation to save a life. Maybe that's why he'd taken to the army. In the army, the only obligations were to your comrades and the mission.

Inside his apartment, he kicks off his shoes, lowers himself on to a sectional couch and settles in to watch a Military Channel documentary on Roman battle tactics. Though he rarely has a chance to use them in his line of work, Carter's skilled with knives. Close-up killing of the kind practiced by all armies until the invention of the gun normally commands his attention. Not this time, though. This time Angel Tamanaka tumbles through his thoughts, invasive as an Iraqi dust storm.

Carter finally gives up at seven thirty, a few minutes before sunset. He decides to visit Angel's neighborhood and take a look around. But there's no way he's going to knock on Angel's door – not without knowing who's behind it. And there's no way he's going up there unprepared. He crosses the apartment, to a walk-in closet in the larger of the two bedrooms. At the darkest end of the closet, he removes a section of floorboard to reveal a metal box nestled between the joists. He takes a .38 caliber revolver, a Colt, from the box, along with a holster, and a Rhode Island license plate stolen from an auto graveyard. Carter likes revolvers for street work because the cartridge casings aren't expelled, as they would be if he used a semi-automatic.

When Carter leaves the apartment, the holstered revolver is positioned just inside his left hip with the handle facing to the right. An unlined denim jacket covers both, though it's not really cool enough for a jacket. The license plate is for the van and Carter attaches it in a few seconds with a handful of magnets. Then he's off, acutely aware of the risks he's taking. New York City's gun laws are draconian. The minimum penalty for carrying an illegal handgun is three years in prison.

Carter takes Fourteenth Street to Tenth Avenue and heads uptown. He runs into heavy traffic near the Lincoln Tunnel, even at eight o'clock, but once past Forty-Second Street, the traffic moves along and he parks the van facing Angel's apartment at eight fifteen.

Carter settles into the back of the van and carefully checks his surroundings, using the windshield and the side mirrors. He's on a block in the very early stages of gentrification. A few doors in from the far corner, a drug crew services cars and pedestrians. In the middle of the block, four Hispanic teenagers, three boys and a girl, lean against a car parked in front of the low-income project on the south side of the street. They're sharing a forty-ounce malt wrapped in a brown paper bag, clowning around, the girl shrieking from time to time. Across the road, Angel's building is one of the block's few bright spots, three tenements renovated to form a single building, its central entrance protected by a wrought-iron gate heavy enough to fend off the Mongol hordes.

Carter's prepared to wait for hours if necessary. He's looking as much for Bobby Ditto as for Angel. He's thinking Bobby, or whoever he sends, will initially do what Carter's done, which is put the apartment under surveillance. But Carter's overestimated the patience of New York mobsters. Not ten minutes after he settles down, the wrought-iron gate swings open to reveal Angel Tamanaka accompanied by two men. The younger of the two walks on Angel's left. He's got a jacket, a woman's jacket, folded over his left arm, which is pointed at Angel's ribcage. His right hand grips the back of her neck.

Fish or cut bait, engage or withdraw. Carter has no more than a few seconds to decide. Then the second man, much the older of the two, reaches out to squeeze Angel's ass, his thin lips parting in a grin as cruel as it is narcissistic. He's got the power, the juice. He can do anything he wants to this disposable human being. Can and will.

Carter exits through the side door of the van. Angel and her escorts, still fifty feet away, are walking right toward him. He ambles in their direction, moving to the outside of the man presumably holding a gun. When he comes within striking distance, he steps in front of the man and pulls the left side of his jacket away from his body, revealing his own weapon. Instinctively, the man brings his gun to bear on the threat.

Carter waits until the gangster's hand moves a few inches before driving his foot into the man's crotch with all the considerable force at his command, a snap kick against which the man has no defense. Almost in the same motion, he draws his Colt and slams it into the side of the man's head.

One down and one to go. Carter levels the gun at the second man, who stands frozen in place, immobile as a department store manikin.

'You move, you're dead,' Carter explains. Then he asks, 'What did I just say?'

'Don't worry. I'm not packing.'

Carter repeats the question. 'What did I just say?'

'If I move, you'll kill me.'

Carter squats and strips the gun, a semi-automatic Glock, from the hand of the first man, who rolls on to his back and groans. Carter ignores the blood running along the man's face and neck. He rummages through the man's jacket and discovers a cellphone. The cellphone goes into his pocket, the gun beneath his waistband.

'Are you the brother?' he asks the older man as he rises to his feet.

'Whose brother?'

The man has a narrow face, a hatchet face, dominated by a sharp hollow nose that reminds Carter of a triangular sail on a racing yacht. He stares at Carter through contemptuous eyes, having apparently concluded that Carter's not going to kill him. But not killing and not hurting are two different things. Carter slaps the man across the face with his free hand, the crack loud enough to arouse the kids across the street. They erupt in a chorus of encouraging whoops.

'Are you the brother?' Carter asks again.

The man's eyes now project rage, impotent rage, helpless rage. But he has no choice. He has to answer. 'No,' he says, 'I'm not.'

Carter doesn't dispute the claim. The man looks nothing like Ricky Ditto. He steps close to him, jamming the revolver into his gut, and pats him down. No gun. Carter gestures to the man on the ground, who's managed to rise to his knees and is now vomiting on to the sidewalk.

'I want you to pick up your buddy and walk to the end of the block. If you turn around before I'm gone, I'll kill you, witnesses or not. And you tell the brother he should heat up the cappuccino. I'll be comin' to visit.'

EIGHT

Angel can't stop shaking. She's shaking when Carter takes her hand, when he leads her to the van and puts her inside, when he drives north to 125th Street, then cross-town and over the Triborough Bridge into Queens. She's shaking when he parks at the Pilgrim Diner on Astoria Boulevard, when he takes her inside, when he orders coffee and apple turnovers for both of them. There's a little voice in her head that keeps saying, 'It's not fair.' There's another little voice that keeps saying, 'So what?'

When she tries to lift her coffee cup, she spills hot coffee on her hand.

'Are you going to say anything?' she finally demands.

That brings a smile to Carter's face, a somewhat lopsided smile that reveals a chipped incisor on the left side of his mouth. 'This is what I get for saving your life? Not to mention your honor?'

Angel doesn't rise to the bait. 'They said they were cops. The older one had a badge.' She shakes her head. 'I never should have opened the door.'

'They probably would've kicked it down. Subtlety's not their thing. Patience either.'

Angel cuts through the apple turnover with the edge of her fork, spears a piece and shovels it into her mouth. 'Damn, this is really good.'

'They do their own baking.' Carter picks up his turnover with his fingers and takes a bite. The crust flakes off beneath his teeth. 'The Pilgrim's been feeding the cab drivers who work LaGuardia Airport for fifty years. Sometimes I come here at three o'clock in the morning just for the smell.'

The only thing Angel can smell is her own fear. 'I don't get it, how you can be so calm? Do you do this every day?'

'No, not every day. But I've done similar things often enough to use the adrenal rush to my advantage.'

'Does that mean you weren't afraid?'

'I was afraid that I'd have to shoot them, which I didn't want to do.'

Angel feels a sudden rush of pure rage. The one with the hatchet face had the cruelest smile she'd ever seen, not to mention the fact that his eyes were filled with lust and he'd threatened to rip her flesh off with a pair of pliers.

'I wish you had,' she says. 'I wish you'd killed both of them.'

'Too many witnesses.' He gestures to her cup. 'Finish your coffee and I'll drop you off wherever you want. By the way, did they tell you who they were?'

'They said something about a man named Bobby. Like I was supposed to recognize the name.'

'That would be a mobster named Bobby Ditto. His brother,

the one who's dead, was named Ricky Ditto. Their actual last name is Benedetti. Somehow, Bobby discovered that you and Ricky had a date that afternoon.'

'How did he find out my name and address? The old guy, the one with the hatchet face, called me Angel.'

'Most likely from your pimp . . .'

'My agent.' Angel sighs. She's finally slowing down and she wonders how far she'll fall. Last time, after Carter shot Dr Rick, she slept for twelve hours straight. She glances around the diner, at all the Pilgrim kitsch. There's a plaster turkey in every corner. 'I have nowhere to go,' she finally says.

'How about your folks?'

'My father's dead and my mother's a drunk. Last I heard, she was living in a shelter.'

'What do you want me to do? I—'

Angel cuts him off. 'I want you to do what you said you were going to do. Go after that . . . that Bobby Ditto.'

'Sorry, Angel, I only meant to worry them. Bobby Ditto's not a threat, not to me.'

'Then why did you interfere?'

Carter's eyes dart to the diner's entrance. Two men have just come through the door. Thickly built, they wear wife-beater T-shirts that reveal jailhouse tattooing on their upper chests and arms. When they take seats at the counter, he turns back to Angel.

'I only came to warn you.'

'But you didn't just warn me. You got involved and I'd like to know why.'

Carter shakes his head. He's not going there. But Angel's not fooled and she's not stupid. He either wants her body or he has a conscience, despite his profession. And it has to be number two because he intends to drop her off. Unless, of course, he wants a quickie in the van. Angel represses a smile. Everything about Carter intrigues her, from his nerdy front, to his stunning (lucky for her) proficiency, to his confidence, to his white-knight heroics.

'Like I said, I only came to warn you.'

'OK, but the fact is that you kicked the crap out of one of them and scared the crap out of the other one. I could see it in his eyes. He definitely thought you were gonna kill him. But you didn't, right? And now you and me, we're joined together in their minds. We're joined together and my name is the only one they know, which means they're gonna keep looking for me.'

Carter's trying to think of what to say – her logic is impeccable – when Angel's cell punches out the opening notes to Lady Gaga's 'Poker Face'. He nods when Angel looks up at him. Her life is no business of his. Then she puts the phone to her ear and her already grim expression darkens.

'What? What? That can't be.'

But it is, because when she hangs up a minute later, Angel hasn't brightened. She tilts her chin up to meet his gaze and Carter realizes that her eyes aren't black after all. They're an impossible indigo that reminds him of the blue of the sky just before dark in the mountains around Tora Bora.

'That was Pierre's wife, Jeanne-Marie. Pierre's dead. As in shot, killed, murdered.' Angel looks down at the table. She's shaking again. 'Holy shit, what the fuck have you done to me? To me and the rest of the girls. Because the only thing they stole was Pierre's computer. And they didn't even take that. They just took the hard drive.'

'You want some more coffee?'

'Is that supposed to be funny?'

'Probably not. So, what about an almond horn? The marzipan filling? It's unbelievable.'

Carter's remembering the first few minutes after a firefight. You were alive and that was enough. Tomorrow morning, you'd wake up on the right side of the grass. Carter's been in dozens of firefights, in Asia and in Africa, and come through uninjured, a blessing he doesn't attribute to his own skills. Better men died before his eyes.

'Do you have a name?'

'Carter.'

'Well, here's the thing, Carter. I left home unexpectedly and I somehow forgot to take my purse. That means I've got nothing, no clothes, no identification, no money, no credit cards, no debit card. I've got nothing and it's your fault.'

'Actually, I'm blaming the whole thing on Ricky's wife and children.'

'Say again?'

'We were both in Ricky Ditto's house because his family was somewhere else. We were there to take advantage of that fact in order to advance our individual interests. Myself, I'd never kill a man in front of his family, and I assume you apply the same principle to your own work.'

'Actually, one guy snuck me down in the basement while his wife was upstairs. He had this fantasy about a sex slave . . .' Angel stops when Carter begins to laugh. So far, so good. 'You said something about more coffee.'

'Sure, you want another Danish?'

'No, too sweet for me. Just the coffee. I have the feeling it's gonna be a long night.' Angel's further encouraged when Carter's eyes narrow just the tiniest bit. As men go, he's a difficult read, but lust is lust and men have a hard time concealing their desire. He wants her. She can work with that.

Angel leans back and stares down at the table. There's an imprint on the tabletop of the Pilgrims landing at Plymouth Rock in a rowboat. The man stepping on to the shore has blond hair and a pointy little beard. He carries a staff in his hand, a staff topped with a Christian cross. Just in case any lurking savages should misunderstand his intentions.

'You have to protect me.' Angel runs a finger over the cross as she remembers one of the maxims placed before her at a seminar entitled 'Reach Out: Life Is For The Taking.' The race, Dr Maureen Lippcott had insisted, does not go to the swift or the strong. The race goes to the nimble. Conditions change. Adjust or die.

OK, so the dying part was a bit overdramatic. But you can't control everything. That was the lesson. Just a few weeks ago, she'd read a story in the paper about a man – she can't remember his name – who'd once been in the mortgage writing business. His company went bankrupt after the market crashed, but he'd read the cards before they hit the table. Within a few months, he opened a company that negotiates with banks on behalf of mortgage holders in default.

'You can't leave me to wander the streets,' she says.

'Don't you have any friends?'

Actually, Angel isn't that close to anyone, which is another part of being nimble. You have to be prepared to move on, at least until you reach your final goal. 'First of all, the girls I know are in the same business I am. Second, what's-his-face, that gangster, has Pierre's hard drive. So what I should really do is warn my friends, not visit them. Hey, weren't you listening the first time? Those gangsters came to get me and ran into you. That means we're joined together in their minds. That means they'll be looking for me harder than ever.'

Angel's encouraged by Carter's nod. He's not disputing the facts. But there's something she's not telling him. Almost from the time she became a woman, Angel's been attracted to bad boys. Her first lover, the last time she heard, was doing fifteen years in a federal pen for bank robbery and kidnapping. Angel's always considered this attraction to be a character flaw, one certain, if indulged, to negatively impact her life plan. But now she's sitting across from the baddest bad boy in New York and she's got nowhere to go.

'You have to protect me,' she declares. 'You can't wash your hands and walk away.'

Carter stares down at his sticky fingers, then wets his napkin and wipes them off. 'You want me to take you home?'

'I . . .' Angel shrugs, then says, 'Yes, you have to. Otherwise, I have no chance.'

'Sure you have a chance. You can go to your apartment right now, pack a few bags and take off.'

'What if they're waiting for me?'

'If a chance was certainty, they wouldn't call it chance.'

'Is that supposed to be funny?'

'OK, Angel, let's suppose I take you back to my home, that we tangle up our lives. What do you think will happen if you become a threat to me somewhere down the line?'

It's a good question, which Angel freely admits. But there's another item on her agenda, one she's not quite ready to reveal, not until she's softened him up a little more. She snaps her fingers. 'I've got an idea. You can train me to do what you do. That way I'll be able to fight back.'

'That's cute, Angel, but it doesn't answer the question.'

'You think I can't do it? Hey, Carter, I've already got the memoir planned. *From Ho to Hit Bitch: A Transformative Journey*. It's guaranteed to be a number one selection of Oprah's Book Club. I'll sell millions of copies and retire to my yacht in the Bahamas.'

Angel nods encouragement when Carter's smile becomes a laugh. That little glimmer of lust she noted before has now blossomed. It's burning white-hot. She looks down at the disembarking Pilgrim and says, 'There's something else, Carter. Ricky Ditto liked to brag. He bragged from the minute he picked me up until you shot him. Along the way, he told me about his houses and his businesses and what a tough guy he was. In my world, the customer's always right, so I encouraged him to a certain extent. Anyway, Ricky made this left turn off Broadway just after we came into the Bronx. There was a hillside covered with trees – it was too steep for buildings – and we were about halfway there when he pointed at this apartment house. Here's what he told me, Carter. Ricky said there was an apartment in that building with three hundred thousand dollars under the floorboards.'

Carter signals to the waitress for a check, which she has ready. The diner's crowded and she's anxious to clear the table. Carter picks up the check and slides out of the booth, with Angel following closely behind. As they wait for the cashier to ring up the check, one of the tattooed men spins on his stool to openly stare at Angel's breasts. Then he looks into Carter's eyes, discovers an even darker version of himself and returns to his meatloaf.

Angel is more beautiful naked than dressed. She's an altar at which Carter can bring himself to worship. But Carter doesn't fool himself. When he runs his mouth along Angel's inner thigh, from her crotch to the back of her knee, he doesn't assume the guttural sound rumbling up from her chest indicates passion of any kind. Same for the twitch of a muscle just below her navel and the pressure of her manicured nails on the back of his head. Feigning passion is a necessary skill in the sex worker business. But then, twenty minutes later, Carter finds himself confronted by the unexpected.

Angel's face reddens, then her neck and her shoulders, the rush of blood leaving her skin the color of a sunburn. They're both soaked with sweat by now, and they're changing positions with the agility of performing dolphins. When Carter finally explodes, his orgasm is as powerful as any he's ever known.

A few minutes later, Carter's lying on the wet sheets, his hand over his eyes, trying to catch his breath, when he feels a second release. Janie's passing? Paulie's email? Carter's ship has sailed without his noticing. He's in the deep water now, and there's no turning back, the shore already lost to sight. Angel's lips are on his throat. Ready or not, here I . . . Well, it might take a while before they get to the last part.

'Tell me the truth.' Angel leans forward, until her breasts fall lightly against Carter's chest. 'Am I worth a thousand dollars?'

'Did you say you wanted the truth?'

'Absolutely.'

'I wouldn't go more than nine-fifty.'

Angel jabs a finger into his belly. 'Damn, you're hard everywhere. It's amazing. The men I've known in my life? If they had a body like yours, they'd be wearing sleeveless T-shirts tight enough to pass for girdles.'

When Carter doesn't reply, Angel jumps up, walks naked across the room and begins to rummage in a chest of drawers. Her movements seem perfectly natural, as if she's totally unaware of the predictable effect her bouncing buttocks have on Leonard Carter. But then she looks back over her shoulder, a wicked gleam in her eyes.

The face of an angel? The soul of a whore? Every man's fantasy come to life? Carter feels like someone nailed his eyes to her ass.

'Here, this'll do.'

Angel spins around to display a summer-weight pajama bottom. She jumps on the bed, her breathing shallow, and works the pajama legs through the slats on the headboard. Then she ties his wrists. This is all play, of course, and Carter knows he can pull his hands free at any time. But then Angel lays a pillowcase over his eyes, tucks the ends beneath his head, and the game becomes more interesting. Carter holds his breath while Angel runs a fingernail across his chest, gently, slowly. Then she takes his left nipple into her mouth and gives it a tug.

Even as the inevitable, inescapable groan passes his lips, Carter's thinking, yes, the ship has definitely sailed; yes, it's in the deep water; no, I can't see the goddamned shore. But then he realizes there's nothing new here. His ship has sailed many times: when he left the military, when he left Iraq after the collapse of Coldstream Military Options, when he left Africa with the blood money in his pocket. No, there's nothing new here, except for Angel, except for him flopping on the bed like a hooked fish.

And then there's the money.

NINE

Bobby Ditto's pissed, as usual. He's pissed about the steady drizzle, the unseasonably low temperatures, the traffic, a car that stalls at every light ('What? I bought a fuckin' Audi for this?') and especially the situation. Bobby's traveling from his home in Bay Ridge, Brooklyn, to Paulie Margarine's house in Astoria, Queens, and he's coming alone, hat in his hand. He's scared, too, though he can't admit it.

Bobby parks the car in Paulie's driveway, a liberty which makes him feel slightly better about himself. Then he walks into the house without being invited when Paulie's kid, Freddy, answers the door.

'You could take a seat in the living room.' A year out of prison, Freddy's not all that impressed. 'My father's with his nurse. He's havin' a treatment.'

And there he is, Bobby Ditto, cooling his heels on a couch that's seen better days, in a room that hasn't been dusted in a month. And no coffee, either. Just sit your ass down, keep your mouth shut and wait.

Bobby only recovers his equilibrium when Freddy wheels

his father into the room. Paulie halfway to dead, maybe more than halfway. His skin's the color of puke and he's so weak he can barely take Bobby's hand.

'So?' Paulie says after Freddy makes an exit. 'What's up that couldn't wait till after my funeral?'

'Hey, Paulie, I'm sorry for your illness. And you could trust me on this, I wouldn't be here if it wasn't important.' Bobby leans forward to place his hands on his knees. An exercise fanatic who ups the ante with a steroid soup injected by his trainer, Bobby's the physical opposite of his deceased brother. He's terminally ambitious, as well, and prefers to get his way through intimidation whenever possible. But he has no juice here, not with Paulie Margarine. Paulie's old school. He doesn't scare. In fact, right now, he seems to be falling asleep.

'Paulie,' Bobby says, 'you still with us?'

Paulie's eyelids part a few millimeters and he smiles. 'Sorry, man, but I took a couple of pain pills and they're just kickin' in. Hey, you wanna hear somethin' funny? The shit they're givin' me, if I had to buy it on the street I'd go bankrupt.'

'I hear you loud and clear. If we were drinkin', I'd raise a toast to the war on drugs.'

'And I'd drink to that toast. If I still had a liver.'

Bobby chuckles. 'Tell me, Paulie, you ever do somethin', somethin' you thought about for a long time, somethin' that seemed a hundred percent right, only it went completely wrong?'

'Yeah, sure.'

'Well, this business with my brother, it's blowin' up in my face.' Bobby stares for a moment at a shelf lined with tarnished bowling trophies. 'Ya know, I had to do something about Ricky bein' whacked. That's our way of life, right? That's what everyone expects.'

Paulie's eyes are closing. 'It's our way,' he agrees.

'OK, so I find out from Ricky's friend that Ricky had a date with this whore on the day he got hit. Then I find out the whore's name and where she lives – I won't say how – and I send the Blade and a kid named Ruben Amaroso to pick her up. So they snatch her in her apartment and they're bringin' her out, no problem, right? Then, outta nowhere, they run into this guy, he's like a fuckin' freak. He kicks the shit out of Ruby, puts a gun to the Blade's head and tells the Blade that he's comin' after yours truly, meaning me. Then him and the whore take off together, only God knows where.'

Paulie takes a long time answering, but he finally mumbles a reply. His pupils are small enough to be a period at the end of a sentence. 'So, why are you comin' to me?'

'You put out the hit.'

'See, Bobby, that's where you're wrong. You were the one who put out the contract. I only connected you to a contractor. The whole thing was your idea.'

Bobby Ditto taps his finger on the arm of the chair. Bobby hadn't exactly *hated* his brother. Ricky was OK, but he was in the wrong business, what with his big mouth. Plus, in Bobby's opinion, he was definitely soft. If the Feds got their hooks into him, he'd turn rat for sure. And he didn't contribute, either, not where it counted. The business they're in, it's all about muscle. They dealt with Mexicans, Colombians, Russians and half the black gangs in Brownville and South Jamaica. Meantime, Ricky hadn't even made his bones.

'I'm not here to put any blame on you, Paulie. I'm here because I need a line on this guy you hired.'

'I didn't hire him, you did.'

'OK, OK, I get it. But how did he get connected to the whore? Because I was thinkin' I'd take out the whore and the pimp, and that would be it. Bobby's been avenged, no harm, no foul. That's what I meant by doin' somethin' you know is a hundred percent right, only it goes wrong.'

Paulie's perking up a bit, the story having caught his attention. 'First thing, how do you know the guy who took the whore is the guy who whacked Ricky?'

'According to the Blade, the guy said, "You tell the brother to heat up the cappuccino because I'll be comin' to visit."' Bobby feels the muscles in his arms and legs tighten. 'Hey, you know me for a long time. I been threatened before. Only before, I knew who was makin' the threats. Before, I could do somethin' about it. Now I gotta sit and wait.'

Paulie knows exactly how Bobby Ditto feels. He was in the same place only a couple of years before, a place called helpless. 'From what you say, it's gotta be our guy who saved the whore's ass. But about the reason I got no idea. None whatsoever. Me and our guy, we don't socialize.'

'I hear ya.' Bobby does hear Paulie, especially the part about *our* guy. Now he'll have to beg when what he'd like to do is yank this fuckin' gimp out of his wheelchair and put a knife to his eyeball. 'What I need, Paulie, is a heads-up. I can't give this guy the first move. I mean, he killed Ricky in Ricky's own house, so now I gotta worry every time I come home about what's on the other side of the door.'

'Or what's comin' through the door while you're asleep.' Paulie raises a hand, palm out. 'But the thing is, my job, as a middleman, is to protect you and him both.'

'And that means you didn't tell him, right? About me?'

Paulie's answer is prompt, since he's already anticipated the question. Plus, Freddy's waiting in the kitchen with a shotgun. 'Most likely this is comin' from the whore. Or maybe our guy did his homework. What's certain is that he's involved with the whore some kinda way. He was probably comin' by for a quick hump when he ran into the Blade and Ruby.'

'Yeah, maybe.' Bobby Ditto rubs his fingers over his chin. He's a heavily bearded man, his five o'clock shadow commonly visible at ten in the morning. 'Look, our guy, he's good, right? Or else you wouldn't use him.'

'He's the best.'

'OK, he's the best. But from what you said, he's not connected to our thing.'

'Also true.'

Bobby takes a thick envelope from the pocket of his sport jacket and drops it in Paulie Margarine's lap. 'I need some help here, Paulie. Otherwise, I'm not gonna see him comin'.' He gestures toward the envelope. 'There's five grand in there.'

'You want me to sell out? That's what you're askin'?'

'It's *our* thing, our *cosa nostra*, not his.'

There's an unspoken threat here, one that Paulie's quick to recognize. Paulie was present at Bobby Ditto's christening.

Back in the day, he and Bobby's father worked together on deals. So it's not a hard choice for Paulie, since refusing a favor of this kind might easily result in a war.

'You know what's gonna happen if our guy puts two and two together?' Paulie answers his own question. 'He's gonna come after me and Freddy. That's a lotta risk. Plus, I don't really know all that much about him. In fact, I hardly know *anything* about him. So, be warned in advance. You might be puttin' out your dough for nothin'.'

'Hey, you gotta have a way to get in touch with him.'

'Yeah, by email, which I send off to a website in Belarus.'

'Bela who?'

'It's a little country near Russia.'

'And that's where he lives?'

'No, Bobby, it's not where he lives, which is the whole point I'm tryin' to make.' Paulie holds the envelope between bony fingers. 'You want, I'll put this in my pocket. You wanna take it back, no hard feelings.'

'Just tell me, Paulie. I got no choice here.'

'He's an American who goes by the name of Carter, which could be his first or his last name. He was a mercenary at some point and he was involved with a British officer named Montgomery Thorpe. That's it . . . no wait. You remember a couple years back when I lost a few soldiers?'

'Yeah, you had a problem with some kinda raghead gang, right?'

'Uh-uh. It had nothing to do with them. What happened to me was Carter, all by himself. So if I was in your shoes, Bobby, what I'd do is take a vacation.'

TEN

Carter's feeling pretty good about the surveillance he and Angel conduct. The rain-speckled windshield conceals their presence in the back seat of the van, while the spatter of rain on the van's roof provides enough white noise to cover their conversation. They could stay here all day without being noticed. Around and behind them, the block is entirely residential, the foot traffic light. Before them, on the far side of the street, a six-story apartment building squats on a corner lot, its double-glass lobby doors in full view. The building is just ornate enough, with its scroll-and-bracket lintels, to have a name – Wilson Arms – set in stone above the doors. According to Angel Tamanaka, there's a buried treasure somewhere inside.

Carter's not entirely convinced. They'd wandered through the neighborhood for twenty minutes before they came upon the building, passing a dozen similar apartment houses, though none situated on a corner. The hill, on the other hand, the one Angel first mentioned, is where it should be, just two blocks away. Covered with trees and brush, and at least a hundred feet high, it's steep enough to pass for a cliff.

The hill is only a small piece of the bedrock that first emerges, like the spine of a half-buried fossil, at 72nd Street on the West Side of Manhattan. This far north, it separates the Latino-dominated neighborhood they're in, Kingsbridge, from the more affluent neighborhood of Scarsdale, site of Ricky Ditto's home. Angel and Ricky might easily have passed this corner on the way to his assassination.

'Do you have a goal?' Angel asks without warning. 'I mean, like a *life* plan?'

Carter doesn't reply immediately. The question feels like an ambush and he can't remember the last time he spoke about his personal life. Carter's the man nobody knows, the invisible man, a shadow in a city of shadows. Still, it's already a time of firsts because now there's someone on the planet, besides Paulie Margarine, who knows what he does for a living. Or used to do.

'I have a today plan,' he finally says, 'and a tomorrow plan.'

'And that's it?'

'Pretty much.'

'Not me. And this could be the end of part one.'

'Which is?'

'Capital accumulation. Remember, unless you have some kind of special talent, which I don't, it takes money to make money.'

'What about your looks?'

'OK, then my appearance is my only gift and I intend to make the best of it. You play the hand you're dealt, right? If you're smart?'

Carter lays his hands on the seat-back in front of him. It's all he can do to keep them off Angel's legs. He's convinced her to forego make-up and dress down, but even in a shapeless K-Mart skirt and blouse, she's still conspicuous.

'What about part two? What are you going to do with all that capital?'

'It's a long story, but if you want to hear it . . .'

'We have plenty of time.'

Carter settles back, remembering night watches in the Afghan deserts and Congo rain forests, nights when his fellow soldiers whispered their tales into the darkness. Over time, he'd come to relish the stories and the intimate setting, nobody going anywhere soon. On moonless nights in Afghanistan, the stars seemed inches above his head. In Africa, the dark was filled with the furtive sounds of nocturnal animals that scurried through the trees or prowled the jungle floor. Did the snapping of a twig signal the passing of a leopard? Or the approach of an enemy?

'How long do you plan to be here?' Angel asks.

'A couple of hours, maybe more.' He smiles when Angel lays her hand on his shoulder, the gesture as casual as it is calculating. 'Unless you think we should go knocking on doors. "Excuse me, but do you happen to have hundreds of thousands of dollars buried under the floorboards?"'

Angel props her knees against the top of the seat-back and her skirt slips to mid-thigh. 'OK, so I began to put my life plan together when I first came to New York. I was barely eighteen and I was staying with my cousin while I looked for a job. Of course—' Angel stops abruptly when the doors open across the street and a man holding a black umbrella steps on to the sidewalk, turns left and heads toward Broadway.

'So, you're staying with your cousin,' Carter prompts.

'Yes, right, and it worked out OK because Rita was a private duty nurse and she did sixteen hour shifts. I hardly saw her. Anyway, New York is a pretty strange place to get used to when the only place you really know about is a Seattle suburb. The dirt, the noise, especially the subway . . . I was like totally unprepared. But New York is awesome, too. There's so much energy, half the time I felt like the city was dragging me around by the collar. I wanted to go everywhere, see everything and I visited all the tourist places, Central Park, the museums, Soho, the Statue of Liberty. I even took a ride on the Staten Island Ferry. Guys tried to pick me up, of course, practically every minute, but Rita gave me this warning when I first arrived, about serial killers and sadistic rapists and how New York men couldn't be trusted, so I stayed by myself a lot of the time. I still do, really. I mostly stay by myself.'

The statement seems worthy of comment, but Carter only shifts on the bench seat. The rain is falling harder now.

'OK, so one night around seven o'clock, I was up by Lincoln Center, hanging around the plaza near the fountain. Lincoln Center just glows at twilight – it's still one of my favorite places – but that night was definitely special for me. All of a sudden, these stretch limos began to arrive, one after another, Lincolns and Cadillacs and Mercedes Benzes, and even a stretch Hummer. I moved over to watch for celebrities, me and almost everyone else in the plaza, but I didn't recognize anybody, which was maybe for the best. The people who got out of those limos and walked into Avery Fisher Hall were kind of ordinary, short and tall, skinny and fat, young and old, except for the way they were dressed. All the men wore tuxedos and the women wore evening gowns made of every color and fabric known to man. It was like a moving rainbow. And the jewelry, especially the necklaces . . . One woman, I swear, had an emerald the size of my fist that bounced on her cleavage. Another woman – she had to be like eighty – wore so many diamonds you couldn't see her chest. Those diamonds were spitting fire, Carter. I swear it hurt my eyes to look at them. They were like alien death rays.'

Angel's little laugh stops abruptly when a BMW pulls to the curb across the street and the door opens. A man carrying a small gym bag steps out into the rain, dashes the few feet to the Wilson Arms' entrance way and disappears through the glass doors. The man is hatless and the white bandage above his left ear jumps across the street, as penetrating, in its own way, as the glitter of diamonds on a dowager's chest.

Angel looks at Carter. He's staring through the streaked windshield with the cold, blank eyes of a predatory fish. Oh look, dinner.

'Carter?'

'Hang on a minute.'

The minute becomes ten, during which Angel considers her options. She likes Carter well enough, and he definitely turns her on. Better yet, the attraction is mutual. But she has to look to the future. Does Carter fit into her plan? Yes, if they're successful and they split the pot. But how does she know he'll pay off? And what is she prepared to do if he doesn't? Is she supposed to trust him? A man with the eyes of a shark? Compared to Carter, Ricky Ditto's black eyes were touchy-feely.

Carter takes a deep breath. 'All right,' he says.

'What were you looking for?'

'A light to come on in one of the apartments. That would probably have told us which apartment he went to. No luck, though.'

'You think, wherever he went, there had to be someone already there?'

'Not necessarily. He might have gone to an apartment with windows in the back. And it's not that dark, even with the overcast. He could be making do.' He turns to look at Angel, his eyes now amused. 'You were right, Angel. The dearly departed Ricky Ditto was definitely connected to the building.'

Angel's pleased when Carter's gaze, as it shifts from her eyes to the van's windshield, briefly settles on her breasts. She's unbuttoned the top three buttons of her dowdy blouse, the better to tease him with. Carter likes to be teased, as Angel likes to tease.

'So, what now?'

'We need intelligence, and I think I know just the cop to get it from. Meanwhile, we sit.' Carter drops his hands to his lap. 'So, you're on the plaza at Lincoln Center and there are all these rich people . . .'

Angel takes a moment. Her story is essentially true, but she wants it to be entertaining as well. 'I think I was dazzled at first,' she finally says. 'But after a while I began to see a pattern that caught my attention. More than half the women were much, much younger than the men, at least twenty years. I saw a lot of men in their fifties with wives in their thirties, and a few in their forties with wives in their twenties, but all of the women had diamond rings – and I'm talkin' big, Carter – on their left hands.'

Angel holds up her own left hand with its unadorned ring finger. 'So, like, they troop inside and go up this flight of stairs to the second floor and then down this long promenade. Avery Fisher Hall has two-story floor-to-ceiling windows and I watched the parade for a while. That's when I realized that some of the women were in their fifties, while the men were really old. I saw two women actually pushing wheelchairs. Amazing, right? But you know what? These women were seeing their husbands into the grave. They were keeping their end of the deal.'

'The trophy wife deal?' Carter smiles. 'That's what you want, Angel? To be a trophy wife?'

'Hey, remember those Marilyn Monroe movies, *How to Marry a Millionaire* and *Gentlemen Prefer Blondes*?' Angel shakes her head. 'Do me a favor, give me the name of a young girl out there who dreams of marrying a poor man. And while you're at it, show me the twelve-year-old who doesn't dream of a platinum wedding in the Plaza Hotel. Instead of a K-Mart wedding at the American Legion Hall.'

Carter's about to concede the point when Ruby Amaroso, still toting the gym bag, exits the Wilson Arms and dashes to his car. When he pulls away from the curb, Carter works his way into the front seat and starts the van.

'So, what do you think, Angel? Is he bringing money in or taking it out?'

'Why? Are you going to steal the bag?'

Carter shakes his head. 'We're not giving up the element of surprise for an unknown reward. Did Ricky say anything about what he did for a living?'

'He hinted that he was some kind of gangster.'

'Gangster covers a lot of ground, but if he was dealing drugs, especially on a wholesale level, he'd have money stashed somewhere, a lot of money. And that stash would most likely be in a place nobody would suspect. But I'm getting ahead of myself. We need more information.'

'Does that mean you're going to do it? You're going to rip them off?'

'It means I'm real interested.'

Carter turns on to Broadway, giving the BMW plenty of room. He drops his hand to Angel's knee and runs a finger along the inside of her thigh. She responds by kissing the side of his neck.

'Tell me more about your gold digger scheme,' he says. 'Tell me why you need capital.'

'OK, my plan is to go to the Caribbean once I have my stake in place – to St Barts or Tobago where you get an international crowd – and open a small art gallery. But suppose I went there broke. How long would I last before I became somebody's mistress? These men, the ones I'm talking about, they know how to play rough, especially if a girl doesn't have options. That's what having your own money really does. It gives you options.'

'I won't argue the point, but I have one question. Have you ever considered a plan B?'

'Which is?'

'Hard work, education?'

Angel doesn't respond and they follow the BMW over the Broadway Bridge and into Manhattan. By the time they pass Columbia University, Carter knows exactly where the gangster's headed. He's on his way to Angel's apartment where he finally pulls to the curb beside a fire hydrant and settles in to watch the entrance to her building. Carter drives on past, makes a right on to West End Avenue, then double-parks.

'What are you going to do?' Angel asks.

'Send a message.'

'A message.'

'I want to concentrate Bobby Ditto's attention. I want him to be more worried about his own skin than his money in the Bronx.'

'Are you going to take the bag?'

'Absolutely not.'

A car slides away from the curb and Carter pulls the van into the open slot. Angel can almost see the neurons firing away in his brain. Without warning, a single thought grabs her own attention: Get away from this man. Even if you have to sleep in the goddamned subway, even if you have to go home with the first jerk you meet in a corner bar. Carter's traveling a road that has nothing to do with Angel Tamanaka and her plans for the future.

'OK, Angel, here's the way I want it to go down. We circle around the block so that we come up behind him. I want you to walk ahead of me, understand? You walk right past him, turn the corner, jump into the back of the van and stay down. I'll take care of the rest.'

'Which is exactly what?'

'That depends. If there are witnesses, I'll have to settle for a beating. If we're alone on the block, I'm going to kill him. You understand, Angel. When he picked up the gun, he lost his right to live. He became a warrior and all wars have casualties.'

Angel doesn't mistake the warning. If she helps him now, she'll be picking up a gun of her own. And she understands what he means about the right to live. You can't take human life and claim your own life to be somehow sacred. And there's one other thing. If she goes along, she becomes an accomplice, an outlaw, in her own eyes and in the eyes of the police.

'Why do you want me to walk past him?'

'First, to distract him. Beyond that? Look, he fucked up last time out. Now he has a shot at redemption. I think he'll try to force you into the car. With a little luck, he won't notice me until I'm on top of him.'

The conflicts ricochet through her mind, the pros and cons, the costs and benefits, the risks and the rewards. Much too fast to be weighed. Angel feels only the ascension of some wild piece of herself, a chained demon suddenly freed and all the more powerful for its long imprisonment.

'Just walk past him, right? Walk past and keep on going?'

'That's right.' Carter leans forward to detach the knife strapped to his left calf. He slides it behind the waistband of his khaki pants. 'Just walk past him and keep on going no matter what. Even if he somehow takes me out, you'll be safe.'

'OK, I'll do it.'

ELEVEN

Carter's time with Paulie has taught him that most gangsters, no matter how tough, are poorly trained and unpracticed. Maybe they'll fight at the drop of a hat, maybe they'll kill you and go to lunch afterward, but they lack the skills to effectively defend themselves. He follows Angel down the block, she beneath a blue umbrella, he on the opposite side of the street and slightly behind, moving in the shadows. The rain is falling hard, the entire block deserted. There's not a surveillance camera in sight.

The gangster produces a double take worthy of a silent movie comedian when Angel walks by, his hand already groping for the door's handle. He opens the door, slides out into the rain and takes a step, the possibility that he's the hunted, not the hunter, never entering his mind.

Carter makes contact before his target reaches the end of the BMW's hood, his left hand grabbing the man's shoulder while his thumb probes for the space between two ribs. Then he punches the dagger's blade directly into Ruby Amaroso's heart, the impact so hard and sudden the man barely manages a grunt before his eyes close and his knees give out.

Carter guides the body, as it falls, between the BMW and the car in front. Then he walks off without looking to the right or the left, or even removing the knife, mission accomplished, Carter just another pedestrian going about his business. Thirty seconds later, he's in the van, buckling his seat belt as he starts the engine. He glances in the rear-view mirror as he pulls away, at Angel Tamanaka, at Angel Face, huddled against the side of the van.

Welcome to the Hell World, kid.

Though aware of serial killers and their predilections, Carter never before associated the act of murder with any variety of sexual charge, not until he and Angel come through the door and begin to yank at each other's clothes. Only then, as she lies beneath him, her heels on his shoulders, he thrusting into her, two animals in rut on the carpet in his sister's living room, does he acknowledge the relationship. This is not a marathon, this encounter, it's a sprint; the both of them going all-out. Angel's lips are pressed together, her eyes narrowed, brow furrowed. She seems angry to Carter, and not without reason. But Carter doesn't care. He just knows that he wants her today and he'll want her tomorrow, and that's the end of his life plan.

They feast afterwards, on tapas from a Spanish restaurant on Woodhaven Boulevard. Avocado toast, chickpeas with garlic and parsley oil, farmhouse toast and figs with ham. They stuff themselves, then shower together before Angel's adrenals finally shut down and she flops naked on to their bed. Carter drops down beside her. He's feeling a kind of buyer's remorse, like an animal who's wandered into a dark space and now smells a trap.

'You want to hear the answer?' Angel says.

'To what question?'

'The one about why I don't choose plan B – hard work and education.'

Carter rolls up on to an elbow. 'You don't have to explain yourself to me. I was only kidding.'

'No, I want to. I want you to know where I'm coming from.' Angel strokes the side of Carter's face. 'My grandfather, Yoshi Tamanaka, was born in Seattle in 1928. Like every West Coast Japanese citizen, he spent World War Two in an internment camp – you'll notice that American historians never say *concentration* camp – along with the rest of the family. Grampa was seventeen at the end of the war and he went to school for a couple of years before opening a lumber yard near Green

Lake, north of Seattle. You might say he got lucky, because the Interstate Highway System came right past the town and linked him to builders in neighboring counties. His business was still growing when he passed it on to my dad in 1988. That would be Hideki Tamanaka. Dad devoted his life to nurturing his inheritance. Ten hours a day, twelve, fourteen – he didn't run his business, or his life, by the clock. Shoulder to the wheel, nose to grindstone. Dad was a grab-your-boot-straps man. He loved Richard Nixon's favorite saying, "When the going gets tough, the tough get going." In his mind, hard work equated to success, one to one. Every failure in life was a failure of will.'

Angel rolls up to sit at the edge of the bed, her feet dangling, her back to Carter. She takes a moment before resuming her tale. 'So, what happens is that Home Depot opens a giant lumber yard twenty miles west of dad's. That's in 2001. Then in 2003, Lowe's opens a store fifteen miles to the north. Dad can't buy lumber at the prices they pay, but he doesn't need their margins to make a profit because he runs his operation more efficiently. So he stumbles along for a few years, holding on to whatever clients he can, until Lowe's and Home Depot decide to increase market share by cutting wholesale prices to the bone. Short-term, they don't care if they lose money at one particular store. They've got a hundred other stores backing them up.

'My father was a jerk, Carter. He couldn't admit that he was wrong, that you could work your ass off and still be crushed. When the business went into the red, he borrowed from the banks. When the banks cut him off, he refinanced his house. When that money ran out, he sold off his stocks and emptied the bank accounts. And when there was nothing left, he put a gun to his head and pulled the trigger. My mother was already a hopeless drunk by that time and I don't remember her crying at dad's funeral, though she nearly fell into his grave. What I do remember is spending the next two years, until I graduated high school, with an aunt, then getting my little butt on the first plane out of town.'

Carter sits up and lays a hand on Angel's shoulder. It's not the best story he's ever heard, but it's good enough for a rainy night in New York. 'There's a moral here, a bottom line. I can smell it.'

'Yeah, there's a moral. Forget the bullshit about hard work and personal responsibility. That's just propaganda to keep the peasants on the farm. God blesses the child who's got her own and I intend to get mine.'

TWELVE

Bobby Ditto's thinking that it doesn't just pour when it rains. It shits all over your head. Ruby Amaroso was the most responsible of the young kids Bobby recruited two years ago. When you gave him a job, he got it done, plus he kept the rest of the jerks in place. Now he's in the morgue with a tag on his toe, and yours truly, meaning Roberto Benedetti, is the chief suspect. The cops have been to visit twice, even though Bobby referred them to his mouthpiece when they first showed up.

And now this, the final insult, he has to turn for help to the goddamned Russians and they send him a slanty-eyed chink who doesn't weigh more than a hundred and fifty pounds. A little pussy-boy with a flat-nosed face carved from stone. They're in the bunker and he's offering the chink coffee, but the chink's not showing the slightest respect, for Bobby or for the Blade, who's standing with his back against the wall. No, the jerk's actually refusing Bobby's hospitality.

'See,' Bobby explains, 'I need to know what you can do for me, if anything. This card?' He holds up Louis Chin's business card: XAO INVESTIGATIONS. 'It wouldn't mean a thing to me, even if I could pronounce it.'

'"Zow." It's pronounced "Zow." But I understand that we've been recommended by people you trust.' Chin's thoroughly enjoying the gangster's obvious discomfort. He's worked with the guineas before. As self-centered as drag queens, they have a hard time coping with people who aren't afraid of them.

'Yeah, that's all well and good,' Bobby says, 'but I gotta

know what you can do for me before I tell you my business. And I don't think I need to explain why.'

Chin steeples his fingers. 'Two basic facts. First, there are nineteen hundred private companies under contract to one or another of the federal government's intelligence arms. Second, more than two hundred and sixty-five thousand individuals working for these companies have a Top Secret clearance, which allows them access to sensitive data. Most of these individuals are honest and hard-working, but not all. For a fee, some are willing to pass along information. A smaller number will actually conduct investigations.'

'So, these guys, they're like traitors? They sell information to terrorists?'

'If that's going on, which I very much doubt, it's news to me. What my contacts do is more like what happens at the Motor Vehicle Bureau or the IRS or the various credit agencies. For a fee, they pass data to private investigators.'

Lou Chin recites the pitch more or less from memory. He's a year out of the Marine Corps where he led a company operating in southern Afghanistan and Pakistan. Chin had loved his job and fully expected to make the Marine Corps his permanent home. But then, one cold, moonless night, a mortar round landed two yards from where he crouched on a roof in Kandahar. His three comrades were killed instantly, while he, himself (except for a minor flesh wound tended by a company medic) was uninjured. Four months later, he accepted an honorable discharge and came home, figuring that some higher power had sent him a strongly worded message.

'Why don't you describe your needs,' he concludes, 'and I'll tell you whether or not we can meet them.'

'And you'll guarantee confidentiality, right?'

'Absolutely. We never compromise a client.'

'No, you just sell government secrets.'

Chin spreads his hands and shrugs. Someone's got his fingers wrapped around Bobby Ditto's balls and the gangster lacks the capacity to unwrap those fingers on his own. That's why he's called on Xao Investigations.

'What about money? What about your . . . your fee?'

'One thousand dollars for this consultation, which you've

already paid. The rest depends on what you need.' Chin smiles for the first time, a thin smile that's gone in an instant. 'Which, I suppose, brings us back to square one. I can't very well price our services without knowing what they'll be.'

Louis Chin's wearing tan slacks, an off-white linen jacket and a copper-colored golf shirt. To Bobby Ditto, the clothing looks expensive and sophisticated, which annoys him all the more. He's thinking Chin (whose forebears in America reach back to the California gold rush) should be serving him wonton soup and egg rolls.

'I need a minute to talk it over.' Bobby stands up and motions for the Blade to follow as he walks out of the bunker and closes the door behind him. They're now standing in the warehouse's storage area, surrounded by rolls of substandard carpet that Bobby expects to unload on the New York Housing Authority. 'Whatta ya think, Marco? Is the asshole legit?'

The Blade rubs his nose, an annoying habit that he simply can't break, no matter how much it pisses off his boss. 'What I'm thinkin', Bobby, is that we gotta do somethin'. We can't afford to have this Carter gunnin' for us, not right now.'

The Blade's referring to an upcoming deal, the biggest in the short history of Bobby Ditto's crew, seven kilos of pure heroin at $71,000 per kilo. Bobby's in the process of putting the $497,000 together and he's still got time – the dope won't reach the US for another week or so – but the last thing he needs is some crazed mercenary out to kill him. And for what? To protect a whore?

'I feel like I stepped into a world where nothing makes sense,' he tells the Blade. 'Like I'm on fuckin' Mars.'

'Ditto that,' the Blade responds. 'But here's somethin' to dream about when you go to sleep tonight. You pay this slant-eyes a few grand, which is chump change, and he tells us where to find this Carter guy. Then we snatch Carter, along with his fuckin' whore, and spend a week givin' 'em exactly what they got comin'.'

'A week?'

'A week.'

Bobby Ditto smiles for the first time in days. 'Ya know why I pay you the big bucks?' he asks as he opens the door to the bunker. 'Because you're worth every penny.'

Chin nods when Bobby Ditto resumes his seat. He's come to sell his services and he knows he's succeeded before his client says a word. A good thing, too, because Xao Investigations' entire workforce is limited to a single man with a good front and better connections, a man named Louis Chin who's pretty much surviving day to day.

'All right,' Bobby Ditto says, 'here's what I know. The asshole's an American named Carter. And don't ask me if Carter's a first or a last name, it could be either. What's definite is that he was a mercenary – or still is – and that he hung out with a former British officer, also turned mercenary, by the name of Montgomery Thorpe.'

'That's it?'

'Yeah, that's it.'

'Well, mercenary's a big category. It covers everything from private contractors like Halliburton to rogue units buying opium from the Taliban.' Chin clears his throat. 'Still, from what you've told me about Carter's skills, he has to be ex-military. That means he also has to be in a DOD database.'

'What's DOD?'

'The Department of Defense.'

'And you can get into their computers?'

'Much more than that. The people I use can access parts of the CIA's many databases, and the National Security Agency's, and others besides.'

'And these people, they don't work for the government?'

'They work for private companies under contract to the government. But the important thing, for you, is that if Carter left the military to become a merc, some agency most likely tracked him. That would also hold true for Montgomery Thorpe.' Chin shuts down abruptly, the message plain. No more freebies. The ball's in Bobby Ditto's court.

'OK,' Bobby says, 'how much?'

'Fifteen thousand to do an investigation. No guarantee on the results.'

'Fifteen grand's a lot of money.' Bobby's voice carries a little edge, not quite threatening, but close enough to make a point which the chink apparently doesn't get.

'First thing, Mr Benedetti, I could go to jail for what I'm

doing. Second thing, I have to spread the money around. I don't have access to any of this data. I have to rely on other people. But why don't we do this: Give me ten up front and the other five when I find something useful.'

'And if you don't?'

'Then we'll call it even.'

Bobby nods to the Blade who crosses the room to open a small metal box. He removes two packets of hundred dollar bills and passes them to his boss.

'One more thing before I fork this over,' Bobby says. 'I can't be waitin' around for an answer. You gotta work fast.'

'Monday morning fast enough?'

Bobby hands over the bundles. 'Monday morning, same time, same place. And one more thing. Abe Abramov personally vouched for you, which means I'll go right back to him if you jerk me off. And if I go to Abe, he's gonna come to you.'

Point made, Bobby leads Chin to the foot of the stairs and watches him until he disappears into the showroom. Then he returns to the office and the Blade, who's sitting in the chair formally occupied by Louis Chin.

Bobby drops into his own chair and says, 'So, where do we stand?'

'We've got the product eighty percent sold, that's the good news. But we're still negotiating a location for the buy.'

'What about the money?'

The Blade flashes that little frown he displays whenever he has to pass on bad news. 'We can't make it on our own. We're gonna have to take front money.'

The front money will come from buyers eager to trade payment in advance for a steep discount. Which, Bobby supposes, makes them investors.

'So, where do we put the money this time?' Bobby's got money stashed in five locations scattered about the city, an elementary precaution, but now he has to concentrate his capital. He's has to be ready.

'We did Bensonhurst last time.'

'And the time before?'

'Little Neck.'

'With the lawyer, right?'

'Yeah, the one who got busted for bribing a juror.'

Bobby runs a finger through his thinning hair. They'd gotten the money out three hours before the cops showed up with a warrant.

'OK, let's do the Bronx this time. Move the money into the Kingsbridge apartment. Handle it yourself, Marco. I don't want any slip-ups. If we're not ready, the deal's gonna walk away from us.'

THIRTEEN

Angel's glad. Glad to be out by herself, glad to be wearing her own clothes, glad for the soft Saturday night. Carter's off on some mission that doesn't include her, this following an afternoon they spent at her apartment where she packed every suitcase she owns with her 'achiever' wardrobe. Not boutique (that will come later), or even all-designer, her outfits nevertheless mark her as upwardly mobile. Tonight she's wearing skinny jeans, a red blouse that reveals a fashionable line of cleavage, a midnight-blue leather jacket, and Cynthia Vincent wedges that add two inches to the length of her already long legs. The True Religion jeans came from Saks, but the top was bought a year ago at Macy's, while the jacket came from a discount leather shop on Orchard Street. Still, she looks good and she knows it.

Along with dozens of unattached twenty-somethings, Angel's walking along Avenue A on Manhattan's Lower East Side. The clubs in this part of town cater to every taste, from ratty punk bars to slick, neon-lighted pubs designed for bottom-rung Wall Street wannabes. Naturally, on a Saturday night, the hormones are flying, male and female, and Angel, who doesn't fear the competition, is in her element.

The compliments, not to mention the outright propositions, polite and vulgar, come from all sides. Although she occasionally plays the hook-up game, Angel ignores the intrusions. Carter's enough to satisfy her bad-boy appetites. Only the night before, he'd briefly taken her into his world, revealing an entirely unsuspected dimension. He'd stripped down to a pair of gym shorts an hour after dinner, then produced an ebony box with African animals carved into the wood, dozens of them. The box was impressive enough, but then he lifted the cover to reveal a pair of ceremonial jade daggers in the shape of fire-breathing dragons.

Carter had carried box and daggers to a room cleared of furniture at the back of the apartment, then put on a show that was half-dance, half-meditation. He'd covered the entire room, a dagger in either hand, his movements fast, then slow, then fast again, now smooth and fluid, now as stylized as a Maori war dance. Later, after the daggers and the box were stowed in the back of a closet, he explained that his workout, culled from a number of fighting traditions, was as practical as it was unique, every movement designed to ward off an attacker.

The physical end – the grace, speed, precision, agility – came as no surprise to Angel. But there was a level of creative sophistication to Leonard Carter that she'd never suspected. The daggers were Burmese and very old – they had to be worth many thousands of dollars. (Carter had only been willing to admit they were paid for in blood.) They were also beautiful, an actual treasure that might have been on display at the Asia Society. And the elaborate dance he'd performed with them, derived or not, was his own creation.

Angel had briefly studied Zen Buddhism at a storefront temple, back when she was a newly arrived immigrant. After only a few weeks, she came to realize that the religion demanded a commitment she wasn't prepared to make, whereupon she dropped out. Now, as she crosses Eleventh Street, she remembers her instructor, a Japanese monk who wasn't above making a pass at her, causally mentioning that Zen's most ardent practitioners in pre-modern Japan were Samurai warriors. Raised a Christian, Angel embraced a gentle-Christ view of religion that didn't include a warrior caste vicious enough to behead peasants for daring to look at them. Carter, apparently, was beyond such delusions, beauty and death playing equal parts in his performance.

Angel's musings are interrupted when five skateboarders in torn jeans and ratty T-shirts fly out of Tompkins Square Park. They tear across the sidewalk and into the street where they play chicken with the traffic on Avenue A. Bemused, Angel watches them for a moment. The Lower East Side is all about diversity, a mix of types that includes Latinos from the housing projects along Avenue D, chess hustlers who dominate the park's south-east corner, ex-patriot Brits who gravitate to faux-pubs like The Clerkenwell. Something for everyone, a new adventure every night. There's even a bar-restaurant, Bondi Road, that caters to Australians.

A few minutes later, Angel walks into Prime Numbers, a dance club on Sixth Street. Barry Martin, the club's owner, stands near a door leading to the basement. Always suspicious, he's supervising a Latino busboy engaged in restocking the bar. The air is filled with techno music piped down from the second-story dance floor.

'Angel, where you been, girl? Me long time no see.' A Jamaican, Barry's voice runs up and down the octaves, his accent far too thick for the Princeton graduate he is. Nevertheless, his enthusiasm's heartfelt. Attractive women are the lifeblood of bars catering to the young.

'Been here and there, Barry. Have you seen Milek?'

'What you want with that boy, Angel? He's no good for nobody.'

'Then why do you let him in the club?'

A good question. Later on, a bouncer will stand guard at the club's entrance, the better to maintain the joint's exclusive image. But Angel doesn't need an answer. Milek Ostrovsky is Prime Numbers' resident coke and ecstasy dealer, tolerated because dance club patrons drink more booze and dance more dances when they're stoned out of their minds.

'Milek's playin' billiards, same as always.'

Angel heads for a large alcove in the back of the club. A full-sized pool table covered in red felt occupies most of the space, with just enough room on the sides to wield a cue stick. Milek is doing exactly that, but he stops when he sees

Angel. They'd hooked up once upon a time, a weekend affair that temporarily satisfied Angel's bad-boy propensities. Now she instinctively compares Milek to Carter and sees him for what he really is: a rapidly aging man in his mid-thirties, his hair thinning, his paunch growing, a threat only in his own mind.

'Hey, baby, what's up?'

'Need to talk, Milek.'

'Sure.' Milek hands his cue to his sidekick, a bulked-up Latino kid so taciturn he might be a mute. 'Finish the game for me, Carlos.' He winks at Angel. 'I'll be back when I'm back.'

Angel follows Milek out the door, on to the sidewalk, then west toward First Avenue. 'You're looking bummed-out this evening,' Milek observes. Angel has yet to crack a smile. 'Is something wrong?'

'I need a gun, Milek. Two, actually, a big one and a small one.'

A short skinny kid walks toward them. His purple hair is moussed into a stiff Mohawk and his bare arms are covered with tattoos. An unleashed pit bull lopes beside him, its pink tongue hanging nearly to the ground. The pit bull outweighs the kid by twenty pounds.

Milek and Angel observe a brief silence as they give the dog a wide berth. Then Milek asks, 'Why are you coming to me?'

'Because you once told me you could get anything.' Angel smiles sweetly, but the challenge is plain enough.

'You're asking me to get you a weapon without knowing what you're going to do with it. If you go home and shoot your boyfriend, I'll be a co-conspirator.'

'If I was going to shoot my boyfriend, I wouldn't be asking for two guns,' Angel says. 'But here's the deal, Milek. I have a thousand dollars in my purse. If you don't want it, I'll find someone who does.'

'Whoa.' Milek shakes his head. 'What happened to you, Angel? You used to be sweet.'

The sweet part was never sincere, but Angel doesn't avoid the underlying truth. She has, indeed, changed, and Leonard

Carter's the agent of that change. This is not a matter she intends to share with Milek Ostrovsky.

'Two guns, a thousand dollars,' she says. 'Yes or no.'

Three hours later, Angel's back in Carter's Woodhaven apartment. Carter's not home yet, which is all to the good. She carries her purchases into the bedroom where she lays them out on the dresser, a .45 caliber Ruger revolver and a .32 caliber Bersa automatic, a sub-compact with a seven-round magazine. Compared to the massive Ruger, the Bersa is nearly weightless.

Angel had examined the weapons in Milek's battered Honda. The workings were simple enough. According to Milek the revolver had no safety. You point and pull the trigger, that's it. The Bersa did have a safety, but all you had to do was flick it up with your thumb. At which point you were good to go.

'One thing, Angel. The .32 probably won't stop a man with a single round unless you shoot him in the head, so I hope you're a good shot.'

'I'm not.'

'Then point it at the middle of his chest – or her chest, for that matter – and keep pulling the trigger until the gun's empty.'

Angel has no specific plans for either weapon. But she's watched Carter over the last few days, watched him head out to practice his marksmanship or his fighting skills, and she doesn't want to be unarmed if Carter should decide to rip her off. She knows she's not his match, but there's always the element of surprise. Angel's good at deception.

Angel hides the revolver beneath a stack of her panties in a bureau against the wall opposite the bed. The little automatic, the sub-compact Bersa, goes into the toe of an insulated winter boot lying in the back of the closet. As it's the middle of May, the boot won't be used again for many months.

Satisfied, Angel raids the refrigerator, piling a scoop of cottage cheese and a handful of blueberries on to a plate. She carries the plate into the living room where she pours herself a glass of Chardonnay and inserts a Ted Allen DVD into Carter's player: *Uncorked: Wine Made Simple.* As Angel understands the trophy wife bargain, she's obliged, or will be, to properly maintain her spouse's household. Meat, potatoes and a bottle of beer just won't do for the elegant dinner parties she intends to throw. Thus, she studies, perfecting her craft as Carter perfects his. Angel is majoring in Art History at Brooklyn College, reads every upscale fashion magazine she can find, attends weekend seminars on antique American furniture and French wines. When the time comes, she intends to be prepared. She will strike while the iron is hot. She will seize the day. She will laugh all the way to the bank.

Or she would, if her attention didn't keep wandering to Leonard Carter. That business with the knives? By the time Carter finished, his body was as chiseled as the daggers he so carefully wiped off. The glistening sweat didn't hurt either. Now she wonders when he's coming home. What's it been? Six hours? It feels like forever.

FOURTEEN

Carter's been sitting on Lieutenant Solly Epstein's house all evening, scrunched into the van's back seat, munching on bag of a Granny Smith apples, drinking cans of Red Bull to stay alert, peeing into an empty bottle when necessary. Carter and Epstein have a history, a past in which Epstein twice attempted to take Carter's life. Epstein hadn't been up to the job, not even close, but Carter let the man live, a favor that now has to be repaid. There are no freebies in Carter's world.

Epstein finally drives up to his small home in Bay Ridge, Brooklyn, at eight o'clock. He parks his Taurus against the curb, shuts the engine and gets out of the car. Before he can lock up, the screen door on his house opens and a little boy, a toddler, runs out to stumble across the grass and into his father's arms.

'Daddy, daddy, daddy.'

Carter's touched, no doubt, and not a little jealous. He will never have this for himself, this simple pleasure. Lo Phet would have laughed if he'd even raised the subject.

'No daddies in Hell World. Only sires.'

Carter watches father and son disappear into the house. If there are no moms and dads in Lo Phet's universe, he thinks, there are definitely men and women. He's smitten and he knows it, his mind instantly calling up the rise and fall of Angel's breasts, the hiss of her drawn breath, an image and a sound, so clear she might as well be in the van. And they'd done that, too, in the cargo area by the rear doors. The windows had fogged over long before they finished.

All of which is not to say that Carter trusts Angel Tamanaka. No, Carter doesn't trust Angel because he doesn't trust anyone. Trust, as Angel might put it, is not Carter's thing. It's not what he does.

Carter settles a little deeper into the seat. There are folks about, dog walkers, a jogger or two, and he doesn't want to be noticed. The address he had for Epstein, now four years old, is still good. That's enough for now.

Carter needs intelligence and Epstein's long-standing assignment to the NYPD's Organized Crime Control Bureau makes him the perfect candidate to supply it. Epstein's sold information in the past. There's no reason to suppose he won't go that route again. The trick is to get him alone, the woman and child being, of course, innocent civilians.

The lights in the upstairs bedrooms, as they're turned on and off, mark the family's progress. First in a room at the east side of the house. The curtains in the room's single window are open, the shade drawn up, and Carter assumes he's looking at the boy's room, that Solly's putting his child to sleep. In any event, the light goes out twenty minutes later.

Another hour passes, with the lights on the lower floor, in the living room and the kitchen, remaining lit. Then the lights go out, the kitchen light first, as lights come on, in an upstairs bedroom and in the bathroom, more or less simultaneously. Carter's thinking he might leave at this point. Tomorrow's another day and there's Angel back in Woodhaven. Hopefully.

But Carter doesn't move, and his patience is finally rewarded at eleven o'clock when the bedroom goes dark as a light comes on downstairs. Epstein emerges a moment later. He ambles to his car, jingling his keys, whistling to himself. Then he's off and running, with Carter following shortly behind.

The trip isn't very long, only a few blocks to a pedestrian bridge crossing Shore Parkway. New York's upper bay is just a hundred yards distant and Carter's nostrils fill with the odor of the sea, though the harbor is screened by trees and bushes. When Epstein pulls to the curb near the overpass, Carter passes by and drives another block before sliding the van into a parking space. By the time he gets out, Epstein has crossed the bridge and disappeared.

Carter jogs to the overpass and takes the steps two at a time. Epstein's nowhere in sight when he reaches the top, and he crosses the bridge quickly, the traffic zinging along beneath him. Carter intends to pursue Epstein, to run him down – this is Carter's big chance to engage the cop in a long, pointed conversation – but the scene before him is too compelling and he stops for a moment. To his right, the towers of lower Manhattan rise like the phalanx of some great advancing army. Lady Liberty, alone on her island and lit from top to bottom, holds her torch aloft as if leading the charge. Across the harbor on Staten Island, single-family homes run in parallel lines across low shadowy hills. To his left, the Verrazano Narrows Bridge, with its lit cables and towers, unites Staten Island with Brooklyn. The Verrazano is the most slender and graceful of the city's suspension bridges, at least in Carter's opinion, despite it being the longest by far.

Carter has been here before, to walk the promenade running between the highway and the water on a bright fall afternoon. When he spots Epstein sitting on a bench nearby, the faint glow of a cigarette in his right hand, he knows exactly why the man has come to this spot. The view is stunning.

Carter drops on to the bench next to Epstein a moment later, but Epstein doesn't flinch. 'I was hoping you were dead,' he says.

'Sorry to disappoint.'

Epstein tugs on his cigarette. He's a short man, barely

five-eight, and bald on top, with a barrel chest and heavily muscled shoulders. 'You'll have to excuse me,' he says, 'Maybe I'm dense. But I don't think I'm in your debt. I think we had a deal and I kept my end.'

Carter had exacted a price when he allowed Epstein to survive the second attempt on his life. Yes, I'll let you live. But only if you put a gun to your partner's head and pull the trigger. With his wife about to give birth any minute, Epstein had complied.

'Benedetti,' Carter says. 'Bobby and Ricky, the Ditto brothers.'

'Like I said, Carter, I don't owe you a thing.'

The cop rises, grinds his cigarette into the pavement and begins to walk south, toward the bridge. Carter follows, not yet ready to pull out the big guns. He will, though, if it comes to that. From their right, the pulsating roar of high-speed traffic assaults their ears, reducing the splash of the waves against the boulders protecting the shoreline to an insinuating murmur.

'How have you been, Solly?' Carter asks.

Epstein laughs. 'I got a kid now, a boy, and another on the way, and then Mr Death shows up. That would be you, in case you're interested. So, how good can I be?' Epstein hesitates, then lowers his voice. 'I know you hit Ricky Ditto. The way it happened, inside the house, the alarms defeated, no sign of forced entry, one shot through the forehead? It had to be you.' Epstein stops suddenly, but doesn't meet Carter's gaze. 'And there were others. A Polish gangster shot through the head from three hundred yards away. A Russian dead from a single knife wound just below his sternum. You already used that one, Carter, in Macy's a few days before Christmas. I thought you were more creative.'

Carter thinks he's now supposed to ask the cop if he, Carter, is a suspect in any of these cases, if his name has come to the attention of the authorities. He doesn't.

'I'm gonna have to invoke my constitutional right to avoid self-incrimination,' he says. 'Mum's the word.'

'Yeah, well I wouldn't sweat it. The FBI and the NYPD are places where nobody knows your name.'

Carter stares for a moment at a line of oil tankers and container ships anchored in the harbor. He wonders if they're waiting to unload, or if they're off to some faraway port with the turn of the tide. 'I've been sitting in the van for the last eight hours. You mind if we keep walking?'

They continue on for several minutes, Carter watching headlights flicker in the superstructure joining the bridge's upper and lower decks. Epstein needs time to adjust and Carter's a patient man. He will not be the first to speak.

'Are you married?' Epstein finally asks. 'You got any kids?'

'No.'

'So, you're completely on your own? Nobody to report to at the end of the day?'

Carter smiles to himself. Only a few days before, he would have responded without hesitation. Now there's Angel Tamanaka.

'What's your point, Solly?'

'I can't make ends meet. That's the point. I can't make the numbers add up, no matter what I do.' He ticks the points off on the middle finger of his left hand. 'The job's cut back on overtime, so I have to make due on my base pay. Sofia's been working for the last year, but child care eats up most of her salary. Now she's pregnant again and she'll be gainfully unemployed for a year, even if she works into her ninth month.'

Epstein glances at Carter, who's staring at the bridge. 'I work in a gas station on my off-days,' he continues. 'I'm the monkey in the booth you have to pay if you don't have a credit card. I make twelve dollars an hour, but only because I carry a gun. The other monkeys get eight.' He shrugs. 'Between the house payments and the car payments – we need two cars now – and the payments for the loan I took out with the credit union . . . Let's just say I'm in over my head, Carter. Let's just say that when Sofia quits her job, me and my little family are gonna sink beneath the waves. Glug, glug, glug.'

Epstein's complaint reminds Carter of Angel's cautionary tale about her father's doomed attempt to save his lumber yard. Hideki Tamanaka had given his all to the struggle, but the forces arrayed against him were too powerful to resist. He'd found a way out, though, by firing a bullet into his head. Epstein, or so it seems to Carter, has other plans.

They walk past a couple, teenagers by the look of them, making out on a bench. Lost in lust, the young lovers appear not to notice the intrusion. Epstein smiles and nudges Carter with an elbow. 'You remember when you were that young?' he asks. 'There was no such thing as enough.'

Carter returns Epstein's smile, though his sexual experiences, before and after joining the military, have been sporadic and brief. 'I'm not out to kill Bobby Ditto,' he says.

'Is he out to kill you?'

'Sure, but he doesn't know who I am, or where to find me, or how to fight me if he did.'

'Then why come to me?'

'I'm coming to you, Solly, because I want everything in the files you cops undoubtedly keep on the Ditto brothers. I want every known associate, every address, what they do, their connections . . . hell, I want the names of their children and grandchildren. I want to be buried in information.'

They continue on for a time, until they're standing in the shadow of the bridge. The towers on this side, the Brooklyn side, rise seven hundred feet above their heads.

'What do you think they did first?' Carter asks. 'I'm talking about the people who built the bridge. What was the very first step they took?'

'Convince the politicians to give them money. Look, it's gettin' late and I need a few hours' sleep. I'm working tomorrow.'

'My cards are on the table. I've got nothing to add.'

'Fair enough, so let me put my own cards on the table. I'm not an idiot, Carter, so I know you're gonna pull a rip-off. Bobby doesn't do hijackings or commercial burglaries. He doesn't run whores or make book or lend money. Bobby Ditto's in the drug business and that means cash, cash, cash.'

Epstein turns suddenly and begins to retrace his steps. Intrigued, Carter follows, certain of only one thing. Something in the cop has changed and the good lieutenant's no longer afraid of him.

'There a bottom line here?' Carter asks.

'Two bottom lines. The first one has you cutting me in, which would definitely be in your interest if you need manpower. The second one has you paying me ten grand for the files.'

Out on the water, an ocean-going tug out-pushes a loaded barge toward the narrow passage between the upper and lower bays. Beyond, the Atlantic Ocean runs all the way to Europe. The barge carries an EPA logo on the side and a cargo of sludge from one of the city's waste treatment plants, a cargo to be dumped long before England comes into view.

Carter nods to himself when the tugboat sounds its foghorn. He's intrigued by Epstein's proposal, but far from ready to make a commitment. He has no idea what resources the operation will call for. That's why he's after the files.

'I can't choose without the files and I'm not giving you ten thousand dollars. The way I see it, you're in my debt.'

'Even though I kept my end of the deal?'

'There was no deal, Solly. What you did was more in the nature of an insurance policy. But the fact is I don't know what I'm going to do with the information, which may or may not answer the questions that need answering. I'm willing to go to a grand to cover the risk you'd be taking, but that's it.'

'What about the first part?'

'Bringing you in?'

'Yeah.'

'I like to work alone, for obvious reasons. But I'll think about it.'

Now Epstein takes a moment to think. He stares across the water at the low Staten Island hills, his lips slightly parted, eyes fixed. Then his expression hardens as he turns to Carter.

'Four,' he says. 'Four grand. I gotta get at least four.'

Carter walks into the bedroom he shares with Angel to find two votive candles burning in ruby-red jars on a dresser. An opened book lies between the candles: *Infinite Island: Contemporary Caribbean Art*. Angel's sleeping atop the bed's comforter. She's lying on her stomach, her right arm stretched out beneath the pillow, her dark hair flowing over her shoulders, one leg drawn up. Carter traces the length of her legs, the curve of her buttocks, the dimples along her spine. He's wondering what she'll do if he wakes her up – Angel's a sound sleeper – when she rolls on to her back and opens her eyes.

'Whenever you leave, I think maybe this time you won't come back,' she tells him as she rubs the sleep from her eyes.

'You worried that I'm gonna leave you?'

'Leave me?' Angel gestures at the bulge in Carter's pants. 'No, what I think is that you might be killed. Nobody's invincible.'

Carter takes off his shoes and socks, then unbuttons his shirt. 'Does that mean you'd miss me?'

'Missing is part of the deal. Sooner or later.'

'Inevitably?' Carter drops his shirt and tugs at his belt. He's asking himself what Lo Phet would make of this world he's stumbled into, if there's a name for it. 'No escape?'

Angel's eyes slide over Carter's body, the slope of his shoulders, the humped biceps, the wormy veins that criss-cross his forearms. The skin on Carter's chest is stretched tight and her hand rises from the comforter just a bit, as though she's already feeling that skin on the tips of her fingers.

'You need to move a little faster,' she says.

'And why's that?'

'Because I hate to squirm.' Her smile is wicked. 'It's sooooooo unladylike.'

An hour later, they're sharing a pint of mango ice cream, sitting atop the covers, when Carter says, 'We'll be moving out of here tomorrow.'

'Where are we going?'

'I have another apartment, in Manhattan.' Carter dips the spoon into the ice cream, places it before Angel's lips and watches her pink tongue capture the offering. 'I can be traced to this address,' he explains. 'Not easily, but it's possible.'

'Then why live here at all?'

'To leave a trail, a false trail. Just in case.'

FIFTEEN

Bobby Ditto feels a bit sorry for the two men, his bodyguards, exiled to the parking lot of the Cross Bay Diner. They've got what in the Caddy? Containers of lukewarm coffee and a few doughnuts? Meanwhile, he's staring at a three-egg omelet stuffed with lox, peppers and onions, sides of dollar pancakes and bacon, and a fruit salad, heavy on the cantaloupe. Altogether, a nice breakfast.

Bobby doesn't use the drugs he sells, or allow his subordinates to use them. The standard penalty for transgressors, rigidly enforced, is a broken kneecap and lifelong exile from the crew. Bobby doesn't drink, either, except for the occasional beer or glass of wine over dinner with family or colleagues. He eats, though, and only his steroid-fueled workouts save him from the morbid obesity he richly deserves.

The Cross Bay Diner rests on a small plot of land facing the cargo warehouses at the ass end of Kennedy Airport. The decorative scheme is retro-aviation. Strung on cables attached to the ceiling, models of a twin-prop Douglas DC-8 and a Boeing 707 sway in a gentle breeze created by the diner's ventilation system. The waiters, male and female, wear brown, two-pocket shirts with epaulets on the shoulders and gleaming silver wings at the breast. Posters advertise the services of long-vanished carriers: TWA, Pan Am, Eastern.

Bobby cuts a slice of bacon in half and puts it into his mouth. The Cross Bay isn't far from his Howard Beach home, and he knows the waiters and the owner, who's sitting behind a cash register. They know him, too, know him well enough to show respect. *Mr Benedetti*. Bobby Ditto likes that.

Bobby eats slowly and methodically, cutting his food into smallish bites, the longer to spend with his meal. He's thinking about the hard drive taken from Pigalle Studios' computer when the Blade whacked the pimp. Finally accessed by Levi Kupperman, Bobby's computer geek, the drive includes the first names of Pigalle's clients, along with the numbers of the credit cards they used. Bobby's pretty sure he can work backwards from the card numbers to the clients' full names. That makes blackmail a definite possibility, Pigalle being a high-end operation. Unfortunately, the hard drive was taken from the computer of a murdered pimp, which presents complications.

Blackmail was not a consideration when the Blade took the hard drive. Bobby was after the whore, Angel Face, and that turned out to be worse than a dead end. Bobby shakes his head. He doesn't want to think about the stupid moves he made, especially the decision to hit his brother, the one that started it all, and he's relieved when Louis Chin pushes through the door.

Chin's wearing dark glasses and a yellow golf-shirt that might be made of silk. Bobby watches him cross the room, his stride athletic, his body language casual, unafraid.

'Hey,' Bobby says, a standard greeting that could easily be mistaken for a grunt.

'Good morning.' Chin slides into the far side of the booth. 'That smells good.'

'Order whatever you want. It's on me.'

'I think I'll settle for coffee.'

Bobby Ditto raises his hand and a harried waitress approaches. In the borough of Queens, Sunday morning is diner-breakfast day and the restaurant's packed.

'Coffee for my friend.' He watches her leave, then turns to Chin. Bobby wants to bring him down a peg or two, to soften him up before they come to the bargaining phase. Chin has some limited information to sell, for which Bobby intends to pay as little as possible. 'You're some kind of special forces guy, right? Like a SEAL in the Navy?'

Chin stares at Bobby for a moment, his eyes curiously blank. 'I don't remember speaking about my past,' he finally says. 'Which is irrelevant to our business together.'

'I know, but that's what I heard from the party that recommended you.' Bobby cuts through his omelet and shovels a forkful into his mouth. He chews for a moment, then adds salt to his eggs. 'But what I'm sayin' is this. You don't look anything like what I thought a Navy SEAL or a Green Beret is supposed to look like. I always thought they were big guys.' Bobby illustrates his point by flexing a massive bicep, a gesture that's met with a sneer.

'Actually, it's more about skill and endurance, and a high pain threshold, than physical strength,' Chin responds. 'Say you're six-six and you can pick up the side of a building. Does that mean you can run forty miles in a day? Or hit a moving target six hundred yards out? I don't think so.' Chin pauses long enough to let the message sink in. 'But as I said, my past is irrelevant to our present business.'

Bobby doesn't react to the veiled threat, any more than Chin reacted to Bobby's little taunt. 'So, whatta ya got for me?'

'A history, a name, a photo.'

'But no address?'

'I have an address, the address Carter used prior to entering the military.'

'What if Carter's not there? What if he's living somewhere else?'

'He is there.' Chin leans back when the waitress arrives with his coffee. Like Bobby, he waits for her to drift off before he speaks. 'I've already checked it out. Carter's been living in an apartment in Queens for the past several years.'

'How do you know this?'

'I spoke to the super, a man named Miguel Romero.' Chin leans forward. 'The information you gave me regarding Carter's background. Carter doesn't know you have it, right?'

Bobby thinks it over for a moment. Paulie Margarine isn't all that trustworthy, not in Bobby's opinion, but he'll keep his mouth shut this time. You don't tell a man like Carter that you betrayed him.

'Yeah, OK. Carter doesn't know I have the information. So what?'

'So he thinks he's safe and there's no good reason for him to move.' Chin leans forward. 'We've got the element of surprise.'

'Ya mean *you've* got the element of surprise. What I got, so far, is hot air.'

Chin sips at his coffee. 'C'mon, Bobby. Money talks, as they say, and so far you haven't said a word.'

'Here.' Bobby takes an envelope from the inner pocket of his jacket and passes it across the table. He's got no choice. Chin's delivering big time. 'Now, let's hear the story.'

'Leonard Carter enlisted in the army on his eighteenth birthday, a raw recruit with an obvious talent. His evaluations were uniformly superlative and he went from basic training to special forces training without skipping a beat. He became a Ranger, first, then was chosen for Delta Force, which is the ultimate. After 9/11, he took his training to Afghanistan, which is where it becomes a little murky. Are you familiar with the kill or capture list?'

Bobby shakes his head. 'Uh-uh.'

'The spooks compiled a list of top Taliban and Al-Qaeda commanders, a kill or capture list, early in the war. As it turned out, the capture part was more like wishful thinking because most of the targets were hiding out in Pakistan or Somalia or Sudan or Yemen. So the task force assembled by the spooks – Task Force 373 – was closer to an assassination squad than anything else.'

'And Carter was on that task force?'

'Yes, along with other Delta Force personnel, Navy SEALs, CIA and NSA agents, and private contractors. But my connections couldn't access where Carter went or what he did. All we know is that Task Force 373 was operating in a number of countries by the time Carter left the military. That would be six years ago.'

Bobby pours maple syrup on his dollar pancakes, cuts the stack in quarters and fills his mouth. 'Secret or not, I got a pretty good guess about what he did. That's because he's still doin' it.'

'I won't argue the point.' Chin shrugs. 'Anyway, the CIA kept track of Carter after he left the army, but the material on him is sketchy. Carter worked for Coldstream Military Options, a private contractor in Iraq, until they went broke. From there, he drifted along the west coast of Africa for sixteen months, teaming up with Montgomery Thorpe along the way. What they did together isn't exactly clear, but it's certain that Carter returned to the United States three years ago. And that's it. Upon setting foot on American soil, Carter disappeared from our radar screen.'

'Until now.'

'Until now.'

'Gimme the address.'

Chin passes over a folded piece of paper containing an address in Woodhaven, Queens, not twenty minutes from where they sit, along with a single photograph. The photo was taken shortly after Carter entered the military. It depicts him in full uniform, his expression earnest, his mouth tight, his chin outthrust, more boy than man.

'You think he looks like that now?'

'Probably not, but every other photo was purged when he entered Delta Force.' Chin clears his throat. 'I know it's not my business . . .'

'You're right, it's not.'

'But if you're planning to . . . to take Carter on . . .'

Again, Bobby interrupts. 'What's my option? To sit on my hands and hope he goes away?'

'No, to hire me.'

'You?'

'A few minutes ago, I told you that my past was irrelevant to our business. No more. I've been where Carter's been. I've walked in his shoes. I know how he thinks.'

Bobby's first impulse is to send the little fuck on his way. He's not forgetting the Blade's fantasy about snatching Carter and the whore off the street. But there's this deal coming up fast that needs all his attention. Bobby Ditto's not only risking his entire stake, he's accepting front money from people who won't sit still if he loses their investment.

'How much?'

'Fifteen.'

'How will I know you pulled it off?'

'What if I bring you his head?'

'That'd do.'

SIXTEEN

Carter doesn't waste time. Ten minutes after Angel leaves their apartment on Manhattan's Lower East Side, he's in her bedroom, searching through her belongings. When he discovers a .45 caliber Ruger beneath a stack of her panties, he smiles. The weapon is way too heavy for Angel, the likelihood of her striking a target more than three feet away remote. Nevertheless, Carter fetches a tool kit and removes the gun's firing pin. Then he wipes the revolver down and puts it back where he found it.

At this point, Carter should continue his search. At another time, he almost certainly would. But now he merely rummages through the drawers in the bureau before pausing to consider two possibilities.

First, are Angel's intentions proactive? Without doubt, she's driven by a need to accumulate money – her every ambition involves money, and lots of it. But Angel's far from stupid and the consequences of double crossing Leonard Carter are obvious enough. She'd have to kill him or be afraid for the rest of her life. Does she have the balls to murder a man?

Again, Carter smiles. He's gotten his anatomy confused. And, yes, Angel definitely has nerve, purchasing a gun big enough to knock down a grizzly bear being proof enough. Still, it seems more likely that the prize is hiding behind door number two. Carter's too dangerous, too unpredictable, and once he gets his hands on the money, he'll have no further need of her. In fact, he has no further need of her right now. So why not invest in a little protection, a little insurance? If things go wrong, at least she'll have a fighting chance.

Carter walks through the apartment, to the window in the living room. He cranes his neck to stare over the building across the street at a gloomy sky. The weather's important to him because he intends to pass the morning and early afternoon squatting on a warehouse roof three blocks from Janie's apartment. Just two years ago, the warehouse was packed with furniture, a bustling enterprise that could only be approached after the doors were locked at night. Now it's empty, another victim of the ongoing economic troubles. Bad news for the workers, good news for Carter. From the roof, he'll have an excellent view of the surrounding blocks.

This morning, when Carter accessed his email account, he found a message from the super at Janie's apartment building, Miguel Romero. The message was succinct: a man, an Asian, had come around asking if Carter lived in the building. Romero's known Carter since Carter was a little boy and they've come to an understanding. If a snooper turns up, Miguel's to cooperate, tell the truth, take any money offered. Then let Carter know.

Meanwhile, there's still the cop. Carter and Solly Epstein are due to meet in an hour.

Carter takes a thin poncho from a closet shelf and slips it into a backpack. He adds two bananas and a thermos filled with coffee, then eases the backpack on to his shoulders. Briefly, he considers and rejects taking a weapon other than the knife strapped to his calf. Suppose the snoop is a cop? True, he identified himself as a private investigator when he braced Miguel, but there's still the chance.

Cautious by nature, trained to caution by the military, Leonard Carter avoids making decisions on the fly. He wants to know who this man is, why he's asking questions about Leonard Carter and who hired him, assuming he's really a private investigator. And Carter wants to accomplish each of these objectives without confronting the man on the street. Not that Carter doesn't have a handy suspect, a likely betrayer, a man he never trusted but always liked.

Carter closes and locks the door behind him. He takes the elevator down six flights and walks out into the damp spring morning. Tulips bloom in a pair of window boxes to his right and the air is faintly scented by a small lilac bush in a townhouse garden across the street. Carter looks up at a sky the color of a prison blanket. He's thinking that he woke up healthy this morning and he's going to spend the night with Angel

Tamanaka. Given the life he's lived, as boy and man, he can hardly expect more.

Louis Chin's been sitting in his rented Camry for three hours, feeling more and more uneasy about the silenced Glock stashed under the seat. Louis's always been a good salesman, but what he sold Bobby Ditto was a bill of goods, at least when it came to his own background. Louis Chin's never walked in Carter's shoes. He led a company, sure, and he was assigned to Intel for a year, which is where he made his contacts. But the military he served was a blunt instrument, whereas Carter's military was finely tuned. No way could Louis Chin operate fifty miles into Pakistan. Or Yemen or Somalia or Syria, for that matter. No way could he execute his mission – which for Carter meant executing human beings – and make it out alive.

Chin taps the steering wheel. The business of being a civilian has turned out to be a constant challenge. As he understands it now, the top-down military model suited him far better than the anarchy of the civilian world, every day beginning with new decisions, new consequences. Following orders was a lot simpler.

Of course, as a front-line Marine in Afghanistan, his life was at risk every day. That was why he quit. And now here he is risking his life again. Nevertheless, he's certain that he has the element of surprise on his side. Even if Carter's a paranoid type, he'll be looking for Italian gangsters, not a well-dressed Asian.

Chin steps out of the Camry and into a light drizzle. He retreats to the shelter of a storefront canopy where he stretches, leaning to his left, then his right, in a vain attempt to loosen the muscles of his lower back. As he does, he glances up at a three-story building, a warehouse of some sort, located on a neighboring block, Myrtle Avenue. If he can get up on the roof, he'll have an unobstructed view, both of the windows fronting Carter's apartment and the main entrance to the building itself. Chin estimates the distance between the warehouse and the apartment building to be a mere two hundred yards. Maybe he isn't the greatest marksman ever to enlist in the Marines, but armed with a rangefinder and a decent rifle, he won't have any problem hitting something as large as a man.

Chin enters the little grocery store to find an Arab running the show. Two Arabs, actually, one by the cash register, a second behind the deli counter. That's another thing about civilian life. Half the little grocery stores in New York are owned by Arabs. When had that come about? Why hadn't anyone told him the hajis were taking over?

When no ready answer to either question comes to mind, Chin picks up an orange soda and a small packet of ibuprofen tablets before heading back to the car. Seated again, he chases the tablets with the first two inches of his soda and settles down. Back when he signed his discharge papers, he'd imagined a warm welcome from the many private security agencies owned by ex-Marines. And he'd gotten a warm welcome – *Semper Fi, BooYah* – but they were laying people off, not hiring. Now . . .

Chin stiffens when he picks up movement in the rear-view mirror. The man approaching the Camry on the street side of the vehicle is ten years older than Leonard Carter, with bull shoulders, a bald head and a cheap suit that has to belong to a cop. This is not good news, not with an illegal pistol under the seat. The silencer, all by itself, could put him in a federal prison for the next five years.

Sure enough, the man raises an open billfold as he comes up to the window, revealing a detective's gold shield and an ID card. The billfold snaps shut before Chin can read a word.

'Lieutenant Epstein,' the cop says. 'May I see your driver's license and registration?'

'Am I doing something wrong, detective?'

'Yeah, you're not complying with a lawful order. Show me your driver's license and registration.'

With no real choice in the matter, Chin produces the documents. 'The car's a rental,' he explains.

Epstein slides a pair of reading glasses on to his nose before scrutinizing Chin's license and the rental agreement. He takes a spiral notebook from his pocket and writes down Chin's name, address and driver's license ID number.

'Mr Chin, will you tell me what you're doing here? You've been parked for the last two hours.'

Chin has the right to refuse and he knows it. He's in a legal parking space and he's not committing a criminal act. But then the cop smiles apologetically.

'I'm not tryin' to harass ya. I got a good reason.'

'I'm a private investigator, detective. I'm on a case.'

Epstein's eyes widen. 'Yeah? A private eye?'

'That's right.'

'And you're licensed, right?'

'Right.'

'Can I see your license?' When Chin complies, Epstein examines the license, then says, 'Mr Chin, do me a favor. Step out of the car and take a look around. Please.'

Epstein's tone is so reasonable, the expression on his face so mild, that Chin simply exits the Camry to stand in a heavy mist that instantly coats his face. He looks around, as asked, discovering a single pedestrian, a massive black man in a red football jersey walking a dog that can't weigh more than two pounds.

'I don't see anything.'

'Ah.' Epstein raises a finger. 'See, that's the whole point. We're lookin' for a serial rapist and we've got this whole area under surveillance. But you don't see anything out of place because the whole point is to stay invisible until the mutt shows up.'

Chin looks at the ground for a moment. He's thinking any port in a storm, any excuse to get himself and the gun out of Dodge. 'You're telling me that I'm messing up your operation and I need to leave?'

'You're definitely conspicuous. I mean, who sits in a car for two hours? People walkin' the street see you, they're gonna make you for a cop. Definitely. Now, I can't order you to leave. You're a private investigator, licensed by the NYPD, and you're goin' about your regular business. But I'd really appreciate your cooperation. We'll be outta here by tomorrow morning, one way or the other. You can always come back.'

Chin accepts with a nod. Of course, he'll cooperate. When Epstein hands over his paperwork, he slides into the Camry, starts the car and drives off. The relief that follows proves nearly overwhelming. Only at the last minute does he notice a stop sign at the end of the block.

Chin comes to a halt in the crosswalk, blocking the path of an elderly woman crossing the street. With the window still open, he listens to the tap of her cane on the pavement as she works her way around the car. Chin's not resentful when she pauses long enough to favor him with a raised middle finger, not at all. He thinks he deserves the salute.

SEVENTEEN

Angel arrives at the Rubin Museum of Himalayan Art ninety minutes before her appointment with Vincent Graham. A dedicated multitasker, she's combining business with business, the first order of the day to choose a painting. Angel has a paper due for her last Art History class at Brooklyn College, a final thesis. She's decided to compare storytelling traditions in Christian and Tibetan art, and to connect both traditions to the illiteracy prevailing in those cultures.

The paper, Angel's certain, will be easy to write, its essential point beyond dispute, yet at the same time original because no one else in the class will think of it. In medieval religious art, candles symbolized holy illumination, flames the fires of hell. The lamb substituted for Jesus, the iris for the Virgin and the dove for the Holy Spirit, while eggs indicated the fertility of nature and chains symbolized slavery. Each of these symbols, and many more, would have been recognized and understood by the general population, just as today we instantly associate the golden arches with McDonald's, or the swoosh with Nike.

Angel works her way up three levels before she comes upon a painting that nicely illustrates her main argument, a *bhava-cakra* or Wheel of Life. There's a printed explanation of the painting's symbolism mounted on the wall beside the work, an explanation the work's intended audience would neither require, nor understand, even if written in the Tibetan language. Prepared as always, Angel removes a pad and a pen from her purse, then fills a page with notes before turning her attention to the painting.

A series of concentric circles, the wheel is held by Yama, a fanged, three-eyed demon tasked with judging the dead. The wheel's outer circle depicts the Twelve Causes and Effects, among them birth, conditioning, ignorance and desire. The next circle is divided into six sections and illustrates the six realms, the Realm of the Gods on top, the Hell World on the bottom. Between them, to the left and right, are the Realm of the Asuras, demigods burdened with every human vice, the Worlds of Humans and Animals, and the World of Hungry Ghosts. From the painting's upper corners, two Bodhisattvas look down at the wheel. Finally enlightened after lifetimes of effort, the wheel no longer turns for them. Which probably accounts for their serene expressions.

Angel puts her notebook away and steps back, for the first time immersing herself in the painting. The colors are bold, the glaring demon, Yama, ferocious enough, with his tiara of human skulls, to thoroughly impress. This is no joke – that's the message any Tibetan, even the most humble peasant, would understand. Since they'd instantly associate the three figures at the center of the wheel, a rooster, a pig and a snake, with the three poisons, greed, hatred and delusion.

After a few moments, Angel lifts a camera from her purse, a Nikon SLR, then meticulously photographs the painting's every detail. She takes more than fifty shots before returning the camera to its case. Angel's thinking, as she heads off to the lobby, that the *bhavacakra* perfectly illustrates all the points she hoped to make. *Bhavacakras* are ubiquitous, as well. A simple computer search will turn up hundreds of examples. No surprise. Transmitting a consistent set of ideas to an illiterate population was the whole point. Or so she intends to claim.

For just a moment, Angel toys with the idea of using twenty-first century symbols to illustrate a swing from religious concerns to a culture obsessed with consumption, a world of hungry ghosts. Then she shakes her head as she tells herself not to be a jerk. She's already got an 'A' paper. There's nothing to be gained by injecting armchair sociology into the equation, no reason to search the bush when the bird in her hand is already made of gold.

Angel spots Vincent Graham in the museum's lobby. He's standing with his back to her and his hands in his pockets, contemplating a Buddha carved from gray stone. He turns at her approach, his expression wary, as well it should be. Angel didn't explain her mission when she arranged the meeting and Graham is a client, a repeat client whose fantasy boiled down to kidnapped-princess-sold-into-slavery. This is a script he certainly wants to keep from his wife and two adolescent daughters, a script Angel can reveal. But Angel hasn't come with blackmail on her mind, far from it. Although he's not Donald Trump or Bruce Ratner, Vincent's a player in the city's ongoing real estate game.

'Angel, it's good to see you again, though I have to admit I was surprised to hear from you.' In his forties, Vincent Graham is short and round. Ordinarily a jolly sort, he's not jolly now.

'Believe me, Vincent, I never would have called you if I wasn't desperate. But I've got a big problem and I know you can help me out.'

Angel's deliberately cryptic statement does nothing to reassure Vincent Graham, but he doesn't object when she takes his arm and leads him up the museum's spiral staircase to a statue of the sleeping Buddha on the second floor.

'Have you heard about Pierre?' she asks.

'Pierre?'

The suspicious note in Graham's voice doesn't surprise Angel. He'd put a move on her at their last meeting, offering to fly her to Costa Rica for a five-star vacation. When she declined, he handed over his business card, just in case she changed her mind. Now he's afraid, and quite reasonably, that she might be recording the conversation.

'Do you want to pat me down, Vincent? Would you like to do a strip search?' Angel allows her smile to expand, revealing the edges of her teeth, the tip of her tongue. It's obvious that good old Vincent would like nothing better, frightened though he is. 'If you recall, Pierre ran Pigalle Studios. He's the man you spoke to when you arranged our dates. Now he's dead, Vincent. Somebody murdered him.'

'I wasn't aware of that. Why was he killed?'

'Well, that's just it. I don't have the faintest idea, and the police don't, either. But I got a call two days ago, a man's voice saying that I know what I did and I have to pay for it. But I don't know what I did and neither do the other girls he's contacted.' Angel tightens her grip on Graham's arm as she leans into him. 'I think the guy's making it up as he goes along. I think he's *beyond* crazy.'

Far from scared, Vincent is noticeably relieved. There's no blackmail scheme happening here. There's only the pressure of Angel's breast against his ribs and a state of arousal that will become painfully obvious if pursued even a little further.

'What do you want from me, Angel?' He raises an apologetic palm before making an obvious point. 'I'm not a tough guy.'

'All I need is a place to go, a room or an apartment, if things get really bad. And I have money, Vincent. I'm not asking for a handout. If you can set me up with a place, I'll be more than happy to pay you whatever it's worth. But I need the keys today. I have to be ready to move.'

Graham waits for a troop of Buddhist monks to pass before he speaks again. The monks wear saffron robes and their shaved heads glisten. They smile and bow as they go by, their hands steepled together on their chests.

'So, where were we?' he asks.

'We were talking about an apartment.' Angel turns to face her benefactor. She stares into his eyes and finds them rapidly filling with a lust she doesn't begrudge. Angel's traded sex for money in the past and there's no good reason for him to think she won't trade sex for some other benefit. 'Like I said, money's not a problem. But I need the key right now.'

'Does that mean you'll be moving in?'

'No, not today, and if I don't use the apartment within the next two weeks, I won't use it at all. But I have to be ready.'

'Then what about my . . . my special place? The studio on Thirty-Seventh Street? Otherwise, I'll have to call Varrier Management and have someone check the inventory. I don't keep track of individual apartments. I own too many.'

The one-room apartment in question is dominated by a gigantic bed and a collection of sexual aids large enough to stock a small porno shop. Angel knows she's not the first woman he's taken there, and that she won't be the last.

'How much do you want?' she asks.

'How long will you need it?'

'No more than a few days.'

Vincent pauses for a moment, then says, 'Let me see if I understand. You're telling me that if you do need the place, you'll need it within two weeks and you won't be staying more than a few days. Do I have that right?'

'Exactly right.'

'Then I can't charge you, not when you're in trouble.'

'Please, Vincent, I'd rather pay.'

'No, I won't hear of it.' Vincent reaches into his back pocket. He removes his wallet and takes a key card from an inner slot. 'This card works the lock on the outer door and the apartment door. Take possession whenever you're ready, but call me as soon as you get settled. Otherwise, I might walk in at a bad moment.'

Angel rises on her toes to offer Graham a kiss that rocks him back on his heels. As she turns away, she thinks of Carter, of his life being little more than an endless preparation for the battlefield. Angel will never acquire Carter's skills. That's a given. But it doesn't mean she's without weapons of her own. Angel's hoping with all her heart that everything works out, that she and Carter emerge triumphant to split Bobby Ditto's money. But Angel's not her father's daughter. She will not put her faith in her hopes. And as for Vincent Graham, there's always the little gun nestled in the toe of a boot, the one that fits her hand so nicely.

EIGHTEEN

Louis Chin's in good spirits as he makes his way along Roosevelt Avenue in the Queens neighborhood of Flushing. For once, he doesn't feel out of place, a sixth generation Chinese-American living in a Chinese-Korean neighborhood dominated by new immigrants. Louis doesn't understand a word of Mandarin or Korean, the languages commonly addressed to him when he enters a shop or a restaurant, and he's truly sick of the contemptuous looks bestowed upon him when he confesses his ignorance. As if the color of his skin and the shape of his eyes somehow binds him to a heritage in which he has zero interest.

Chin's spent the last two hours in a bar with a war buddy, Nelson Flanagan. Flanagan's in the private security business, running a start-up company in a hostile economic climate.

'Every day's another firefight, Louis. That's the beauty of it.'

Nelson doesn't march with the real players. He's not Kroll Associates. L&L Security's clients manage third-tier office buildings in obscure, outer-borough neighborhoods. Their needs are commonly limited to a single security guard stationed behind a table in the lobby, a guard whose main function is to prevent the homeless from taking up residence in the hallways.

Once upon a time, Louis and Nelson were responsible for a combat unit operating near Kandahar, Louis an officer, Nelson his sergeant. They'd shared the same foxhole, ducked the same bullets, mourned the same dead.

'This business, it's like another war. It's combat all over again. Only now you fight with money instead of bullets.'

Chin responded with an appropriate '*Semper Fi*', but his thoughts had already shifted to another factor. The dollars Nelson put in his pocket, week by week and month by month, were a hundred percent legit. He wasn't looking over his shoulder, waiting for the cops to snatch him off the street. At worst, he'll end up in bankruptcy court. Instead of a prison cell.

Chin's thinking that the law of averages will catch up with him if he trades in secrets long enough. He's thinking the Feds will come down on him like a ton of bricks. He's thinking he needs to find another way.

The good news is that Nelson's landed a top-tier client in the form of Grantham Management. Grantham wants L&L Security to staff a ten-story commercial property about to open near City Hall in lower Manhattan. The contract, according to Nelson, is all but signed.

'Come in now, Louis. I'm talking about partners. See, you've got a presence that clients are definitely gonna love. It's that officer thing, right? People not only respect you, they assume you're smart because you're Asian. Me, I'm a jarhead and I always will be. I take orders. I get the job done. With you out front and me watching your back, we can't fail.'

Chin hesitates as he turns from Kissena Boulevard on to Barclay Avenue. For just a moment, he stares at a six-story apartment building halfway up the block, his building, home sweet home. A red-brick cube devoid of architectural detail, the building's as plain as a low-income housing project, as plain as a prison. Chin figures that's only reasonable because the structure was originally built for working-class New Yorkers a paycheck away from poverty.

Nelson asked Louis for an answer by the end of the week, but Chin's already made up his mind. The encounter with the cop has him spooked. The bulge under the arm, the handcuffs dangling from a belt loop. Louis's parents would die if he got himself arrested. His father's an engineer, for Christ's sake. His mother's an accountant.

So, that's it. Chin heads for home, imagining himself a businessman fretting over the accounts receivable, wondering how in the world he'll make the next payroll. Maybe ten years from now, if he works enough seventy hour weeks, he'll be reasonably compensated. Maybe.

Chin hesitates before the inner lobby door. The lock is broken, the door slightly ajar, a common occurrence that never fails to annoy Chin. The lock wasn't damaged by vandals or thieves. Pragmatists to the core, the residents are themselves responsible. The intercom hasn't worked in six months, which means you have to come to the lobby when you have a visitor or receive a delivery. Or you would if the lock wasn't broken.

There's a bottle of white wine in Chin's refrigerator, a half-assed decent Chardonnay that calls to him as he presses the button for the elevator, as the door opens and he steps inside. Only when the elevator begins to move do his thoughts turn to Leonard Carter. Another ten grand and he'll have the cushion he suspects he'll need for his transition to legitimacy. Chin's not suicidal. He's not intending to confront Carter one on one. But there's that warehouse two blocks away, the one he noticed while the cop examined his ID. Chin had driven past the building on his way out of the neighborhood, a matter of pure chance. The structure was vacant, its doors and windows covered with sheets of plywood. Late at night, access to the roof would involve only a minimum of risk. Chin's almost certain the roof overlooks the windows of Carter's apartment, all of them.

If Carter believes himself to be safe, Chin thinks, if he fails to take elementary precautions like keeping the shades drawn, if he foolishly exposes himself . . .

Chin keys the two locks protecting his door, steps inside his apartment, locks the doors behind him and flips on the light. Big mistake. If he'd reversed the last two steps, if he'd turned on the light first, if he'd seen Leonard Carter standing in the kitchen before he locked the door behind him, he might have had a chance. Maybe not, though. Carter's holding a gun in his right hand, a silenced, .22 caliber semi-automatic, an assassin's weapon. His eyes are calm and cool, his stare unwavering.

'Walk further into the apartment,' he says.

Chin counts off the steps – one, two, three, four, five – until Carter orders him to stop.

'Strip down. Toss your clothes across the room.'

Well, there it is, Chin thinks. What goes around, comes around. In Afghanistan, he'd ordered suspected Taliban to strip down shortly after taking them into custody, ostensibly because their garments and bags had to be searched. But a naked prisoner is a compliant prisoner, reduced in his own eyes, and everybody knew it, including the prisoners. Humiliation by design, caution the excuse, a naked exercise in power relationships. Forgive the pun.

'You want to hear a joke?' Chin asks as he strips off his briefs to stand naked.

'Sure.'

'What happens when a Chinese man with a hard-on runs into a wall?' Chin gives it a couple of beats before delivering the punchline. 'He breaks his nose.'

Carter doesn't laugh. 'I want you to sit down with your back against the wall, your feet crossed at the ankles. Do it now.'

Chin complies, but then asks, 'Would you mind telling me what this is all about?'

Carter responds by shooting him in the right knee, the pain so overwhelming that Chin's vision is instantly replaced by a wall of fire, as if he was staring into the heart of a blast furnace. He wants to scream, but he knows better. Then the fire recedes and he watches Carter raise the .22 until the barrel is pointed at his forehead.

'I have a low tolerance for bullshit,' Carter explains.

Unable to speak, Chin stares for a moment at the blood flowing from his knee. Then he wraps his hands around the punctured bone and feels the shattered bullet trapped beneath the skin. This is exactly what'll happen if Carter pulls the trigger again. The round will shatter as it penetrates his skull, leaving each tiny shard to track a different path through his brain.

'What do you want me to tell you?' he finally mutters.

'First, how you found me.'

'Do you know who Bobby Ditto is?'

'I know.'

'He had information on you, your last name and your involvement with a man named Montgomery Thorpe.' Chin pauses for breath. 'I have a . . . a contact with access to sections of the CIA's database.'

'Classified sections?'

'Yes, classified data. I discovered Thorpe first, then you as a known associate. From there it was a matter of working backward until I found the address you gave when you enlisted.'

'And Bobby Ditto knows my name and address?'

Chin's wishing that Carter's expression would change. He'd prefer righteous anger to the man's eerie calm. 'Look, I'm just a clerk. I trade in information. I'm not a threat.'

'Then why did you put my apartment under surveillance? And why do you have a scoped Remington 30.06 in your closet?'

'I'm a hunter, a deer hunter.'

'No, you're not. You don't have any hunting equipment, not even a pair of boots. You hunt humans, Chin. Which leaves you without any right to complain when your prey fights back. I've searched your apartment and I know you've been to war. So, unless you're that rare atheist in the foxhole, it's time for you to make your peace.'

But Chin doesn't pray. Instead, he begins to cry, the tears running from his eyes in a little stream. Not that it helps him. Carter has responsibilities now, to Angel and the cop. If he risks himself, he risks them, and Chin, given his military experience and his access to state secrets, is a genuine threat.

'One day it'll be my turn,' he explains. 'Today, it's yours.'

Paulie Margarine's fully awake when Carter steps into his bedroom, yet he sees or hears nothing until Carter reaches the foot of his bed. Paulie's awake because he's in pain, despite a patch on his chest that leaches a steady dose of Fentanyl on to his skin. The cancer is everywhere, including his bones, and he has little time left. Now, looking up at Carter and the gun in his hand, Paulie knows that he has even less, that his journey is almost complete. And the amazing part is that he still wants every minute, that he doesn't want to surrender a single second.

'Carter?' The word is barely audible and he swipes a dry tongue over dry lips before repeating himself. 'Carter?'

'Yeah, Paulie, it's me. The man you never expected to see

again.' Carter shakes his head. 'How much, Paulie. How much to sell me out?'

'I never . . .'

'Bobby Ditto connected me to Montgomery Thorpe, which he couldn't have done without your help. I just want to know how much.'

Paulie's too ashamed to admit the truth. Five thousand? Given the cost, the gain was pitiful. 'Fifteen grand, but the money wasn't the point. My family and his, we go back a long way. I couldn't refuse him. But I swear, I never thought he'd actually find you. I never thought you'd let yourself be traced. I thought you were too smart for that.'

In fact, Carter might have sold Janie's apartment at any time over the past few years, knowing she'd never use the place again. Instead, he deliberately left his back trail in place, the better to see who was coming up behind him. 'Tell me why Bobby came to you? What made him think you could help him?'

Paulie tries to raise himself up far enough to slide a second pillow beneath his head, only to be greeted by a sharp pain that runs in a jagged line from his right shoulder to his fingertips.

'Holy shit, I feel like my arm's on fire.'

Carter leans forward to lift Paulie's head, to prop up the pillows, to lay the old man back down. 'You want something?'

'The docs say if I take any more painkillers, they'll kill me instead of the pain.' Paulie laughs, surprising even himself. But he's not a man to be victimized by illusions. He took a chance when he sold Carter out, though he truly believed the odds against the information he bartered leading to Carter were astronomical.

'So, my question. Why did Bobby come to you, Paulie? How did he know who to ask?'

'If you're thinkin' I advertised our relationship, you're wrong. Bobby Ditto knew to come to me because it was Bobby who put the hit on his brother. He told me that Ricky was a snitch, but that was bullshit. Ricky wasn't worth squat and Bobby was proppin' him up. What I think, Bobby got tired of doin' all the work for half the profit.'

'But you didn't ask?'

'Business is business.'

'Yes, it is.'

Paulie shifts his aching knees, turning on to his side. 'What about Freddy?' he asks. 'What about my son?'

'Gone,' Carter says. 'I couldn't leave him out there to hunt me down.'

'It's what I woulda done.'

Paulie looks through the window at a full moon hanging just above the birch trees in the yard outside. He finds himself wishing he could sit outside one more time, sit in full sun, listen to the birds sing, watch a robin search for insects in the grass. This entire spring – his last spring – has been about the birds. Starlings, robins, sparrows, an occasional blue jay, once a cardinal, once a red-tailed hawk that circled overhead for almost an hour. There were days when he looked forward to their songs as eagerly as a baseball fanatic to opening day.

'Are you a Catholic, Paulie?'

'Yeah.'

'You want a minute to pray?'

Paulie considers the offer. 'I made confession two days ago for the first time in forty years, to a Nigerian priest named Father Owegnu. Once I got started, I couldn't stop. I had to tell him everything. Hey, credit where credit is due. The priest didn't interrupt and he didn't get moralistic on me. He didn't give me a penance, either. He just told me to keep on prayin'.'

'And you've been doing that, Paulie? You've been praying to your maker?'

'Yeah, I had to because I knew I was gonna be seein' Him soon.'

Carter raises the .22. 'Then say hello for me.'

NINETEEN

Carter pushes into his apartment at three o'clock in the morning. Still awake, Angel's on the computer. Carter lays the package he's carrying on a table as she approaches. He's expecting to take her into his arms, but Angel doesn't reach out to hug him. Instead, she punches him in the chest.

'Why didn't you call me? I was worried sick.'

And what can he say to that? I was busy murdering three people and it slipped my mind? Angel's standing in front of him, hands on hips, cheeks flaming. She's wearing a T-shirt that reaches to mid-thigh, no bra and some marvelously erotic perfume that might be successfully marketed to victims of erectile dysfunction.

'If you wanted a worry-free life,' Carter finally says, 'you should have gotten out of the van when I offered to let you go.' He raises a hand to caress the side of her face. 'The criminal life, it's not given to serenity.'

Carter goes into the kitchen and takes a black, industrial-grade trash bag from the pantry. He strips out of his clothes and stuffs them in the bag. Then he marches naked into the living room where he retrieves the package he laid on the table. The package contains Louis Chin's hard drive, along with several printed documents that outline Carter's military, and post-military, careers. Carter's already tossed the .22 automatic (but not the silencer) into the East River. Tomorrow, he'll dump everything else, including the clothes and the shoes he wore.

As he flips the switch on a paper shredder next to the computer workstation, Carter glances at the computer's monitor. The figure that stares back, some sort of monster clutching a giant wheel, more or less compels his attention. The monster's three eyes bulge from his head and he wears a crown of five human skulls.

'What's that?' he asks.

'It's Tibetan, a Wheel of Becoming.' Angel lays a hand on Carter's bare shoulder. 'I have a paper to write, my last Art History paper, and I'm going to compare this painting with religious art of the Middle Ages.'

Carter begins to feed the documents into the shredder, but his attention remains on the image in the monitor. 'What's a Wheel of Becoming?'

'I'm not a Buddhist, Carter, but I think it's supposed to be about the different worlds and how we get into them. See here, these are the worlds, in the second circle. On top, the World of the Gods. On the bottom, the Hell World.'

'The Hell World? In Africa, I worked with a mercenary from Nepal. His name was Lo Phet and he claimed we were already living in the Hell World.' Carter examines the segment at the bottom of the wheel more closely. He finds cold and hot hells, humans boiling away in a cauldron. A dog tears at the flesh of a man impaled on the branch of a tree. And, yes, it does remind him of Africa where the boy soldiers routinely amputated hands and feet, arms and legs, noses, lips and ears. Where mass rape was the norm and enslaved villagers mined for diamonds under a sun hot enough to substitute for hellfire.

Carter finishes shredding the documents, then destroys the hard drive before adding what remains of both to his clothes in the trash bag. Finally, he puts the bag next to the front door and heads off to the shower. Close-in head shots produce blowback in the form of blood droplets and minute particles of bone. Carter can see bloodstains on his right forearm, and he assumes there's trace evidence on his neck and in his hair. He doesn't think himself pursued, but he's taking no chances. Better to be sure.

Ten minutes later, Angel's leaning against the towel rack, her eyes fixed on Carter's soapy chest. 'You're pretty quiet tonight,' she says, a clear invitation to unburden himself.

But Carter's not about to confess – he's not even tempted. He squeezes a dab of shampoo into his palm and begins to work it into his hair. Right now, he's trying to feel something. Regret, triumph, relief, he doesn't care. But that's not happening. Maybe later.

Carter steps out of the shower to find Angel standing with a towel in her hands. Somehow, when he wasn't looking, she ditched the T-shirt.

'Why do I have the feeling,' she asks, 'that you're going to be mean to me?'

Carter's not mean to Angel. He revels in her beauty instead, as though, after many, many throws of the dice, nature had finally gotten it right. There's no millimeter of her skin he doesn't taste. His hands are everywhere, tracing the contours of her body, the arch of her breasts and her hips, the folds of her ears, the hollow spaces between the vertebrae on her spine. At one point, lost in his own pleasure, he thinks he might be imagining her.

Moments later, Angel re-establishes her corporeal nature by heading off to the bathroom, then to the kitchen. She returns with a container of peach yogurt, not the ice cream Carter was hoping for.

'So,' she asks as she settles, cross-legged, on the bed, 'what's it like in the Hell World?'

Carter mulls the question over, wondering exactly where to go, or whether to go anywhere. Angel's Great Adventure. That's what it's about for her, a stepping-stone to her ultimate goal, a point of passage. Carter's intimately familiar with points of passage. He knows that some of them are one-way only, and he decides to warn Angel.

'There were eleven of us in Liberia,' he begins, 'chasing down a warlord named Tama Youboty and the blood diamonds he stole from another warlord named Togaba Kpangbah. I say warlord, but lord is too big a title for Youboty. He had about thirty men under his command, boy soldiers, none more than sixteen, a few no taller than the AK47s they carried.

'Our commander was a Brit named Montgomery Thorpe who claimed to be educated at Sandhurst, the British Royal Military Academy. Some way, he got us out ahead of Youboty, so that we were waiting for the warlord when he drove up to this deserted village in the Nimba Mountains. I was stationed at the entrance to the village, me and two other men, Jerzy Golabek and Paul Ryan. We were concealed behind rocks on a hillside. Thorpe and the rest of our men, eight in all, were on the other side of the village. You understand, there were eleven of us and we were going up against thirty fighters with superior arms. Our advantages were concealment and surprise, but they were no guarantee.'

Carter leans against the headboard, his eye moving to the ceiling as he organizes the details. The boy soldiers have haunted him for years, the memories surfacing in bits and pieces, an image here, an image there, triggered by the face of a bewildered gang-banger on a perp walk, or the odor of blood in a butcher's shop.

'The plan belonged to Thorpe and it was simple enough. We'd let Youboty and his technicals—'

'What's a technical?'

'Technicals are unarmored pickup trucks, usually Japanese, with large caliber weapons mounted in the beds, in this case fifty caliber machine guns. Anyway, the plan was to let Youboty turn into the village, then open fire from behind with small arms and a mortar. We were hoping that he'd retreat through the village and into an ambush on the other side.'

Carter stops long enough to accept a spoonful of yogurt. 'The village was in the Nimba Mountains, above eight hundred meters, where the jungle bleeds into a mix of pine forest and grasslands. This was in midsummer, in equatorial Africa, and we were completely exposed to the sun, a ragtag collection of mercs from every continent except Antarctica. Even in the mercenary world, we were the lowest of the low, like the bandit Samurai in that movie. We served no master.

'I remember the wind hissing over the rocks and a family of jackals that searched the huts in the village, one by one, and the sweat running from my hair to my toes, and the hours ticking by. Thorpe had made an educated guess, but a guess is still a guess. If Youboty took a different route – and there were others open to him – we'd have to fight our way back to the coast with nothing to show for the risk.

'But Thorpe was right this time. Youboty and his boy soldiers arrived at two o'clock in the afternoon, crowded into four technicals. Youboty was in the cab of the lead vehicle. The boy soldiers were huddled around the fifty caliber machine guns in the truck beds. They wore rags and their eyes were hollow, their faces gaunt. I knew they were vicious. I'd seen, first hand, what they did when they happened on an occupied village. They were cruel, needlessly cruel, but there was a method to their cruelty. Little bands like Youboty's had no access to supplies. They pillaged to survive.

'Anyway, the first part went exactly as planned. Golabek fired off a mortar round just after Youboty's technical cleared the first house. As luck would have it – bad luck – he scored a direct hit. Youboty and his lieutenant were blown to pieces. See, the boy soldiers couldn't fight, even with their master alive. They had no training and no real experience defending against soldiers who did. That's why they panicked when Paul and I eliminated the machine gunners with our M16s. Instead of retreating through the village, away from our fire, they jumped out of the technicals and ran into the mud huts.'

'I think I might have done the same thing,' Angel declares. 'Duck for cover.'

'The cover was an illusion because the roofs had fallen in and they were completely exposed to mortar fire from both ends of the village. The huts were death traps. But they still had options. They could have massed and attacked my position, or they could have dug in, forced us to come for them, or they could have surrendered. But they didn't, Angel. No, what they did, in ones and twos and threes, was dash into the open and fire off their weapons. I don't know what they expected to hit – not a single round came anywhere close to our position – but standing out in the open, only a few hundred yards off, they were as unprotected as targets on a shooting range. As far as I could tell, I never missed, not once.'

Carter pauses to ease the pressure in his diaphragm. He's having trouble drawing a breath. Angel's watching him, eyes wide, mouth open. She's never seen him like this, and she doesn't know what to make of his story. Carter doesn't help matters when he finally says, 'You know the expression that mob guys use? Making your bones? Like you're one thing before you kill for the first time, then you become something else?'

'Yeah, sure.'

'Well, I killed children for money, Angel, and not because they were vicious murderers, which they were. I killed them for the diamonds they were guarding. What does that make me?'

TWENTY

Bobby Ditto grunts with each upward thrust of his arms. He's on the deck behind his home in Howard Beach, Queens, only a few miles from Kennedy Airport on Jamaica Bay. Bobby's doing bench presses, pushing two hundred and fifty pounds into the air with each rep. This is a workout weight, and far from his best efforts, which reach beyond three-fifty.

The Blade stands behind the bench, his hands beneath the weight bar as it rises and falls. At a signal from his boss, he guides the weights on to the bench's hooks. Unburdened, Bobby sits up, dropping his feet to the ground as he lifts a pair of forty-pound dumb-bells and does a set of rapid-fire curls. Just after dinner last night, one of his favorite whores injected a mix of human growth hormone and steroids into his left buttock. His ass is still sore, but the rest of his body's humming along, all gain, no pain.

Except when he thinks about Paulie Margarine and his boy, Freddy. Bobby has a half-assed connection in the NYPD, a sergeant named Casey, who he called as soon as he heard the news. According to Casey, Paulie and his son were discovered in their beds, shot once through the forehead. There was no sign of forced entry, despite the house being alarmed, and no physical evidence was recovered. Nevertheless, given Paulie's long-term mob affiliation and the kid's being released from prison only a year before, the cops are looking at the usual suspects, including Bobby Ditto.

Right after hanging up on Casey, Bobby used a throwaway cellphone to call Louis Chin. No answer on the first, second or third attempts. Goodbye, Mr Chin.

Levi Kupperman's face appears in the sliding door leading

from the deck into the house. 'I'm done,' he says. 'The house is clean.'

Bobby lays the weights down and stares at the kid, standing there with his little meter in his hand, hollow eyes pleading, a bag of bones. Bobby's thinking that Levi's usefulness is coming to an end, that maybe his addiction has reached a terminal phase. The kid looks like death warmed over, like he's waiting for someone to open the lid on his coffin so he can climb in and make himself comfortable.

'Take care of him,' Bobby tells the Blade. Then he gets up and strolls to the edge of the deck. Located on a channel leading to Jamaica Bay, Bobby's home is on stilts, the better to avoid the inevitable flooding when nor'easters push the Atlantic Ocean in his general direction. Below him, tied to a wooden pier, his pride and joy bobs in the swells, a twenty-two-foot SunDancer with enough cabin space to bed a pair of whores, or hide several bodies. Bobby keeps the SunDancer fueled and ready to go from early April until mid-November.

'OK, boss, he's gone.'

Bobby turns to his most trusted advisor – the Blade's as close to a father as Bobby's ever known – and smiles to himself. Right this minute, two of Bobby's men are sitting in the living room, looking through the windows. As if they could stop – or even slow down – Leonard Carter.

'See, Marco, what I can't figure is why I'm standin' out here in the sunshine.' He jerks a thumb toward the sky. 'Instead of bein' up there, tryin' to explain my life to St Peter.'

'You'd need a hell of a shyster to bring that one off,' the Blade responds.

'Is that what you figure? That we're gonna burn, no questions asked?'

'No, what I figure is that when you're dead, you're dead, and that's the end of it. But what could I say? To each his own.'

'OK, but the question I'm still askin' is why I'm not dead.' Bobby walks back to the weight bench. He picks up a pair of thirty-pound dumb-bells, leans back and begins doing flys, his arms fully extended.

The Blade follows Bobby over. He positions himself at the

foot of the bench and folds his arms across his chest, but says nothing. The Blade's wearing a royal-blue track suit with white piping on the arms, a high-end knock-off. The Blade never buys retail, not if he can help it. He figures legit manufacturers are even bigger crooks than the factory owners churning out the fakes.

'I've been thinkin' along the same lines as you,' the Blade finally says, which is not the truth, not at all. The Blade's been primarily focused on their upcoming deal.

'This guy, Carter?' Bobby lays the weights on the bench. He's breathing a little harder and his massive chest is slick with sweat. 'He's like a magician, right? Like he walks through fuckin' walls? Hey, face the facts. Paulie was nobody's asshole, and neither was his kid. Meanwhile, they got whacked in their beds.'

The Blade's quick to agree. 'The man's good. I seen for myself what he can do, like first hand. Know what I think? I think the army trains these guys to be supermen. Like the Jews, ya know? Like the Mossad. They could track down anyone, anywhere. Like they're fuckin' invisible.'

'Then why am I still walkin' around, Marco? How come I'm not sittin' in the morgue, waitin' to be sliced and diced?'

'All I know for sure is that he said he was comin' for you.'

'But when? What's he waitin' for? Think for a minute. Carter shoots Ricky. Then he takes the whore away from you and Ruby. Then he whacks Ruby right on the street, takes out Paulie in his bed, and most likely the Chink's gone, too.' Bobby lifts the weights to his chest, lies down and starts another set of flys. 'I don't get the timing, Marco. I don't get the timing at all.'

The Blade's thoughts come together before Bobby completes the set. First, his boss is right. If Carter wanted Bobby dead, he would've made an attempt by now. Yeah, they've been careful, but they're not exactly hiding. 'I'm thinkin' that he wants somethin'.'

'But he's not tellin' me what it is.'

'No, and he has Ruby's cellphone. The number for the warehouse is on it. He could've called any time.'

'So, then what?'

Once the Blade's mind begins to move in the right direction, his logic follows the same path taken by Solly Epstein. Outside of Bobby Ditto's life, there's only one thing he and his boss have that anybody *could* want.

'What we gotta do, like right away, is bring the money into the bunker.'

'The money?' Bobby drops the weights to the deck and sits up. The basic question – why am I still alive? – was as far as he'd gotten, that and the fact that the payments to Chin were wasted money. Now he's thinking he could be ruined forever. 'Where do ya get that from?'

The Blade takes a deep breath. 'Follow the connections, Bobby. Carter connects to the whore. The whore connects to your brother. Your brother – who had a big mouth, which everybody knows – connects to the money.'

'Fuckin' Ricky.' Bobby stops at the approach of a small boat. He walks over to the rail and waves to Vince Capporelli, who lives two houses away. Vince holds up a bluefish that must weigh fifteen pounds.

'You need to get out in the bay,' Vince calls. 'The blues are feeding close to shore. The water's boiling.'

Bobby can remember a time when he would have packed his fishing gear, filled a cooler with beer and sandwiches, and been out the door fifteen minutes later. Now he spends his days in a bunker.

'OK,' he tells the Blade, 'get the boys together, pick up the money and bring it to the bunker. I want you to use at least three men and make sure one of 'em is Donny Thorn. I'm gonna put him in charge.'

Donny Thorn is Donald Thornton, an Irish kid who grew up with Bobby and his brother. He's quick, tough and gets the job done, the perfect choice to replace Ruby.

'A harp? The boys ain't gonna like that.'

This is not something Bobby needs to be told. The rest of his men are Italian. Taking orders from an Irishman won't come easy. So what? Bobby returns to the weight bench and lies down. All this bullshit, it's ruining his workout.

'Just get it done, Marco. And tell the boys to bring a change of clothes and a toothbrush. They won't be leavin' that basement any time soon.'

TWENTY-ONE

When the Blade steps on to the sidewalk, Carter and Epstein both respond with a muttered 'Fuck.' More ladylike, Angel settles for, 'Oh, shit.' The Blade went into the building unburdened. Now he's carrying a small, hard-sided suitcase. And that's not the worst of it. No, the Blade's accompanied by three younger men whose heads swivel back and forth as they hustle over to a Ford Expedition with appropriately darkened windows. A minute later, they take off.

'Does this mean what I think it means?' Put off by Solly Epstein's sudden appearance, Angel's been sulking all day. She wants to know why she wasn't consulted before Carter added a full partner to their little enterprise. Of course, Carter may very well be planning to eliminate the cop and his share of the loot, all in one fell swoop. As he might be planning to eliminate Angel Tamanaka. There's no way to know.

Carter ignores Angel's question. 'They're spooked about something. If I follow them, we'll be spotted.'

'I think I know where they're going,' Epstein says. 'I think they'll take the money to the bunker. Work your way back to Harlem River Drive and head south.'

Angel bristles again when Carter meekly complies. 'What's the bunker?' she asks.

'Bobby owns a rug warehouse in Brooklyn,' Epstein replies. 'He's got a room in the basement, soundproofed, no windows. It's where he does business.'

'A bunker?'

'That's what he calls it.'

'And you think the money's in the suitcase?'

'I can't see another reason why he'd send four men to get it.'

Earlier in the morning, before they set up the surveillance, they'd begun to comb through the hundreds of items in OCCB's file on Roberto Benedetti. A quick review of known associates yielded immediate results. Bobby Ditto's godfather, Vincent Pugliese, rents an apartment, 5B, in the Kingsbridge section of the Bronx. In poor health at age seventy-four, Pugliese lives alone, his wife long deceased, his children scattered. He walks with the aid of a cane and is said, by an NYPD registered informant, to be uniformly polite to his neighbors.

Armed with that bit of information, all three had driven to Kingsbridge. That was four hours ago. Now they're on the road again.

'Why would he move the money?' Angel's watching her elaborately constructed fantasy, the one that has her opening a little art gallery on Tobago just in time for the winter season, dissolve before her eyes. 'Is he on to us?'

But there are any number of possibilities out there and Angel barely listens to Epstein as he dissects each of them. She's wondering exactly what she's going to do if there's no money to steal, no goal to achieve. A return to normalcy seems unlikely, given that Bobby Ditto now believes her partially responsible for two murders.

Angel starts to speak, but then looks over at Carter. His features are composed, his expression almost serene, this despite Bobby Ditto's knowing his name. Angel's annoyed at first, but then skips to an obvious bottom line. No matter what happens to the money, Bobby's fate has already been determined. No need to worry.

The drive to the Red Hook section of Brooklyn takes more than an hour. They're plagued by heavy traffic on FDR Drive along the East River, on the Brooklyn Bridge with its perpetual renovations, most of all on the notorious Brooklyn-Queens Expressway. The delays cost them nothing, nothing that hasn't already been lost. The SUV's sitting in front of Benedetti Wholesale Carpeting, a long, two-story building located a few blocks from the waterfront.

'The bunker's in the basement,' Epstein explains. 'To get there, you have to come down a narrow flight of stairs.'

'How do you know so much about the set-up?' Angel asks.

'An informant.' Epstein's crouched in the cargo space behind the van's rear seat. He's thinking that it's someone else's turn to bounce up and down on the plywood floor. Somebody with a bigger ass. 'The informant's name, a major source, by the way, was Ruby Amaroso. Unfortunately, someone put a knife in Ruby's back last week. I'm not sayin' I know who that somebody was, but I got my suspicions.'

Angel laughs, but Carter's expression doesn't change. Finally, she says, 'The good thing is that we know exactly where the money is. If we can't get to it right now, they have to bring it out, sooner or later.'

'That won't necessarily help us, even if we happen to be watching at the time,' Carter responds. 'The Ford's armored.'

'Seriously?'

'First, the vehicle didn't settle on its springs when four men got inside. Second, the guard on the front passenger's side of the SUV let the window down. It was two inches thick. Third, even though the driver turned slowly, the truck still pulled away from the turn. That's because of the weight. Armored vehicles stop bullets – some of them will stop an RPG – but they don't handle well.'

Carter doesn't wait for a response. He's not discouraged, not yet, but there's plenty of work to be done. 'Look, I'm going to check out the warehouse for soft spots. There's no need for you to be here. I want you to take the subway back to the apartment and work your way through the files. You'll be looking for the same thing I'm looking for, a soft spot.'

Bobby Ditto holds the phone away from his ear. He never should have taken the call – he's got way too much on his mind. But Dealie told his secretary that it was an emergency, so when he tried to back off, Evangeline shook her head, folded her arms across her chest and nearly shouted, 'No way, Bobby. The woman's nuts, as in whacked-out crazy. You handle her.'

Dealie is short for Delilah, Bobby's ex-wife, now living in depressed Las Vegas. Back when Bobby was sixteen and horny enough to hump a goat, Delilah had lived up to her name. Not so after she became pregnant, after they married, after she dropped the first and the second little rug rat. Not after she gained sixty pounds, after she developed a fondness for roulette wheels and designer wardrobes. Bobby has a girlfriend – a mistress, really – stashed in Rego Park, a half-hour from his Howard Beach home. He doesn't intend to let her get five minutes closer.

The emergency of the week concerns Bobby's oldest, George, age thirteen. Little Georgie's been fighting in school again, been suspended again, and is again being threatened with outright expulsion. The problem's Bobby's fault, of course. If he'd been there for his family, if he'd been a real husband, a real father, little Georgie would be a candidate for Pacifist of the Year.

Bobby Ditto allows Dealie five solid minutes of abuse before he interrupts. 'You need to get to the point,' he tells his wife. 'I got business here, business which I need to conduct if I'm gonna keep sendin' that good old child support every month.'

Wrong tactic. Before she finally gets to the point, Dealie unloads a torrent of accusations centered on his missing a payment two years ago.

'Georgie needs a private school, Bobby, along with serious counseling. And I'm not talkin' about some jerk from the Board of Education. I'm talkin' serious here. As in real fuckin' *serious*.'

'When you say private school, do you mean like Catholic school?'

'No, I'm talking like a military academy in Arizona that specializes in problem kids. They got the program and the counselors.'

At this point, Bobby's supposed to inquire into the costs, but he's not biting. Bobby's thinking maybe he'll take his kid for the summer. That would be the cheapest way out. But, no, the last time he saw his children was Thanksgiving, and he liked them about as much as they liked him, which wasn't much at all. Plus, there's always the possibility that Dealie blew the rent money in one of the casinos and her landlord's threatening to evict her. Dealie lies at the drop of a roulette ball.

A blinking red light on Bobby's desk offers the perfect excuse to end the conversation. 'I gotta go,' he tells his ex, which is true. 'Call me next week, give me an update.'

'But I'm not finished,' Dealie wails.

Bobby hangs up, but not fast enough to escape a parting threat: 'I'll call ya tonight.'

The flashing red light alerts Bobby to an incoming call on his personal phone, which he never answers. He jots down the number on the caller ID screen, picks up a throwaway cellphone that can't be traced to him and heads off. This is the bad news about the bunker. The walls are too thick for cellphones. If he wants to make or receive a call, he can try the basement outside the bunker, which sometimes works, or go to the yard where the company trucks are parked at night.

Bobby heads for the yard, passing through the outer basement where Donny Thorn greets him with an enthusiastic nod. Thorn's two companions, Albert Zeffri and Nino Ferrulo, look up, their expressions anything but happy. Ruby's death left the crew with a vacuum each had hoped to fill. Meanwhile, Zeffri has the brain of a frog and twenty-year-old Nino has yet to master his impulses. Bobby knows for a fact that the kid's been knocking over liquor stores. And not because he needs the money.

The beautiful spring day catches Bobby off-guard and he stops in his tracks, disoriented. The sky is bright blue and sprinkled with small puffy clouds. The sun is warm enough to erase all memory of a truly miserable winter. For just a second, he imagines himself on Jamaica Bay, the small lush islands covered with grass and brush, the SunDancer bobbing, a hooked bluefish fighting to the bitter end. Maybe there's a broad along, somebody new, and a cooler full of beer, and a light breeze, and a blazing sunset.

Bobby shakes his head in disgust. Given everything that's happened over the past couple of weeks – given Ruby and Ricky and Paulie and the Chink, not to mention Paulie's fucking kid whose name he can't remember – this is no time for daydreaming. He punches a number into the cellphone and raises the phone to his ear. The man who answers, Elvino Espinoza, speaks English with only a trace of a Spanish accent.

'Good to hear your voice again,' he says.

'You, too.'

'We're looking at the weekend. I'll come by to say hello on Friday morning.'

And that's it, short and sweet. The deal will be consummated on the weekend, probably late at night. Exact time and place will be revealed to Bobby on Friday morning. Be ready.

Bobby folds up the cellphone and puts it in his pocket. Attracted by the scream of wood on a saw blade, he glances across the street at a custom woodworker's small factory. The owner's name is Abel Kousamanis, a Greek immigrant who styles himself a furniture artist. There's a limo parked in front of Abel's shop and Bobby can see him through an open truck bay, talking to a woman in a blue business suit.

Back to the cave, Bobby tells himself. He looks around him, at a truck backing through the roll-up door on the front of the warehouse, at a forklift pulling an enormous roll of carpet from the back of a trailer. Bobby's workers are really hustling. That's because it's after four o'clock and they won't be going home until the trailer's unloaded.

Bobby, as he trudges off, never thinks to look up at the roof where Carter's crouching next to a ventilation pipe, only his forehead and eyes exposed. Good thing. If Bobby had looked up, if he'd spotted Carter, he'd already be dead.

TWENTY-TWO

Carter finally makes an appearance at the East Village apartment a few minutes before midnight. He finds Angel and Solly Epstein seated at a dining room table covered with files and cartons of Chinese food. Angel's hopeful expression fascinates him, as always. She's relentlessly optimistic. But he's got little good news, though he takes her in his arms when she crosses the room in search of a hug. Epstein's grinning from ear to ear as his eyes occasionally drift to Angel's well-rounded buttocks.

Released, Carter picks up a pair of chopsticks and a microwave-safe container of beef in black bean sauce. His instructors would have called it opportunistic feeding. Take your calories and your sleep whenever and wherever you can

– you might be a long time finding another chance. Carter hasn't eaten since they left the apartment in the morning.

'Anything good?' Epstein asks. 'You've been gone a long time.'

Carter responds by snatching a container of rice. He brings the container to his lips and shovels cold rice into his mouth with the chopsticks. The black bean sauce was highly spiced. His tongue is on fire.

'I told them extra hot,' Angel explains.

'Thanks for sharing.'

'Maybe I should go first,' Epstein says. 'What I have to say won't take that long.'

Carter accepts a glass of water and nods. 'By all means.'

'You said to look for a soft spot. We only found one, a kid named Levi Kupperman who sweeps the bunker for listening devices. This information comes, by the way, from Ruby Amaroso. I didn't work with Ruby, or with the joint task force investigating Benedetti, but I do know that Ruby was facing a couple of hundred years on federal narcotics charges. It seems he was dealing on the side and wasn't as careful as his boss. Bottom line, he had every reason to tell the truth.'

Epstein pauses long enough to sip at his beer. He looks from Angel to Carter, finds both attentive, then continues. 'Kupperman's a cocaine addict. The way Ruby put it, "I'm givin' him a year, at the most, before his brain is totally fried." Junkies can be reached by withdrawing or bribing them with their drug of choice, or with some combination of the two. That makes Kupperman a weak spot.'

'If he can find bugs, he should be able to plant one.'

'Planting a bug is the easy part,' Epstein explains. 'Look, there are two general types of eavesdropping devices. The first transmits a signal in real time. You sit outside the bugged site with a receiver and you hear everything that goes on. That won't work in the bunker, which was designed to defeat transmitters. The second type records information on a chip and you have to go back to retrieve the device. Even assuming another trip is feasible, how do you know if anything significant was recorded? You could end up with a five hour conversation centered on broads and baseball. Keep in mind, you take a certain risk in approaching Kupperman. He might run back to his boss.'

Carter glances at Angel. He notes the still hopeful look in her dark blue eyes and has to resist an urge to caress her. Still, he doesn't try to sugar-coat the problems.

'There's a yard next to the warehouse where they park company vehicles overnight, including the armored Expedition. Attaching a GPS device to the SUV will be easy. If I can defeat the alarm, we can also bug the interior.'

'You got into the yard?' Epstein's tone is admiring. The chain-link fence surrounding the yard was topped with razor wire.

'The warehouse isn't well-protected. There are security cameras in front of the roll-up doors and the office door, but not in the back of the building. I was able to access the roof while the warehouse was still open. It would be easier at night when the neighborhood's more or less deserted.'

Carter picks a dumpling from a container, dips it in a brown sauce that might or might not have been intended for that purpose, and slides it into his mouth. He chews slowly, his eyes on Epstein. The cop appears to be impressed, but accessing Benedetti Wholesale Carpeting was no great feat. Compared, say, to operating for a week in the hinterlands of Yemen.

'Look, I don't have much in the way of good news,' he finally says. 'I was able to enter the warehouse through a skylight shortly after the business closed for the night. By then, Bobby and the man we saw with the suitcase—'

'That would be Marco Torrino,' Epstein interrupts. 'He's called "the Blade" because of his nose.'

'OK, Benedetti and Torrino left together a little before six. But not the three men we saw with Torrino in Kingsbridge. They stayed behind.'

'How do you know they didn't leave before we got to the warehouse?' Angel asks.

'Because I came down those narrow stairs that Solly described. There's a locked door at the bottom, a very flimsy door as it turns out, but I could hear a television going, a woman's voice screaming, "Oh, yeah. Oh, yeah. Yes, yes, yes. Give it to me. Give it to me."'

Angel and Solly both laugh, as Carter intended. Then Epstein asks, 'How did you get into the building?'

'There are two skylights on the roof, neither locked down.'

'And you what? Flew down and back up?'

'Actually, I gave up on superpowers a long time ago.'

'So, how'd you do it?'

'I went to a hardware store and bought thirty feet of rope.' Carter pauses, but Epstein's out of questions. 'Look, I can probably neutralize the men inside the basement, but if the money's locked in a safe, we've shown our cards for nothing.'

'Maybe it's just sitting there,' Angel suggests. 'In the suitcase.'

'A little information,' Solly interrupts. 'According to Amaroso, the basement's divided in half. The part at the end of the stairs is used for storage. The bunker's at the other end of building. According to Ruby, it's protected by a thick wooden door consisting of two slabs of oak and an electronic lock that reads a bar code imprinted on a key card. I'm not saying the bunker can't be penetrated, but you'd be a long time getting past that door.' Epstein glances at his watch. 'Time to call it a night. I'm on vacation as far as the job's concerned, but there's no vacation from your family. I better get home.'

'I'll walk you to your car,' Carter says, already heading for the door.

The East Village sidewalks are quiet, even on Avenue A in the heart of the club scene. It's after midnight and tomorrow's a working day. A few smokers stand outside the clubs, indulging their ten-dollar-a-pack habits. On the street, a horde of empty cabs flies past, reminding Carter of a military convoy double-timing through hostile territory.

'So, what's up, Carter? What couldn't we talk about in front of your girlfriend?'

'Your family's up.'

Epstein eyes his companion, but Carter's expression reveals nothing. In his plaid shirt, brown pants and scuffed athletic shoes, he appears entirely inoffensive. 'Say that again.'

'Face the facts, Solly, we've lost the element of surprise.' Carter pauses for a moment. 'This business started as a quick snatch-and-run in Kingsbridge. With a little luck, we could have entered the apartment when the resident . . .'

'Vincent Pugliese.'

'Pugliese, yes. We could have stolen the money when he was out of the apartment, there and gone. That's not the case now.'

Epstein leans against his car. There's a slight chill in the air and the skies above are streaked with flat clouds the color of soot in a fireplace. Like any other New York cop, Epstein's spent enough time on the street to predict the weather more accurately than most TV meteorologists. It'll rain tomorrow, all day.

'How do you think they got on to us?' Epstein asks.

'I don't know that they have. We saw money delivered to the apartment on several occasions. There were no guards when the deliveries were made, just Torrino. Now we see money coming out, this time guarded. Maybe there's a deal going down and Bobby's concentrating his capital. Or maybe he came to the same conclusion you did. Or maybe both things are happening simultaneously. I'm only sure that it doesn't matter, either way, because the rules have changed. There's no getting to that money without spilling blood.'

Both men pause at the approach of three kids, two boys and a girl, none more than sixteen. The kids are Latino and they toss Epstein and Carter hard looks as they pass by. Epstein answers the challenge with a cop glare of his own, but Carter simply ignores a threat he deems non-existent.

'You have a family,' he tells the cop, 'a pregnant wife and a child. Time to walk away.'

Epstein thinks he should be angry, but in fact, having come to the same conclusion about the blood part, he's relieved. 'That's it? You're dismissing me?'

'Not completely. I still need a tracking unit. And maybe a little help on how to install it. I assume they don't run on batteries.'

'Yeah, they do, as a matter of fact.'

Finally, some good news. 'How long do the batteries last?'

'That depends on how often the vehicle is used. Weeks, for sure, sometimes for months. You can buy these things anywhere, by the way. They cost about four hundred dollars.'

At the corner, a couple in search of a cab slips into a passionate clinch. When the girl attempts to back away, she loses her balance and falls into a sitting position on the sidewalk. Her drunken laughter echoes up and down the block.

'I can supply the tracking unit, no problem,' Epstein continues, 'and I think I can bug the Ford, too, even if it is alarmed. But there has to be a bottom line, for the unit and the files. I'm sure this is something you already considered.'

'Yeah, I have. Five thousand up front, Solly. Another fifteen if I bring it off. But I might take my own advice and walk away. I'm not given to assaulting impregnable positions.'

Epstein offers his hand. 'I can't figure you out. One minute you're this, the next you're that. But I'm grateful anyway. That wife and kid? I love the hell out of 'em. My favorite home movie is an ultrasound video of the fetus in Sofia's womb.'

Angel doesn't have a ready response when Carter describes his conversation with the cop. After all that talk about blood diamonds and the hell world, Carter's done a good deed. Two good deeds, actually, because now they won't have to split the take with Epstein. So, maybe she underestimated him. Maybe he's not the bad boy she took him for.

'Am I next on the dismissal list?' she finally asks.

'No.'

'Why not?'

'Because someone has to drive the van.'

'Ah, there's the Carter I know. Practical, practical, practical.'

Carter proves her doubly right when he adds, 'Cops are no good in a firefight, Angel. They usually panic and empty their weapons as fast as they can pull the trigger. If Solly had worked on a SWAT team, I would have kept him on, family or not. As it is, except for the technical part, he's pretty much useless.'

'Like I said, practical, practical, practical.'

They're in the apartment's living room, sitting on a sleek leather couch that mirrors the furniture throughout the apartment. A celebration of glass, chrome and blond wood devoid of adornment, the furnishings are not to Carter's taste, or Angel's, either. But they're not in it for the ambiance.

'You know we'll never get out of prison if something goes wrong,' Carter says.

'Like what?'

'Like if a police cruiser happens to cruise by at just the wrong time, or an unknown witness calls them, or if I should happen to come out on the losing end of a firefight. You can plan all you want, but there's no certainty in war, not for the individual soldier. How old are you, Angel? Twenty-three, twenty-four?'

'Twenty-three.'

'I think life expectancy for women is around eighty-three years. That would leave you staring out through prison bars for the next six decades. I told Solly to consider his family. You need to consider the family you might never have.'

Angel snuggles up against Carter. On the one hand, she's touched by his concern. On the other, he's misjudged her badly. For one thing, blood's already been spilled, Ruby Amaroso's blood, and she was there to play her part. Did the gangster have a wife and children, a mother and a father, uncles, aunts, nephews and nieces? Angel doesn't really care. She's slipped into a place she's been avoiding for a long time, a walk on the wild side from which (and she knows this, too) she might never return.

'I'm going to take a bath now, Carter. I need to shave my legs.' Angel runs her fingers along Carter's thigh, producing a satisfying twitch. 'Unless you want to shave them for me.'

Carter harbors no desire to put a sharp blade to Angel's flesh, even a safety razor, but he agrees to observe the process. The outcome, unfortunately, is less erotic than he hoped. Though Angel pursues the mechanics of bathing and shaving diligently, she speaks mostly about the underdeveloped island of Tobago, part of a two island nation called Trinidad and Tobago.

'Trinidad and Tobago have lots of oil, Carter. And I mean lots. They have a stable government, too, something like Costa Rica's, so you don't have to worry about rebellions and coups. Trinidad takes care of the oil part and it's fairly industrialized, especially in the south and around the capital, Port of Spain. Tobago's a different story. There's a mountain rainforest in the center, the beaches are all white sand and turquoise waters, the fishing is superb and the reefs are almost pristine. This is exactly what you want in the Caribbean.'

'You sound like a tourist video.'

Angel doesn't dispute Carter's assessment. To a certain extent, when she compares Tobago with other high-end resort islands, like St Barts or St Kitts, she has to play the advocate. As it turns out, Tobago's low population density is the island's biggest plus. There's plenty of room for villas and yachts and every other accoutrement that might attract the rich.

'Final points.' Angel leans forward to pull the drain plug, then rises to her feet. She doesn't have to ask for a towel as Carter's already holding one. 'Tobago's almost on the equator, so when it's summer in the USA, it's winter in Chile and Argentina, and vice versa. You can fly from Buenos Aires or New York to Port of Spain in under seven hours. And did I mention Trinidad's carnival? It puts Rio's to shame. Trinidad is the home of calypso and steel drum bands that play every kind of music from soca to classical.'

Carter wraps Angel in the towel and pulls her against him. The heat of her body runs through him in a nearly painful wave. 'Didn't you say something about a *final* point? After which we'd revert to sign language?' Carter slides his hand beneath the towel to cup her breast, a gesture that affects him more than it does Angel, though she covers his hand with her own.

'I want you to come with me,' she tells Carter. 'When I make my move.'

'To the Caribbean.'

'Yes, to the Caribbean.'

'In exactly what capacity?'

'Pool boy, with privileges.'

Carter lifts Angel off the floor and carries her toward the bedroom. 'I don't think pool boy works for me, but I can promise you this. I'm more than comfortable with the privileges.'

TWENTY-THREE

Carter enters River Avenue Storage in the south Bronx, a 24/7 facility, at one o'clock on Thursday morning. He rides the elevator to the third floor and walks to a door at the end of a long deserted hallway. Dropping to one knee, he works the dials on the two combination locks securing the door, then rolls the door up, steps inside and slides the door back down before turning on the light. Carter rents the ten-by-twenty space under an assumed name, having paid with cash for the one year lease.

The room is empty except for two large trunks pushed against the back wall. Carter approaches the trunk to his left. He keys the padlock securing the lid, opens it wide and removes a flat case that resembles cases designed to carry musical instruments. But there's no guitar inside, no keyboard. The case has been specially fabricated to hold an Israeli sniper rifle, an M89SR. It took Carter a year and several thousand dollars to secure the weapon, but the rifle has virtues he couldn't ignore. The M89 weighs only ten pounds and is less than three feet long. It uses 7.62 NATO rounds, which are easy to acquire. Best of all, it came with a detachable silencer designed specifically for the M89. Unlike home-made silencers, this one actually works.

Rifles are much noisier than handguns – there's no confusing the crack of a long gun with a car backfiring, or a kid setting off a string of firecrackers. That's not a big deal in combat situations. The position of a sniper several hundred yards away simply can't be determined on the basis of sound. The opposite principle applies to assassins operating in an urban environment where potential witnesses might be anywhere. True, gunfire is routinely ignored in some inner city neighborhoods, but Carter has no desire to bet his life on community indifference. Silence being the assassin's best friend, he prefers to rely on a well-engineered suppressor.

As he did on the day he acquired the weapon, Carter brings the M89 to his shoulder, and as on that first day, the stock molds to his shoulder, the pistol grip to his hand, the sights to his eyes.

Smitten, he decides. That's the word for what happened to him, with the gun and with Angel, both equally beautiful in his eyes. There's a difference, though. While Carter doesn't know what to do with Angel Tamanaka, he knows exactly what to do with the rifle. Or what he hopes to do.

Carter returns the M89 to its case and sets the case on the ground. He pulls an empty backpack from the trunk and half-fills it with a variety of materiel that might or might not be useful, depending on the set-up. Only a few hours before, he and Epstein accomplished a pair of ends. Without setting off the alarm, they attached a magnetized tracking unit beneath the Expedition's right rear fender, along with a listening device that reached into the vehicle's interior. Epstein accomplished this last trick by drilling a small hole in the underside of the SUV, then inserting the head of a bug through the hole. As the hole was drilled beneath the front seat and the bug only a quarter-inch wide, the odds against accidental discovery are great.

The operation hadn't been without its discomforts. It had rained all day and the yard, no more than earth covered with a thin layer of gravel, was cold and muddy. Epstein had volunteered to crawl under the car and plant the devices by himself, but Carter had insisted, despite the conditions, on observing what he deemed to be a teaching moment.

Carter drops a pair of night vision goggles into the backpack, along with a coil of rope, a ball of netting, a pair of walkie-talkies, a set of lock picks, a box of shotgun shells and a box of hollow-point 7.62mm cartridges. There are other items he might need in the trunk, and more items in the other trunk. A bar of plastic explosive, Semtex, virtually beckons to him. Carter had used Semtex on a job in Houston, wiring a crude explosive device into the ignition of a 700 Series BMW owned by Samuel Reed, a pedophile who seduced the wrong man's son.

Carter settles the backpack on to his shoulders, picks up

the gun case and walks to the door. He puts his ear to the metal surface and listens for a moment before making his escape. Five minutes later, he's back in the van and headed north to a Wal-Mart in Westchester County. Carter's not a Wal-Mart hater. Ordinarily, he enjoys the chain's industrial slant, the bare bones displays and the sheer magnitude of the stores. But tonight, as he walks the long aisles, his thoughts turn to Angel and a remark she made just before he left.

'Face it, Carter, if it wasn't for you riding to the rescue, I'd be decomposing in a New Jersey swamp. No, I take that back. If you were the cold, calculating killer you think you are, you would have shot me along with Ricky Ditto. There are no codes of honor in the Hell World.'

But Carter's sick of the whole discussion. The Hell World thing was Lo Phet's idea, not his. Carter doesn't believe in any world he can't presently see and touch. He doesn't believe in rebirth, either. And as to his being cold and calculating, he and Epstein had enjoyed an intimate conversation just before the cop went back to his family. Epstein proposed that they become partners, just as Paulie had a few years before, this time in the business of ripping off drug dealers. He, Epstein, will provide the intelligence. Carter will supply the muscle. If they choose their targets wisely, and leave the narcotics behind, the risks will be minimal.

'See, Carter, I'm pretty sure that you whacked at least six mob guys over the last few years. Meanwhile, no one's looking for you. OCCB and the FBI? They're into these line charts that run from some bullshit don to the capos, to the soldiers, to known associates. I have to admit the charts look nice and neat when you display 'em to a jury, but they're useless when someone acts outside the box. Like you.'

Carter buys five items at Wal-Mart: an X-Acto knife with a set of blades, a packet of coarse sandpaper, a box of strike-anywhere kitchen matches, a tube of glue and four shrink-wrapped ping-pong balls. He pays in cash, then heads back to Manhattan. His route takes him to the East River where he watches the moon play a game of peek-a-boo with a tattered layer of flat gray cloud, alternately casting a glow on the dark waters, then vanishing. Quite deliberately, as deliberately as he keeps the van within five miles of the speed limit, Carter pushes all consideration of Lo Phet's cosmic scheme from his mind. The truth is that Carter's always liked combat – death the ultimate risk, survival the ultimate reward – an unnamed world, however brief, without questions, without conflict, without longing.

A police cruiser's flashing lights dance in the van's rear-view and side mirrors. The cruiser's coming up fast, weaving from lane to lane, siren blaring. When Carter eases the van into the right lane, the cruiser speeds past, then suddenly cuts in front of him to exit at Forty-Ninth Street. Carter's forced to hit the brakes hard and he wonders, for just a moment, what emergency prompted the two cops in the cruiser to risk the lives of ordinary citizens going about their business. With no ready answer, his mind shifts to something even more unpleasant. Life and death are not the only possible outcomes, not here, not in his particular brand of combat. There's another outcome that will leave him caged for the rest of his life, a potential outcome he described to Angel Tamanaka, an outcome worse than death.

Carter asks himself what he'd do if surrounded by cops, a heavily armored SWAT Team perhaps, with no hope of escape. Surrender? Fight to the bitter end? Briefly, he imagines charging into the open, guns blazing, a boy soldier embracing his inevitable fate.

Angel shakes her head in wonder. Vincent Graham's given his love nest a makeover since she last visited. He's shifted his porn collection from the drawers of a triple-dresser to a cabinet that runs along the wall closest to the bed, a cabinet that must have been custom designed. He's also broken his collection into categories, from BDSM and BBW to Gang-bang and Swingers. Common to thousands of Internet porn sites, the list goes on and on, leaving Angel to wonder if Vincent believes they excite the women he brings here. In truth, she finds the display pathetic, as she finds Vincent Graham pathetic, as she finds most of her clients (*former* clients, she reminds herself) pathetic.

Angel glances at a giant TV screen lying flat against the ceiling just beyond the mirror above the bed. At the push of a button, she knows, the screen will descend, at the push of another button, the hi-def show will begin. Angel can't help but contrast Vincent's sex life to the one she and Carter share. Talk about losers.

But Angel's not here to critique Vincent Graham's sexual predilections. Angel wants to make sure the keys work and that Graham hasn't installed a security guard in the lobby, or a camera above the lobby door. He hasn't – probably because he doesn't want his trysts recorded – and the keys do work. That's enough for now.

Angel reaches into her purse, sliding her hand through layers of detritus, old letters, crumpled tissues, two wallets, a lipstick and a compact, three combs and a small brush, dozens of store receipts, a mini-umbrella and a pair of scratched, multi-tone sunglasses. At the very bottom, her fingers curl around a small automatic, the one no longer in the toe of a boot at the back of her closet.

Angel replaces the little automatic, sliding the pistol beneath a folded dish towel at the very bottom of the bag. She withdraws her hand, gives the bag a shake, then jabs her hand into the depths, burrowing past the mess, using the towel as a guide, until her fingers once again cradle the weapon and her thumb slides up to engage the safety. How long? Two seconds? Three? Not fast, not by Carter's standards. She'll just have to practice.

Back on the street, Angel decides to walk the mile back to the apartment she and Carter share. The air is cool and damp, but it's finally stopped raining. Angel's wearing jeans and a scoop-necked top, a cotton pullover, the jeans tight enough and the top low enough to attract the attention of three males in a jumped-up Toyota SUV. Angel's used to every kind of intrusion, from catcalls to polite good-evenings, but this gang's persistence digs beneath her skin. The Toyota's slowed down to match her pace, a bad sign.

'Get in the car, baby. We'll give you what you really want. I promise.'

Their crew-cuts, pimples and sleeveless muscleman T-shirts, not to mention the Jersey license plate, mark them as terminal hicks. Their slurred voices mark them as drunk.

'We'll use a lubricant,' the one in the back seat declares. 'It won't hurt a bit.'

Angel slides her hand into her bag, slides it through and between the many objects between her fingers and . . . and her equalizer. That's what guns were called in the Old West, equalizers, because they made a little man the equal of a big man. Or a little woman, for that matter.

Angel doesn't acknowledge the comments. She continues on, placing one foot in front of the other, eyes forward, as though walking on empty streets in one of those post-apocalypse movies, the only human being left on Earth. But her thoughts move in another direction. Angel's thinking how easy it would be to pull the little automatic, to place it against each of their skulls, to pull the trigger. Bang, bang, bang. In fact, Angel's hoping they get out of the car.

TWENTY-FOUR

It's not a happy morning, not for Bobby Ditto. The Blade's telling him the warehouse, which just happens to be his home base, isn't secure. Somebody might have been inside and who knows where they went, and maybe his world's coming to a fucking end. Meanwhile, Elvino Espinoza's scheduled to arrive in a couple of hours to make final arrangements for the biggest deal of Bobby's young career. Espinoza's even more paranoid than Bobby. At the first hint of a problem, he'll vanish.

Bobby's thinking how it's not fair, how he's worked his butt off these last few years, never asking for a single special favor. He's thinking he deserves better than a run of bad luck that won't come to an end no matter what he does.

'Tell me again how you came to this conclusion, Marco? I gotta hear this again. Enlighten me.'

The Blade shifts from one foot to the other, but he doesn't back off. Messenger is one of his jobs, good news or bad. 'There's this puddle of water under one of the skylights, thank God it didn't spoil any carpet.'

'So what? It rained all day yesterday.'

'True enough, Bobby, only we been here for two years and the skylight never leaked before.'

Bobby shakes his head. 'Tires don't go flat until they go flat. Your heart keeps beatin' until it stops.'

'OK, I get the point. Maybe it's nothin'. Maybe I'm gettin' paranoid in my old age. But I still hadda check it out, which I did. I went up on the roof myself, boss. That skylight, it ain't locked down.'

'Which means what?'

'Which means somebody coulda got in.' The Blade takes a step back. 'How 'bout,' he suggests, 'you come up on the roof and take a look for yourself. This is not somethin' we could ignore.'

'I haven't had coffee yet and you want me to climb up to the roof?' Bobby fixes his second-in-command with his most ferocious glare, but the Blade doesn't react. Now Bobby has to vent on the only game in town, the three kids in the outer basement.

'You hear the news?' he asks Donny Thorn.

'What news?'

'We had somebody in here last night.'

Donny Thorn's a handsome kid. He's got those Irish good looks, the clear eye, the square jaw, the spray of freckles. Now his head swivels back and forth, as if he's seeing the basement for the first time, which irritates Bobby all the more. That's not Donny's intention and he says, 'Nobody's been in here.'

'I'm not talkin' about here, ya dumb fuck. I'm talkin' about upstairs.'

The words are on the tip of Donny's tongue: *But you told us to stay in the basement. You said for us to keep the door locked no matter what.* Somehow, he manages to hold them back.

'They musta been real quiet, Bobby.' He looks to his companions, Al Zeffri and Nino Ferrulo. 'You guys hear anything?' When both shake their heads, Donny spreads his hands apart, 'But one thing I can say definitely. No one – and I mean nobody – came down those stairs.'

'How do ya know that, Donny? Did you open the door like I told you under no fucking circumstances not to do?'

'No, boss, we didn't.'

'You sure?'

'Absolutely one hundred percent. We didn't go nowhere.'

'And you didn't invite a couple of broads in for a little party?'

Donny Thorn makes the Sign of the Cross on his breast. 'Catholic honor, Bobby.'

Bobby Ditto finally turns away. He feels better now. Donny's not lying. The boys stayed in the basement and the money in the bunker was protected at all times. Bobby follows the Blade through the warehouse and out to the yard where he finds an extension ladder propped against the wall.

'Ya know, Bobby, what you told Donny and them, about someone breaking in last night? That's not the way it happened. If it happened at all.'

'How so?'

'If somebody broke in, they woulda had to do it before it started raining. Otherwise they would've left footprints.'

'So, you're talkin' Wednesday night?'

'Or Tuesday or Monday.'

Bobby's eyes bulge in his head. Monday? Before he installed his security detail? There could be ten thousand bugs in the goddamned bunker. Somebody might be listening to every word.

'Get the freak down here,' he tells the Blade.

'If you're talkin' about Kupperman, I already called him.'

'Good.' Bobby stops to allow a forklift carrying a roll of Berber carpet to pass. 'So, this intruder, how'd he get on the roof? You think he brought a ladder with him? Like the one you're asking me to climb?' Bobby's eyes sweep the yard, moving over the trucks and the SUV, finally settling on the fence with its glistening razor wire. 'And how'd he get over the fence? Did he fuckin' fly?'

The Blade feels like he's been saying the same thing all day, like he's back at Mary Immaculate, in the confessional booth with Father Binnelli. 'I don't know, boss. Only this guy, Carter, if he was some kinda special forces freak like the Chink said? I think he woulda learned how to get past razor wire.'

There it is, Carter's name spoken aloud. Bobby's real good at hating, but he's never felt anything close to what he feels now. No one disrespects Bobby Benedetti. Everywhere he goes – a restaurant, a bar, a wedding, a funeral – men of honor shake his hand. Bobby runs his fingers over his face. He feels like somebody spit on him.

'My day will come,' he tells the Blade. 'Let's take a look on the roof.'

The ladder buckles under Bobby Ditto's weight, but doesn't break as he climbs to the roof and marches over to the nearest skylight. When it swings up on a pair of rusty hinges, he folds his hands across his chest.

'How can this happen? I thought the building was secure.'

'Secure against theft,' the Blade responds.

The skylight is approximately four feet square, way too small to allow the gigantic rolls of carpet in the warehouse to pass through, even if they could be raised the twenty feet between the floor and the ceiling. So what if the skyline offers access? You can't open any of the doors from the inside without setting off an alarm. There's nothing to steal.

Bobby looks around, as he did while standing at the foot of the ladder. The view over the low-rise buildings in the neighborhood is spectacular. He can see downtown Manhattan and the sparkling waters of the harbor and the massive cranes on the docks in Bayonne. Clouds roll overhead, driven by a stiff breeze that riffles through Bobby's hair. From this very spot a decade earlier, Bobby had watched the towers of the World Trade Center burn and collapse. But he's not thinking about the past. He's looking for proof, any proof, that somebody used the skylight to gain access. Proof that isn't there to find.

'This Carter, this prick,' Bobby observes. 'He's got us runnin' around in circles. This is not the way I wanna live, Marco.'

This is another of the Blade's jobs. As Bobby's advisor, he's expected to offer a plan of action, especially when problems arise. Meanwhile, he hasn't got a clue.

'All right, let's suppose somebody got inside. Let's even suppose they got into your office. What did they actually accomplish? The money wasn't even there, right? And if they installed bugs, the cokehead will find them. Hear what I'm sayin', Bobby? Let's not freak out.'

If Levi Kupperman nearly jumps out of his skin when Carter takes him by the arm, his eyes virtually explode when Carter flashes the gold shield of a New York City Detective in his face. He's thinking how it's funny that you know something will happen, absolutely, without doubt, yet you're still unprepared when a cop shoves your hundred and thirty pounds against the side door of a van. And you're even more unprepared when that door suddenly opens and you're tossed inside, when you're on your back looking up at the face of the woman you've been imagining ever since you started jerking off fifteen years ago.

Levi's glimpse of paradise is short-lived. Carter flips him on to his stomach and rummages through his pockets, turning up a packet of cocaine tucked behind an expired credit card in his wallet.

'Look at me,' Carter says.

Kupperman complies – he has no choice – but he doesn't like what he sees, not at all. He might as well be looking into the eyes of a dead man. Levi's hands were already trembling, a by-product of terminal cocaine addiction. Now his entire body quakes. Carter's witnessed this effect before, so often that he now counts on it.

'Tell me what you do for Bobby Ditto? Are you on the way to his warehouse?'

Levi glances at Angel, but somehow those beautiful tear-drop eyes have lost their seductive luster, if they had any to begin with. The woman's not sympathetic, not at all. She's excited.

'Please, I'm not a . . . a gangster. I'm a—'

Carter interrupts the little man's plea by slapping him across the face, a hard crack that spins him into the side of the van. 'Do yourself a big favor, answer the questions I ask.'

'OK, yes. I'm on my way to Bobby's and what I do is

sweep his place for bugs. But that's all I do. I'm a businessman, not a gangster. Swear to God, I don't deal drugs.'

'You're right on part one. You're not a gangster.' Carter examines Kupperman's driver's license for a moment, then slips it into his pocket. 'You're a drug addict, Levi, and you're in over your head. Way over your head. Do you disagree?'

Levi gulps down a breath. His mind is working a little better, true enough, but the messages tossed up by his coke-fried brain do not encourage him. First, this guy is not a cop. This is the guy Bobby Ditto's been worrying about for the last week, the guy Levi heard Bobby and the Blade talking about when he swept Bobby's home.

'I won't argue the point,' he tells Carter.

'Smart move. Now tell me what you do for Bobby. Tell me exactly and don't leave anything out.'

'Like I said, I sweep the place . . .'

Carter leans forward. 'I asked you to be exact. I'm not gonna ask you again.'

'OK, OK. Bobby's has an office in the basement of his warehouse. He calls it his bunker and what I do is sweep the bunker every couple of days. Any kind of recording device, video or audio, digital or analog, I'm supposed to find it. Not that I ever have. I mean, found anything.'

'And that's it?'

'I swept Bobby's home a few days ago. It's the first time he asked me.'

'And what else?'

'Nothin' else. I don't have anything to do with his operation, whatever it is. I do my thing and Bobby pays me off . . .'

'How much does he pay you?'

Kupperman sweeps his hand across his nose. His nostrils are closing fast, a sure sign he needs another hit. 'Bobby pays me off in powder. That's the whole story, OK? I sweep his office. He feeds me. I'm a dog on a leash.'

Levi's thinking that his little speech was eloquent, but Carter spins him on to his stomach and drives a fist into his left kidney. The resulting pain has him flopping on the floor of the van like a hooked fish.

'I've got a big decision to make, Levi. I've got to decide

whether or not to let you live. Trust me on this. You don't advance your case when you lie to me.'

'I didn't. I swear . . . No, wait. I forgot. Every once and awhile, I sweep the armored car.'

'What armored car?'

'Bobby's got this Ford SUV. It's armored up somehow. The door's gotta weigh a hundred pounds.' Kupperman presses his hand to his back. 'Bobby keeps the SUV parked in the yard, but he doesn't use it very often because it burns too much gas. Every coupla months, he tells me to check it out.'

Carter took a chance snatching Kupperman, a chance that's paid off. With a possible deal coming up and Carter the ultimate wild card, Bobby's certain to check the vehicle. Better to know in advance.

'Tell me about the bunker, Levi. Describe it to me.'

'The bunker's where Bobby takes his . . . I don't know what to call 'em. Business associates? Co-conspirators? Customers? See, what with the sweeps and how hard it is to get in there, Bobby figures he can talk business and not worry the cops are listening to every word. The door, I swear it's as heavy as the doors on the SUV.'

Carter's smile is encouraging. 'Go on.'

'OK, let's see. Bobby's computer's in there, the company computer, but it isn't attached to the Internet. He's got two phones, one for the carpet business and another one he never answers. When it rings, he goes outside to call back.' Kupperman sits up and wraps his hands around his knees. 'The phones are on his desk and there are three filing cabinets against the wall. Also a card table where Bobby plays rummy and poker with the guys.'

'What else? Think hard.'

'Shelves on the wall with office supplies, a liquor cabinet, a bathroom with a shower, a couple of closets.'

'Do you sweep inside the closets?'

'Yeah. I especially sweep in the closets.'

'What's in them?'

'One is for clothes, the other for cleaning supplies. There's a set of golf clubs in the clothes closet.'

'What else?' Carter taps Levi's knee. 'Think, Levi.'

'The rug? I can't think of anything else.'

'Nothing? Nothing at all?'

'Fluorescent lights overhead? The pictures on the walls? Wait, one more thing. Bobby keeps tropical fish. The tank's on one of the filing cabinets. And that's it. I swear.'

Carter responds to Kupperman's oath by pulling a K-Bar knife from its scabbard and laying the blade alongside the man's head so that the point rests alongside his right eye. Carter doesn't intend to kill a hapless cocaine addict. Levi's not a gangster and he's not a threat. If worse comes to worse, Carter will call off the operation and Bobby Ditto's big deal will go forward. But Levi Kupperman doesn't know that and his suddenly diminished prospects have induced a state of near paralysis.

'There are two surveillance devices in the Ford,' Carter explains, 'a bug installed through the floorboard and a GPS unit attached to the right rear fender. Are you listening?'

'Yeah, two devices, one on the floor, one beneath the fender.'

'You're not gonna find either one of 'em.'

'Bobby'll kill me.'

'Bobby's day is done, Levi. And here's something else to think about. If you cross Bobby, there's a chance he won't find out. If you cross me, I'll know it by the end of the day. Unless you think I'm bluffing.'

Carter lays the edge of the knife across Levi's throat and pulls the man's head back. 'Do you think I'm bluffing, Levi?'

With his head yanked back and his throat stretched, Kupperman finds it difficult to speak. He glances to his left and happens to meet Angel's gaze. Her mouth is open, the look in her eyes wilder than ever.

'No, no. I don't. I swear.'

Carter pulls the knife away and sits back, the show definitely being over. From the look of things, Angel's been royally entertained. Carter drops the little packet of foil-wrapped cocaine in front of Kupperman, who's lying on his side, crying.

'Do some of this,' Carter says. 'You've got to go to work.'

Drugs are nothing new to Carter. While still in Iraq, he'd entertained two offers, one to raid the coast of Africa in search of diamonds, the other to smuggle morphine through India to the port of Mumbai. He doesn't flinch when Levi unfolds the packet and shovels cocaine into both nostrils. He's not even put off when snot begins to run from those nostrils. He opens the door, half-tosses Levi Kupperman outside and signals Angel to pull away. Another job well done.

Carter slides into the front seat alongside Angel, who's staring straight ahead, her expression grim. 'Why'd you let him go?' she asks, her tone blunt. 'What if he spills his guts to Bobby?'

'For one thing, if Kupperman doesn't show up, Bobby will just hire someone else. There are hundreds of private security firms in New York with the expertise to sweep an office and a car.'

Angel turns from Fourth Avenue in Brooklyn on to Ninth Street and crosses the Gowanus Canal, an open-air sewer that passes for an industrial waterway. A moment later, they pass a complex of stumpy brick apartment buildings, The Red Hook Houses, that once sheltered the stevedores who unloaded ships docked at the nearby piers. The jobs are gone now, along with the ships, but the destitute endure.

'Also,' Carter continues, 'you have to consider the risk you take when you transport a dead body. This neighborhood?' He gestures to a wall covered with gang tags. 'An undercover unit could easily mistake us for suburbanites on a drug run and decide to search the van. A body would be really hard to explain.'

Angel finds a halal food truck parked on Columbia Street a few blocks from the Benedetti warehouse. With the Expedition bugged, they no longer have to keep the vehicle in sight. Carter contents himself with an orange soda, but Angel loads up on the calories, ordering a deep-fried falafel platter with rice, salad and extra white sauce.

'We're going to know soon,' she tells Carter as they return to the van. 'One way or the other, we're going to know.'

'Are you worried?'

Angel doesn't answer right away. She slides across the van's back seat and stares for a moment at the equipment, the two receivers, one for the bug and one for the GPS unit, installed by Solly Epstein.

'If we don't pull this off,' she finally says, 'you'll just go on doing what you've been doing. But me? I have nothing to go back to. When Bobby killed Pierre, he wiped out my past.'

TWENTY-FIVE

Bobby Ditto gets lucky. Elvino Espinoza shows up a few minutes after Levi Kupperman pronounces the bunker free of surveillance devices. Bobby's skin has been crawling for hours, as if the imagined bugs in the wall were bedbugs out to feast on his blood.

Bobby serves the older man Cuban espresso in a demitasse cup imported from Italy, a matter of respect. Espinoza claims to be Cuban, though he represents a Mexican smuggling operation with outlets in a dozen American cities. He even dresses the part: off-white linen suit, skinny black tie, narrow-brimmed straw hat, brown sandals.

'So, Bobby, how have you been?' Elvino asks, his voice carrying the merest trace of a Spanish accent.

'Except for the ex-wife and the kids makin' my life miserable, I can't complain. And you?'

'My health is good. At my age, I ask for no more.' Espinosa takes a photograph from the inside pocket of his jacket. He lays the photo on Bobby's desk. 'My latest granddaughter.'

Bobby picks up the photo and nods, though as far as he's concerned, the infant with the scrunched-up eyes and nut-brown skin looks like just another wetback. 'How many does that make?'

'Eighteen.'

'Nine children and eighteen grandchildren? Must be fun at Christmas.'

'I have only begun, *amigo*. My two youngest girls are at university and still unmarried. But I have no complaints. *La familia*. It's the reason we live.'

It's not the reason Bobby Ditto lives, but he keeps his

thoughts to himself while Espinoza replaces the photo with a slip of paper. Bobby unfolds the paper and reads the day, time and address listed. Essentially, he and Espinoza have identical aims – they want to hold product for as short a time as possible. Bobby is to appear, money in hand, at a trucker's garage in Greenpoint at nine o'clock on Sunday night. He can bring two associates with him and they can be armed, but displays of firepower are unacceptable. That means no shotguns, no assault rifles.

The terms are fine with Bobby. The people Espinoza represents can put fifty soldiers in the field for every member of Bobby's crew. If they decide to rip him off, there's nothing he can do about it. But they won't because they're businessmen. The drug world is filled with bullshit artists who make one excuse after another. Long ago, Bobby decided not to be one of them. He shows up on time and the money is always right.

'No problem,' he tells Elvino. 'I'm ready.'

'Very good.'

Espinoza unlocks a leather briefcase and removes a small lacquer box. He places the box on the desk. Inside, Bobby will discover four grams of heroin on which he can run whatever tests he desires.

Their business essentially done, Espinoza lingers for only a few moments before making an exit. For a few minutes more, Bobby gets to lean back in his chair, satisfied. He gets to think, for those few minutes, that nobody's been inside the warehouse, that the leak was a coincidence, that he's free and clear. Then the Blade's face appears in the doorway.

Even when he's happy, the Blade's lips are no more than two smudgy lines between his long thin nose and his square jaw. Now they've disappeared altogether, as if he forgot to put in his teeth this morning. The Blade's been wearing dentures since he was seventeen. That's when he made the mistake of punching a cop inside a Washington Heights precinct.

'Bad news, boss. The Expedition's bugged.' The Blade taps his leg with his fingertips. 'And the freak's been talkin' to Carter.'

* * *

Bobby's expecting to find Kupperman standing in a puddle of his own urine, shaking like a beaten puppy. Levi's too stoned for that. He thinks he's the hero of the story. Not that he's thrown all caution to the wind. He's arranged to make his well-edited confession before witnesses. Only fifteen feet away, two of Bobby's drivers are changing the front wheel on one of the trucks.

'There was nothin' I could do,' he tells his boss. 'One minute I'm walkin' down the street. The next I'm inside this van with a knife against my throat. There were two of them, a guy who had a grip like steel and some Chinese broad. I couldn't do nothin'.'

'And you were just walkin' along, mindin' your own business when this happened?' Bobby's tone is soft, almost soothing. 'Innocent as a newborn babe?'

'I was on my way here, Bobby. I mean, you called and I came. How could I know there'd be somebody waitin' outside?' Kupperman stares up at his boss for a moment. 'The woman never spoke a word. The guy did all the talkin'. He told me there were two devices in the SUV, a GPS unit under the back fender, and a bug under the front seat. He said if I told you about them, he'd kill me.'

'But you told me anyway.'

'Yeah, see. I'm like protectin' your interests. That's how come you pay me, right?'

'Right.' Bobby rubs the palms of his hands against his chest. He looks at the Blade, then gestures at the workmen changing the tire.

The Blade moves off to shoo the men back into the warehouse, leaving Bobby and Kupperman alone. Levi's shaking again. When he decided to play the loyal employee, he'd assumed that Bobby would be grateful, that he might even be rewarded. But that's not the case. Eight inches taller than Levi and a good hundred and fifty pounds heavier, Bobby's leaning forward, his weight on his toes, ready to close the gap between them. Still, when he speaks, his tone remains soft.

'So, what next, after he tells you about the bugs and threatens you?'

'Nothin'. He just kicked me out.'

'He didn't ask you anything about how I conduct my business?'

'Uh-uh.'

'Didn't ask about my office, or how I protect it?'

'Not a word.'

'Didn't even tell you his name?'

'No, he didn't say his name and I didn't ask. This guy, Bobby, he woulda killed me in a minute.'

'A real badass.'

'Exactly. When—'

'So what I'm wonderin', Levi, is how come you're still alive?'

Levi's mouth hangs open. Now painfully obvious, the question somehow never occurred to him, most likely because he stopped three times on the way over to fuel his determination.

'See,' Bobby continues, 'if it was me pulled you off the street, I woulda definitely whacked ya. That way you couldn't tell nobody nothin'. So, this guy, maybe he's not the cold-blooded killer you made him out to be. Tell me, have you pulled the bugs yet?'

'Uh-uh. First thing when we came outside, I told Marco what happened.'

'Then maybe we're crappin' our pants over nothin'. Let's take a look.' Bobby nudges Kupperman with a fingertip. 'You got the remote?'

Levi keys the remote as they walk the twenty feet to the SUV, unlocking the vehicle and shutting down the alarm. He opens the front door on the passenger side and leans in, laying his head on the carpet. At first, he sees nothing, the contrast between the sunlit yard and the shadows beneath the seat rendering him functionally blind. But then his pupils adjust and the bug jumps into focus, a thin black cable extending two or three inches above the floor.

'Here it is. Right here.'

Though Levi's voice betrays a measure of triumph, these are, in fact, the last words he'll ever speak. His rage finally unleashed, Bobby's fingers wrap around Levi's skinny neck and he presses down with all his weight. Kupperman's hands rise instinctively to grab Bobby's wrists, but the fingers encircling his throat only tighten. He kicks out, scraping Bobby's knees, and tries to roll away. The results are no more encouraging. Lying half-in, half-out of the car, his shoulders wedged between the seat and the firewall, he's helpless. And Bobby's not stopping, not even slowing down. He's slamming Levi's head against the floor and he's talking out loud.

'Hey, Carter, you listenin' to this, you cocksucker? You listenin', huh? I'm gonna run you down. I don't care where the fuck you go. I don't care if it takes me until the last day of my fuckin' life. I'm gonna cut your balls off and make you eat 'em. I'm gonna dig the eyes out of your head. I'm gonna take a baseball bat and break every bone in your body, startin' with your fuckin' toes. You listenin' to this? Huh, you piece-of-shit, fuckin' scumbag? Huh?'

'The one good thing to come outta this bullshit is that the freak couldn't have told Carter about the money.' Bobby lays a hand on the Blade's shoulder. 'That's because he didn't know about it.'

'You think Carter asked him?'

'Don't be a jerk, Marco. Carter definitely asked him about the money. Not only that, he most likely asked the freak to bug my office. That's why I'm talkin' to you out here.' They're standing in the shadow of a twenty-foot truck, their backs to any observer. 'I want you to get someone out here tomorrow morning, a pro, to sweep the bunker. The Ford, too. If Carter's listenin', I gotta know.'

The Blade's no happier than Bobby. Now they've got a body on their hands. Given all the other details to be handled before Sunday night, this is a problem he surely doesn't need. The freak didn't know anything about their upcoming deal. Bobby should have let him go home. Instead . . .

'Do you want my advice, Bobby?'

'Yeah.'

'You need to calm the fuck down.'

Bobby Ditto rises up on his toes. He doesn't care to be spoken to as if he was a child. But the Blade's grim expression stops him. 'I hate this guy, Marco.'

'Well, stop hating him. He's doin' what he's doin' for the same reason you do what you do. Our thing, his thing – there's no difference, Bobby. Hatin' Carter is like hatin' the weather. When it's rainin' you don't look to kill the weatherman. You carry an umbrella.'

'I suppose you happen to have this umbrella with you.'

'I got a plan, which puts me one step ahead of my boss.'

Bobby Ditto can no longer stand still. He turns and leads the Blade to the back of the warehouse, shoving his hands into his pockets as he rounds the corner. The day's turned cold and the wind is up. The cloudless sky is the clean blue of the coldest, midwinter days. Across the street, six men push a school bus into the bus company's dingy garage. At least three of them give orders at the same time, every other word an epithet.

'All right, Marco, you made your point. But what's done is done. Plus, the freak had to go, sooner or later, and we both knew it. Let's move on.'

'OK, first thing, if Carter's after anything, he's after the money. I just can't make myself believe he has a market for the product. That means, once the deal is done, he'll go away. What he has with you, it ain't personal.'

Bobby stops as they approach the far corner of the warehouse. He looks from the razor wire on the fence to the roof twenty feet above his head.

'You're wrong, Marco. I know too much about Carter. He's not gonna leave me on the street. It's the same for me. I got his name and address. Sooner or later, I'll run him down. I don't care what it costs. I'm gonna find this prick and I'm gonna kill him unless he kills me first. But you go ahead. If I fuck up this deal and lose the front money, I'm dead anyway.'

'I hear you, Bobby.' The Blade raises a hand. 'Put another man in the basement right away. If the Expedition comes up clean, leave it inside tomorrow night. We'll load it on Sunday, a half-hour before pickup. Espinoza doesn't want to see more than three men, but there are no rules about the ride over. I want to use at least two cars and I want to put our best men in them. You, me and Donny will be in the Expedition – remember, it's armored – so the money will never be out of sight. Afterward, we take the product to the Queens Village apartment and leave enough men there to protect it.'

Bobby nods along when the Blade makes his final points. Carter wouldn't have bugged the Expedition if he knew when and where the deal would go down. And even if he's within sight of the warehouse when they set out for Greenpoint, what can he do to stop them? Bring in a tank? Fire rocket-propelled grenades? No, in order to stop the Expedition, he'd have to destroy the money, which he'd never do. That's the underlying truth, according to the Blade. Carter's not crazy. He doesn't kill for the fun of it. Present him with an obstacle he can't overcome and he'll back off.

'I don't have a problem with any of it,' Bobby says. 'Just make sure nobody leaves that basement before Sunday.'

'Consider it done.' The Blade lights a cigarette. 'What about the freak? Whatta you wanna do with him?'

'Bring him to the house tonight. I see an ocean voyage in his future.'

TWENTY-SIX

Angel's leaning so far forward that her chin almost touches the steering wheel. She's driving on Fourth Avenue in Brooklyn, weaving through traffic, her breath coming in short heaves. Carter lets her go, at least for the present. He's remembering a night he spent at a forward base camp in Afghanistan with two CIA spooks and a merc from Blackwater. Earlier that day, a twenty-year-old Marine had somehow wandered off the base and been captured. Now they can hear his screams in the distance, carried to them on a light breeze, faint enough to be the cries of a night bird.

Carter had wanted to do something – darkness, after all, is the covert operator's friend – but he was quickly overruled. The team had a mission to perform and the base was only a way station. So, he sat up and listened, along with every other soldier on the post, to the slow, painful death of a brother.

Levi Kupperman's death, by Carter's standards, was neither horrific, nor especially painful. Not even as painful as Angel's naiveté. She wants to do something, anything, to alter a past that can't be altered. She wants to shed the burden. Kupperman's death rattle had echoed in the van long after Bobby Ditto yanked the bug.

'Did we kill him?' Angel asks.

'No, we didn't. But you're gonna kill us if you don't stop for this light.'

Angel slams on the brakes and the van fishtails for a moment before coming to a stop. 'I need to slow down,' she admits.

'You're taking this too hard, Angel.' Carter lays a hand on Angel's shoulder. 'Montgomery Thorpe once told me that human history is a voyage over a river of blood. Blood makes the trip possible, human blood. Thorpe considered himself a deep thinker.'

'What happened to him?'

'First I killed him, then I cut off his head and presented it to an Italian gangster from Queens. A gift of sorts.'

Angel finally takes a deep breath. 'Get serious, Carter. I'm not in the mood for jokes.'

Carter smiles. 'Kupperman took his chances when he chose Bobby over us. That doesn't come as any surprise, by the way, an addict siding with his dealer.'

'But why did Bobby kill him if he was loyal?'

'Bobby needed to hurt somebody and I wasn't available. But that's the difference, Angel, between thugs and professionals. Bobby indulged an impulse that only placed him in greater danger.'

Angel shudders, imagining, for just an instant, what the gangster will do to her if she falls into his hands. 'Does Bobby worry you?' she asks.

'Given the information Bobby already has, he'll probably find me if he works at it long enough. I intend to handle that problem by killing him. But I'm seriously pissed off, too. Bobby had no reason to harm Levi Kupperman, no reason at all.'

Angel guides the van on to a ramp for the Brooklyn-Queens Expressway, only to find traffic at a near stop. Sighing, she works the van on to the roadway, then into the left lane where she watches traffic moving in the opposite direction zip past.

'We're finished, right?' she asks Carter. 'Now that Bobby pulled the bugs?'

Carter doesn't answer right away. He's too busy weighing the obvious cost of going forward, his life, against a set of benefits that elude him. Angel will be gone within weeks if she gets her hands on the money, gone for good. Carter doesn't intend to become anyone's pool boy. So what will he do, besides dump his end of the loot in an already fat bank account?

'Nothing to say?'

Carter waits for Angel to merge with the traffic in the center lane. Up ahead, a man sits on the trunk of a stalled Toyota, his chin in his hands, no doubt enjoying the fine spring day.

'You should have paid closer attention, Angel.'

'To what?'

'To Levi Kupperman.'

'What did he say that can possibly help us?'

'It's what he didn't say that matters. If you remember, the main problem with lifting the money from the bunker had nothing to do with the men guarding it. They're a problem, all right, but a problem I can overcome.'

Angel's smile is nearly beatific. 'The safe, of course. You were worried about the money being in a safe you couldn't open.'

'I had Levi describe the contents of Bobby's office while I held a knife to his throat. Since he couldn't know what I was after, he had no reason to leave anything out.'

'And he never mentioned a safe, which means the money's probably sitting in a closet.'

'Probably?'

'Well, he could have moved it.'

'And I have to kill three men in order to find out?'

But Carter's teasing. He's decided there's only one benefit to be gained from this particular operation. Call it the thrill of combat. Carter can almost taste the moment, almost smell the blood as it trickles into Montgomery Thorpe's river.

All the hours of handgun practice at Carl Maverton's gun range? He'll soon be putting the skills he developed to the ultimate test, a challenge unrelated to Angel Tamanaka, as beautiful as she undoubtedly is, as much as he undoubtedly wants her.

Carter glances at his watch. Two o'clock in the afternoon and plenty of work to be done. 'Head for the Home Depot, the one in Flushing,' he tells Angel. 'I'm going in tonight.'

Carter lays out his equipment on the living room rug: the M89, a holstered 9mm Glock, a combat knife in its scabbard, a hooked pry bar, a two-pound hammer and a wood chisel, a ski mask, thirty feet of rope with a grappling hook attached to one end, a Grade II bulletproof vest, a small bolt cutter, a propane torch and a pair of two-way radios.

'Do you know how to use these?' Carter hands one of the radios to Angel.

'They look like someone dragged them up from the Stone Age. You sure they're not petrified?'

'Walkie-talkies have been around for a long time, but they have certain virtues. First, they communicate directly with other radios. They don't need the phone system or a satellite. Second, they're set to a specific frequency that helps to maintain privacy. But we're not going to use them to talk to each other. Press that button on the side, the large one.'

Angel complies, producing an audible click in the second radio. 'That's it?'

'You're going to drop me behind the warehouse at three o'clock in the morning, then find a parking space within sight of the front entrances. When I need you to pick me up, I'll key the radio three times. If Bobby or any of his people show up before I come out, you do the same thing, one click for each person. If the cops show up, click four times fast. But don't speak, Angel. Don't give me away.'

Angel clicks the radio several times, then drops it beside her on the couch. 'Something has to happen before you go, between us.'

'Fine with me.'

'I'm not talking about sex.' Like Carter, Angel's been guarding her privacy for a long time. She has acquaintances, but not friends, partners, but not lovers. Yet Carter's somehow defeated her security system, as he intends to defeat Bobby Ditto's.

'What if I forget about the Caribbean?' she asks. 'What if I was willing to stay here?'

'Are you asking me to go steady?'

Angel's right foot lashes out, catching him midway between knee and ankle. 'One day you're going to have to come out of that closet. You can't hide in there all your life.'

Carter rubs his shin. 'Isn't that your plan? To hide inside a rich man's wealth for the rest of your life?'

'Actually, I was counting on him dying young and me becoming a fabulously rich widow, after which I'd marry the man of my dreams. But my failings aren't the point. I'm asking about you.'

'Listen, Angel, what I do . . .? Let's just say my occupation doesn't lend itself to a long-term outlook. Or to intimate friendships. As for you tossing away your life's ambition? If I was you, I'd think twice. Sooner or later, probably sooner, I'm going to be killed or caught. I know I've made these points before, but they haven't changed.' Carter's smile is wicked. 'Unless, of course, I settle down, become a member in good standing of the moral middle class. Maybe I could open a small business, stop working out, gain thirty pounds, learn to fall asleep on the couch after dinner.'

'What are you saying?'

'No risk, no gain.'

Angel grimaces. Not only has she failed to make her point, she's not certain that she even knows what it is. Carter's concentration is so intense, as he packs his gear, that she finds herself envious. He's an athlete before a championship event, or maybe an addict contemplating his drug of choice, knowing that he'll be stoned by morning. Stoned or dead.

Finally satisfied, Carter retreats to the dining room table where he lays out the items he purchased at Wal-Mart, the wooden matches, the sandpaper, the X-Acto knife, the glue and the ping-pong balls. Alongside, he places two shotgun shells, a sheet of newspaper and a pair of kitchen shears.

'Let me show you a trick.' Carter motions Angel to stand

next to him. 'I learned this in the military, part of my super-secret advanced training. But then I came home to find thirteen-year-old nerds posting how-to-make-a-flash-bomb videos online.'

Carter fits a blade into the X-Acto knife and cuts one of the ping-pong balls in half, leaving only a tiny strip to act as hinge. He bends the two halves back, creating a pair of small cups, like the halves of an eggshell lying on end. Into each cup, he glues strips of coarse sandpaper in the shape of a cross. The matches come next. Carter cuts off the heads, roughly divides them in two, then lays them on the sandpaper strips.

'There are three men in the basement, untrained and undisciplined. I'd bet my life savings against a quarter that they have no concerted plan of action if the basement door is breached. How much experience and practice they have with handgun combat is also suspect. Remember, they've been in that basement for several days and nothing's happened. Are they psychologically prepared for combat? I don't think so, Angel. But I don't mind giving myself another edge anyway.'

Carter breaks down the shotgun shells, extracts the gunpowder and wraps it loosely in newspaper. He lays the packet on top of the matches in one of the cups, then closes the ping-pong ball.

'I want you to glue the edges together,' he tells Angel. 'Nice and even now. Let the glue drip slowly.' Carter rolls the ball against the tip of the glue tube, describing a neat circle. He blows on the glue, a long slow breath, again turning the ball. Finally, while the glue is still tacky, he covers the seam with a strip of tape and lays what now looks like an ordinary ping-pong ball on the table.

'If you throw this against a hard surface, the sandpaper will ignite the matches and the matches will ignite the gunpowder. There won't be an explosion because the gunpowder isn't packed down. What there will be is a flash of light intense enough to blind someone for about five seconds.' Carter smiles, remembering Gentleman Jerry Miculek. Gentleman Jerry could take out an entire platoon in five seconds. 'That should be enough time.'

TWENTY-SEVEN

Whereas before Angel felt both thrilled and frightened, now she's just frightened. They're in Red Hook, she and Carter, cruising past a long-abandoned factory, its peeling stucco façade reminding her of an elderly aunt whose incurable skin disease kept her indoors for the last several years of her life. Above the van, a bone-white moon edges from the shadow of a raggedy cloud to stare, accusingly, through the van's windshield.

Carter's behind her, in the rear of the van, strapping the Glock to his thigh, donning the vest, checking and rechecking his gear. His expression remains neutral, almost casual, throughout. Angel feels like she's seeing him for the first time, what he is, what she can never be. She's thinking this is a good lesson, though it's a bit late in the game to be learning that you're not cut out for robbery and murder. But, of course, Carter would never use the word murder to describe his plans for the gangsters in Bobby Ditto's basement. No, he'd probably say something like 'Combat related deaths, by definition, are not murders.'

'You having buyer's remorse, Angel?' Carter's tone reveals a hint of amusement that Angel instantly resents.

'Is it that obvious?'

'You do seem a bit nervous.'

Angel shakes her head. They're passing through a narrow park that extends along either side of the road. Baseball fields, a makeshift soccer field with sagging nets at either end, an expanse of greening grass that runs the length of a block and appears silver in the moonlight. A cigarette lighter flares on the edge of the park closest to the Red Hook Houses, illuminating a dozen men gathered together in spite of the hour. It's now three o'clock in the morning.

'Nothing's happened yet,' Carter adds. 'We can still call it off.'

'Is that what you want?'

'I need you steady, Angel.'

Carter lays the coil of rope and the grappling hook on the bag containing his equipment. He slides both toward the door, then pulls on the tea-dyed gloves he'd worn on the day they met. 'Look, you're going to sit in back of the van, in the dark, until I call for you to pick me up. That could take a lot of time, since I'm not sure what problems I'll encounter once I get inside. At some point as you sit there in the dark, your imagination will kick into overdrive. Did Carter's luck finally run out? Is he wounded, helpless, even dead? Is he coming back? How long do I wait?'

'You said an hour.'

'That's only an estimate.' Carter leans forward to kiss the back of Angel's neck. 'I need you steady,' he repeats.

'Are you worried about something?'

'The inner door, the one to Bobby's office. It's a thick slab of wood protected by a deadbolt, keycard lock. Eventually, I'll get through it, but I can't be sure how long that will take. I have to know you'll be here when I come out. Taxis are hard to find in this neighborhood.'

Angel takes a left. Two blocks ahead, she can see the fence surrounding Benedetti Wholesale Carpeting's truck yard. 'How do you plan to get through the door?'

'I'm going to burn it down . . . with a very small flame.'

'Are you joking?'

Carter's not joking, but there's no time to explain. 'If you want to take a pass, just keep driving. I won't be upset, not at all. But once the operation begins, once I'm in the field, I need to know you'll be waiting for me.'

Angel makes a right turn on to the cobblestone street running along the back of the warehouse. 'Tell me where to stop.'

'Up ahead, just in front of the fire hydrant.'

'An hour, you said?'

'If it's going to be more, I'll try to call you on the walkie-talkie.'

'I'll be there.'

Carter waits until the van comes to a stop against the curb, then slides the rear door open and hops out. He reaches back into the interior to lift the bag and the rope, and closes the door. He offers no memorable goodbye, no parting comment, but merely crosses the sidewalk to the chain-link fence, the first barrier, and goes to work.

Chain-link fencing is delivered in rolls, then wired to vertical fence posts and horizontal rails. Carter begins at one of the posts, using the bolt cutters to slice through the links wired to the post. Made of soft, galvanized metal, the fencing offers minimal resistance, and Carter's able to force it back and slide underneath twenty seconds after leaving the van. He returns the bolt cutter to the bag, ties the loose end of the rope to the bag's handles and tosses the grappling hook over the parapet edging the roof. When the hook pulls tight on the first toss, he shows a bit of emotion, a tiny smile that just touches the corners of his mouth. Meticulous preparation has always been his strong point.

The rapid fire, hand-over-hand climb to the top leaves him breathless, but Carter doesn't pause to recover. He pulls the bag up behind him and steps back into the shadows. Carter fears most what he can't control, like the remote possibility that a police cruiser would turn on to the block while he was halfway up the rope. Hanging there, he'd be entirely helpless, escape impossible. He couldn't even shoot his way out. Now he's invisible from the street. He can take his time.

He walks first to the skylight, the means of his initial entry, only to find it secured with a high-end padlock. The padlock's shackle is made of hardened steel and more than a match for the bolt cutters, which comes as no surprise to Carter. If he didn't have a back-up plan, he wouldn't be here.

Carter walks directly to the south-western corner of the building where the tarnished, sheet-metal chimney of a defunct ventilation system rises a few feet above the tarred roof. The ductwork, along with a cap to protect the system from rain and snow, is joined by sheet-metal screws. Carter finds a slot head screwdriver inside the bag and fits it into the nearest screw. Rusted in, the screw gives off a little screech of protest before it begins to turn. Carter's not particularly worried about making noise. Even assuming the guards below aren't asleep, the basement has no windows and the floor of the warehouse is thick enough to support the weight of loaded trucks. Still, once the cap pulls free, Carter leans into the opening and listens for a moment, his eyes closed, his expression serene despite the intense drumming of his heart.

Bobby Ditto's freezing his ass off as he pilots the SunDancer beneath the Cross Bay Bridge after a two hour trip. Not the Blade. No, the Blade's wearing a sweater so thick it might still be on the fucking sheep, which makes good sense because it's early May and the water temperature's only fifty degrees. The air temperature isn't much to write home about, either, not at three o'clock in the morning. The air temperature's maybe fifty-two.

The good news is that there's no wind and no chop to the water. The bad news is that a moving boat makes its own wind. Bobby had pulled a life jacket over his T-shirt a few moments after they dumped the freak's body over the side, an XL jacket so tight it might have passed for a corset. The Blade had the good manners, and the good sense, not to comment, but the facts were on the table. He'd looked stupid, not to mention ridiculous, not to mention pitiful. Plus the jacket was coated with dried salt spray and it's irritating his skin.

The SunDancer emerges from the shadows beneath the bridge into the moonlit waters of Jamaica Bay, traveling east toward the vast expanse of Kennedy Airport. If New York is the city that never sleeps, JFK is the airport that never sleeps. Bobby first hears the swelling whine of jet engines, then watches a 747 lift off the runway, headed straight out to sea as it gains altitude.

'Ya know what?' he asks the Blade.

'No, Bobby, what?'

'I'm wishin' I was somewhere else. I'm wishin' I was on that plane. For the first time in my fuckin' life.' Bobby turns to port and eases back on the throttles as he guides the SunDancer toward Hawtree Basin, a narrow canal flanked on both sides by equally narrow houses. 'But I got a question, pal, and it's this: What does the prick already know?'

'You talkin' about Carter?'

'No, I'm talkin' about the man in the moon.' Bobby points to the silver disc above them. 'Right up there.'

'C'mon, boss.'

'Just answer the question. What does he know?'

'That we're doin' a deal?'

'What else?'

'Bobby, I'm not a mind reader.'

'Then explain how he knew about the freak? Tell me how he knew to bug the Ford? Tell me what he was doin' inside the warehouse?'

At last, an easy question. 'He was after the money.'

'Yeah, right.' Bobby slows to a crawl as he enters the canal. 'So, how did he know the money was there?'

'He didn't, at first. He knew the money was in the Bronx because your brother told the whore.'

'So why didn't he grab it right then? Bein' as he's fucking Superman and Vinny's seventy years old?'

'Actually, I been thinkin' about that.' The Blade pauses to let Bobby ease the SunDancer into a slot alongside his dock. Then he hops on to the wooden planks, ties off the bow rope and straightens.

'So, what did you think?' Bobby asks. 'When you were thinking?'

'First, that we got a rat in the crew. That would be the worst. But then I thought that maybe Carter was outside when you decided to move the money. Maybe he followed it to the warehouse. Maybe he just got lucky.'

Bobby cuts the engines, strips off the life jacket and steps on to the dock. 'But there could be a rat, Marco. And if there is, it's gotta be one of those assholes I put in the basement. One of the jerks who's supposed to be protectin' our interests.'

'That was my thought, too. But there's a problem. Carter connects with the whore and the whore connects with Ricky, who's dead and gone. There's no connection between the whore and anyone else in the crew.'

'That we know about.'

'That we know about,' the Blade quickly agrees.

'Look, Carter's been one step ahead of us, right?'

'I can't deny it.'

'So let's get one step ahead of Carter. We're gonna go get that money, right the fuck now, and bring it back here.'

The Blade hesitates – Bobby's home is lot more exposed than the warehouse – but the look on his boss's face is plain enough. As far as Bobby's concerned, the deed's as good as done. 'Yeah, fine,' he says. 'You want me to call ahead, make sure the boys are awake and ready?'

'No, Marco, you're missin' the whole point, which is security. That's why I'm not gonna call until I'm comin' through the door, and why I'm gonna take away their cell-phones. No more leaks, no more bullshit.'

Message delivered, Bobby heads for the house and a fleece-lined jacket in the hall closet. He pushes a key into the lock on the back door, but then hesitates. 'I swear, Marco, I feel better already. Now, even if Carter's a goddamned psychic, he still has to come through me. I can't tell ya how much I want a shot at that guy. There's no way even to measure it.'

TWENTY-EIGHT

There's no ductwork beneath the sleeve Carter disassembles. Removed long ago, the metal was undoubtedly sold for salvage. The sleeve and cap might have been pulled at the same time, pulled and sold, but that would have necessitated patching the hole in the roof, an expense apparently foregone.

As Carter anticipated, the resulting hole is just big enough to accommodate his shoulders and the equipment bag. He lowers the bag twenty feet to the concrete floor, repositions the grappling hook and slides down the rope to land in a corner behind stacked rolls of carpeting. Briefly, and not for the first time, he considers pulling the M89 tucked inside the bag, only to decide that the weapon's more likely to hinder than to help. Handguns, like the Glock with its fifteen-round magazine, offer a distinct advantage in close range battles, increased mobility more than compensating for the loss in firepower. It would be a different story if the M89 was a fully automatic weapon, but unlike assault rifles, it has to be fired one shot at a time, the same as the Glock.

Carter unties the rope, opens the bag and removes the little flash bomb and the ski mask. He tucks the bomb into his shirt pocket, pulls the ski mask over his head, then hefts the bag and carries it to the stairway leading to the basement. The bag's going to remain behind, at least for the present, and he lays it on the floor before descending. His tread is light, a matter of habit, not necessity. The stairway is made of poured concrete, virtually eliminating the possibility of his footfalls making any sound at all.

At the bottom, Carter takes the flash bomb from his pocket and cradles it in his palm. Then he shuts his eyes for a moment, the better to visualize the sequence to follow, the better to find his own center. He can die here and he knows it. The trick is to replace fear with acceptance, to reach a state of pure purpose, to become a machine designed for battle, a machine indifferent to outcome.

Carter opens his eyes, committed now. He feels nothing inside, not even excitement, his focus too intense to allow for emotion of any kind. A yard away, the flimsy, ill-fitting door between himself and his objective beckons. Carter swivels his right hip back and bends his knee slightly. When his balance is perfect, he comes forward, running the energy from his hip, through his thigh, his calf, his ankle, and into the lock itself.

The door crashes open, the wood around the lock splintering, as Carter knew it would. He slams the flash bomb on to the concrete floor inside, then covers his eyes with his left hand and draws the Glock with his right.

The flash, when the gunpowder ignites, is so intense that it bleeds through his fingers. Darkness follows a split second later and Carter leaps through the doorway. Before coming to an abrupt stop, he takes four running steps into the room, his head swiveling left and right. He first registers a man directly in front of him. The man wears brown boxers and a wife-beater T-shirt and his unseeing eyes stare up at the ceiling. To his right, a second man lies sprawled on a half-inflated air mattress.

His hands cover his eyes and he's muttering the word 'motherfucker' over and over again. Behind him, a third man reaches for a semi-automatic handgun lying on a table. Carter shoots this man first, pulling the trigger twice, a classic, center of mass double-tap. The rounds impact the man's chest within an inch of each other and he drops to the floor, leaving his weapon behind.

The man on the mattress comes next. He's lowered his hands at the crash of the gunshots, but his eyes are looking off to Carter's left when Carter again pulls the trigger twice. The man raises a hand to the wounds on his chest, catching the first few drops of blood. Then his eyes roll up into his head and he falls back.

The third man, the man standing directly in front of Carter, has recovered his sight. He appears to be in his early twenties, a tall skinny kid with a mop of black hair that's standing straight up. The crash of gunfire still echoes in the confined space and the sharp odor of cordite is thick enough to sting his rapidly blinking eyes.

'Hey, I'm not fuckin' armed. Take what the fuck you want. Take the fuckin' building. I don't give a fuck.'

Carter's impressed. Four fucks in four sentences. Meanwhile, the kid's staring at his friends. They're not moving, not even groaning.

'Anybody else here?' Carter asks.

'Nobody, I swear.'

A door on the far side of the basement flies open before Carter registers the lie. The man who steps out has a gun in his hand and he's pulling the trigger as fast as he can, Gentleman Jerry minus the part about aiming. As Carter spins to face the threat, a bullet slams into his body armor on the left side, a matter of pure chance. The round doesn't penetrate the Kevlar fabric, but the pain is ferocious. Carter ignores it, as he'd once ignored the roundhouse kicks delivered to his lower ribcage by a mixed martial artist named Chappy Jorgenson. He raises the Glock, sights in on the man's chest and fires twice. Both shots strike home and the man sags into the door frame, still holding on to his weapon, an unacceptable result. Carter fires for a third time and the bullet punches a hole in the man's face just below his right eye. Game over.

Carter spins on his heel to face the last man standing. Or the next to last, if he includes himself. The kid's eyes are wide enough to pass for headlights. Though his lips tremble and his jaw hangs open, he doesn't make a sound.

Carter lets the silence build for a moment, then wags a finger and says, 'Liar, liar, pants on fire.'

'What, what?'

Out in the field, on capture or kill missions, prisoners were never taken, nor witnesses left behind. But Carter's got work ahead of him, physical labor, and he's pretty sure at least one of his ribs is cracked, if not broken. Every breath produces a jet of pain that he's struggling to mask.

'Cat got your tongue?' he says.

'Don't kill me.'

Carter likes that, a simple plea, with no excuse offered for the lie. 'What's your name?'

'Al.'

'OK, Al. Walk to the foot of the stairs, sit down, put your hands under your ass and cross your legs. Don't make me ask you twice. Do it now.'

Al Zeffri's a simple man. Certainty appeals to him and he's happiest when he only has to think about one thing at a time. Right now he believes, with all his heart and soul, and quite correctly, that his life is hanging by a thread. If he does anything at all to antagonize the man with the gun, his parents will be forced to bear the costs of a funeral they can't afford. He obeys Carter, retreating to the foot of the stairs, assuming the position.

Carter lets the Glock fall to his side as he moves from one fallen enemy to another, checking for a pulse, pronouncing each man dead. That task complete, he approaches Al.

'You're in over your head,' he explains. 'I'm better than you, better trained and better prepared. Do you understand that?'

Zeffri glances at his buddies as he performs a simple calculation. Four men assigned to guard the basement, three of them dead, one attacker who's calm as a fuckin' robot. 'Yeah,' he says, 'I get it.'

Carter touches the Glock's barrel to the top of Al's head as he skirts the man to climb the stairs. He retrieves his tool bag and half-drags it back down, finally dropping it into Al's lap.

'You're going to break into Bobby's office.'

'The Bunker?'

'Yeah, the Bunker.' Carter's ribs are on fire, but his tone conveys certainty. 'If you do a good job, if you work real hard, I'm going to let you live. You want to live, right?'

'Yeah, I do.'

'Good. Now carry the bag to the office door, put it down, then kneel down beside it. Understand? Carry the bag, drop the bag, kneel. Do it now.'

Carter follows Al across the basement. The kid's shoulders are slumped and his head's slightly bowed. He's apparently surrendered. Carter finds himself annoyed. Keeping his promise will entail logistical problems – there's no convenient place to confine the gangster and there are guns everywhere – problems he doesn't have time to resolve. Carter glances at his watch: eighteen minutes.

When Al drops to his knees, Carter issues a series of commands, pausing between each until the task is completed.

Take the rifle out of the bag and hand it to me. Take the propane torch out of the bag and place it next to you. Take the pry bar out of the bag and lay it next to the torch. Take the hammer out and lay it next to the pry bar. Take out the chisel and lay it next to the hammer.

Al obeys each command. He doesn't protest, doesn't ask any questions, doesn't say anything until Carter instructs him to close the bag. Then he manages a wistful, 'OK?'

'Yeah, so far, so good. But it gets a little tricky now. Have you ever used a torch?'

'Yeah, I used to work demolition.'

Carter tosses him a cigarette lighter. 'See, what we're gonna do is burn away the wood around the lock so the door will open with the lock still in place. But what I want you to do right now is run your finger around the lock. Do it.'

Al's right forefinger traces the edge of the lock. Then he looks up, his dark eyes reminding Carter of a puppy's.

'Good, Al, very good. That's the part you're going to burn. Only there's a problem. Can you guess what it is?'

'You're afraid I'll try to burn you?'

'No, that's not it. If you move on me, I'll kill you without hesitation. I think you know that. The problem is that the door might catch on fire. See, there are no windows in the basement and the dinky ventilation system won't handle the smoke, so we can't have a fire. You with me so far?'

'No fire.'

'Exactly. Use the propane torch to char the wood . . .'

'Char?'

'Blacken. Use the propane torch until the wood turns black, then use the hammer and the chisel to gouge the black part away. After you gouge out as much as possible, use the torch to blacken some more.'

Carter positions himself fifteen feet to Al's left and slightly behind him. Now he can watch the kid and the stairway at the same time. If there's to be an intrusion, it will have to come down those steps.

'Start now, Al. Light the torch.'

The process is slow, as Carter expected even before he came down the stairs. Perhaps three inches thick, the door is made of seasoned oak. It shows little tendency to char, much less burn, and Al's forced to wield the hammer and chisel again and again. Five minutes pass, then ten, then fifteen, with Carter urging his captive to work harder. The pain in Carter's ribcage has eased off, but he's not all that confident about his ability to re-climb the rope and haul up two heavy bags afterward.

'OK, Al, you've done good work. You're almost through. Now, stand up and kick the door in.'

Al's as slow and uncoordinated as he is big and strong. The remaining wood around the lock splinters, but doesn't break on his first, second or third kick. Carter decides to motivate him.

'If you don't break through that door, and I mean right the fuck now,' he declares, his tone matter-of-fact, 'I'll kill you and do it myself.'

Al launches himself at the door, slamming his shoulder and his head into the wood. Somehow, he misses the lock, which remains attached to the frame when the door crashes open, offering next to no resistance. That leaves Al to land in a stunned heap on the brown carpet in Bobby's office.

Carter glances at his watch: forty-two minutes. He follows Al into the office, flips the light switch and looks around. There's nothing – no suitcase, no box – large enough to hold the sort of money he's hoping to find. That leaves the room's two closets.

'Get up, Al.'

'I think I hurt my head.'

'Get up, Al.'

Al presses a hand to the right side of his head and staggers to his feet. 'I did what you asked me. I did it.'

'True enough, but you're not quite finished.'

Carter's reminded of the game show, *Let's Make A Deal*. Is the prize behind door number one or door number two? In this case, he's allowed to try both, which doesn't mean, of course, that he won't be zonked. Which doesn't mean that he hasn't killed three men for nothing.

Carter points to the closet door furthest away, the smaller of the two, and says, 'Open that door.'

Al complies, a half-assed smile on his face. His usefulness has pretty much come to an end and he knows it. Shelves dominate the closet's interior, from top to bottom. There's a mop, a bucket and a vacuum cleaner jammed between the shelves and the door, but no suitcase.

'The other one now.'

Despite his outward calm, Carter releases a held breath when Al pulls the door open to reveal a suitcase next to a bag of golf clubs. That it should be unprotected seems impossible at first glance, at least to Carter, but there's a simple explanation. Bobby never kept money in his office because his office would be the first place searched by the cops if he became the target of an investigation. Carter's emergence forced him to bring the money where he could protect it with muscle, a perfectly rational decision. If he'd left the money in the Bronx, it would already be gone.

'Take out the suitcase, lay it on the desk and open it.'

Carter half-expects the suitcase to be locked, but it's not. Opened, it reveals stacks of banded hundreds and fifties. Carter looks down at his watch: forty-six minutes.

'I need you to move a little faster, Al. First, close the suitcase. Then put the tools back in the bag and carry the suitcase and the bag to the stairs. Do it now.'

'Please . . .'

'Do it now, Al.'

Al's expression is glum, but he doesn't protest. He repacks the tool bag, picks up the bag and the suitcase and walks toward the stairwell. Carter's now thinking that his night's work is almost over, but it's not to be. As Al lays his burdens down, the radio strapped to Carter's belt clicks twice. Bobby Ditto's come to play. He's come to play and he's brought a friend along, hopefully the Blade.

Carter waits until Al turns to face him. In combat, this kind of decision, whether to kill a prisoner, was beyond his pay grade. Now he displays the enlisted man's first instinct, which is to cut through red tape. He puts a bullet into Al's right knee, then silences the kid's scream by slamming the Glock into the side of his head.

TWENTY-NINE

Carter was right about everything. Damn him. The minutes are dragging, every second an opportunity for self-torment. Angel's sitting in the back of the van, in the dark, surrounded by the cop's useless tracking equipment, her galloping imagination leaping from one catastrophe to another. Just now, her attention has turned to the walkie-talkie, the one strapped to Carter's belt. Walkie-talkies have a limited range, as Carter explained when he instructed her in their use. If the men inside the warehouse defeat Carter – if they *kill* him, let's be honest – the next item on their agenda will be whoever's on the other end of the walkie-talkie. That would be Angel Tamanaka, thank you.

Angel fishes through her purse, pushing the detritus aside, until she finds the little automatic tucked beneath the dish towel. She takes the weapon out and stares down, the sight of it producing a rueful laugh as she remembers how powerful she felt when she first cradled it in her palm. Now she's envisioning Carter's Glock, envisioning his Glock while she imagines the assault rifles and street-sweeper shotguns available to the gangsters inside the warehouse.

Well, she finally decides, the little gun definitely has one practical application. She can put it to her head and pull the trigger before allowing herself to be captured.

Angel's itching to make a hasty retreat. The van's key is in the ignition. She need only give it a little twist, need only turn the wheel slightly to avoid the graffiti-covered panel truck in front of her, need only step on the gas and . . .

Angel's train of thought comes to an abrupt stop, as if that train had jumped the tracks to slam into the side of a mountain. Two blocks away, a car turns on to the block, its headlights so bright in the side-view mirror that Angel can't tell the make or the model. But then the vehicle passes beneath the only working street lamp on the next block and the light bar spanning the roof leaps out at her. Cops.

Angel's mind kicks back into high gear, the transition between stunned and warp speed too brief to measure. What if Carter shows up right now, a suitcase tucked beneath his arm and who knows how many bodies left behind? What if the cops are responding to a silent alarm inside the warehouse and they catch him off-guard? What if they decide to check out the van? What will she tell them when they find her crouched in the back?

Driver fatigue is responsible for soooooooooooo many accidents. I just had to take a nap.

Yeah, that'd work. Angel can almost feel the cuffs settling around her wrists, almost hear the cops radio for back-up. Which leads her to another question. What if a judge sentenced her to spend the rest of her life in a cage? How would she feel, standing there, listening, her lawyer's attention already straying to the next defendant on her list? This is a question Carter's already posed, a question she left unanswered.

Paralyzed by fear, Angel doesn't move. A good thing, too, because the cops are simply patrolling the sector assigned to them, their mission as innocent as a donut run, and just as routine. Angel hunches down as the patrol car slides past. Now she can see the cops in silhouette, a man and a woman, both on their cellphones. At the corner, they take a right and head toward the Ikea box store on the waterfront.

Angel doesn't have to check her pulse. Her heart's thudding against her ribs, the beats coming so fast she's unable to count them. And the saddest part is that risk is what she signed up for, the great adventure, a walk on a side that's proving much too wild for the likes of Angel Tamanaka. And still no sign of Carter, no signal from the man who warned her, again and again, that he wasn't invulnerable, had no super powers, and might not survive his next violent encounter.

Angel extends her wrist into the front seat where there's enough light to read the hands on her watch. Forty-one minutes. It might as well be forty-one years. She falls back against the seat and methodically surveys her surroundings. All quiet, except for her out-of-control brain, which again poses a series of what-if questions.

What if she panicked when the cops turned on to the street two blocks away? What if she jumped into the front, started the van and tried to flee? What if she signaled Carter and he now believed, wrongly, that the cops presented a threat? What if he aborted the operation? What if he came out shooting?

Enough, enough. Angel covers her ears and shakes her head violently, her hair whipping the sides of her face hard enough to sting. Somehow, a memory surfaces, something a cop boyfriend told her a few months after she arrived in New York. Fight, flight or fright, he'd insisted, are the only possible reactions to a sudden threat. You ran away, or you raised your fists, or you just plain froze. Angel had taken the third path, that was obvious, and she didn't fault herself. But her cop lover had been wrong. There was a fourth way, a way embodied by Leonard Carter. Fear leads to panic, he'd insisted, and panic is the ultimate enemy. Stay calm, fight well.

Angel's attention is drawn by movement on the left side of the windshield. Across the street, a wharf rat makes its way along a corrugated fence. The creature slithers a few yards, its back hunched, then stops to raise its snout and sniff the air before dashing forward again. Initially repulsed, Angel watches the animal until it comes upon a small gap in the fence and wriggles through.

Somehow, the rat's manifest caution serves to calm Angel. Though subject to no imminent threat, it had remained supremely vigilant, nose twitching, head turning, as if surrounded by enemies. Angel checks her watch before settling down. Forty-five minutes. Fifteen lifetimes to go.

In fact, only three lifetimes pass, three minutes, before Bobby Ditto's armored Ford describes the same left turn made by the cops five minutes before. Angel recognizes the car immediately, but this time she manages to check a rising panic. She signals Carter first, then drops the radio on the seat and tells herself to think carefully. There are two men in the vehicle that slides past the van, its sound system blaring, Bobby Ditto and the other one, the one who grabbed her ass as they walked down the street on the day Carter rescued her. The one who spelled out exactly what sadistic games he intended to play with her in the hours preceding her death.

Angel slides the side door open and gets out before the Explorer comes to a stop in front of the warehouse. Her eyes criss-cross her surroundings, evaluating risk and reward. Crouching, she dashes across the street, exposed for a few seconds, until she finally drops to a knee before the corrugated fence previously traversed by the rat. She raises the little gun and focuses on the end of the block, fifty feet distant. If she was spotted as she crossed the street, Bobby and his buddy – the Blade, that's his name – will have to come around the corner to stand directly in her line of fire. Not that she's likely to hit anything from this distance with a poorly manufactured .32, but one thing is clear to her. She didn't freeze and she didn't flee. That means Bobby and the Blade have to be incapacitated, at the very least, for her and her partner to survive. Fight being the only option still on the table.

Angel gets to her feet, takes a few steps and comes to a stop, the gun held out in front of her, steeling herself against a sudden assault, prepared as Carter might prepare, or so she hopes. She pauses long enough to draw a breath and release it slowly, then continues to advance, in fits and starts, until the sound system in the Explorer suddenly cuts off and she hears Bobby Ditto shout, 'What the fuck, what the fuck, what the fuck.'

The Blade echoes his boss. 'What, what, what?' he asks.

'Get around here!'

'Get around where?'

'Get around here, ya fuck. Just do it.'

Propelled by his boss's exasperated tone, the Blade circles the car. 'You wanna tell me what's happenin'?'

'Donny's not answerin'. And don't tell me he's not gettin' a signal. I spoke to him this afternoon.' Bobby punches Donny Thorn's number into his cellphone for the second time. He listens through four ringtones, all the way to the faggy message at the end: *Hi, this is Donny. I can't come to the phone right now, but if you'd care to leave a message, I'll get back to you as soon as I can.*

'Bein' as it's four o'clock in the morning, maybe Donny shut off his phone,' the Blade suggests. 'I mean, the alarm on the front door is still set. You can see the red light blinkin' from here.'

Bobby looks at the light, his mind still whirling. 'What about the roof? Did you lock down the skylights?'

'Yeah, with case-hardened padlocks, but even if Carter beat the locks some way, there's still four men protectin' your money. Unless you think Carter broke through the door in the basement and whacked four men before they could even warn us. I mean, we're not talkin' about punks.'

Bobby's heart rate drops a notch or two, but he doesn't move. The armored Explorer now stands between him and the warehouse, which is just the way he likes it. Carter might be anywhere, he might be nowhere. Bobby draws the H&K .40 cal tucked into his waistband as he studies the truck yard and the roofline, his gaze intent. But there's little to be learned, what with the moon having set and working street lights few and far between. The trucks in the yard are parked haphazardly, creating impenetrable shadows, while the ledge on the roof, long in need of repair, is as broken and irregular as the Blade's teeth after the cops worked him over.

'Tell ya what, Marco,' Bobby says. 'How 'bout you stroll

through the front door and check it out for yourself? Here, I'll give ya the fuckin' keys.'

The Blade's face reddens, but he doesn't take the challenge, in part because he's not armed. 'All right, Bobby, I get the point. So, now whatta we do? Wait for somebody to come out?'

'No, lemme try one more thing.' Bobby slides the gun inside his waistband, then scrolls through his phone's call log. 'I know I called him a couple of weeks ago,' he tells the Blade.

'Called who?'

'Al Zeffri.'

'I got his number.' The Blade takes out his own cellphone, runs through his contact list for a moment, then presses the call button. He holds the phone aloft and both men listen to it ring four times before Zeffri's voicemail kicks in.

'Shit.' Bobby again surveys the warehouse. If anything, the shadows are deeper. But it doesn't really matter. He can't lose the money, his own or the money fronted to him. If he does, he's as good as dead.

'I gotta go in,' he says. 'Simple as that. I gotta go in.'

'I'm not armed, boss.' The Blade's gaze is intense, but his tone is apologetic. 'We were just supposed to dump the freak tonight. I didn't know we were comin' here.'

Bobby instantly corrects his lieutenant. 'What we were supposed to be is ready for anything.'

'What can I say? You get caught with a gun, it's three years minimum. And it wasn't like the freak was gonna put up a fight.'

Bobby drops the cellphone into his pocket and fishes for his keys. He's thinking that his life has been a battle from the day a federal judge sentenced his father to a sixty year bit. Bobby had been what? Fifteen years old? Yeah, fifteen years old and responsible for a morbidly obese mother who cried from morning to night, and a dimwit brother who got beat up every other day.

'Boss?'

'What, Marco? What the fuck do you want now?'

'It ain't what I want. It's what she wants.'

* * *

Despite everything, despite even the gun in her hands, Bobby Ditto is taken with Angel Tamanaka's beauty. The teardrop eyes, the glossy black hair, the rounded mouth and the determined little chin. Too determined. The gun's moving between himself and the Blade, and her hand isn't shaking.

Bobby Ditto knows the difference between a genuine threat and a bluff. Angel will not only pull the trigger if attacked, she's only a heartbeat away from pulling the trigger right this minute. That's OK with Bobby. He feels better now that there's an enemy standing in front of him, and better still when the little gun settles on the Blade.

'Remember me?' Angel asks.

'Yeah, I remember you.'

'Remember all those things you said you were going to do to me?'

The Blade's mouth opens, closes, opens again. 'I was only tryin' to scare you.'

'Scare me into doing what?'

'Into telling me where your partner was.'

'Ah, so that means you weren't going to tie my wrists to a ceiling beam? And that thing with the pliers? That was an empty threat? You were planning to let me go?'

Bobby's measuring the distance between himself and Angel, maybe fifteen feet, two strides and a leap. The little automatic's not a man stopper. Unless she gets real lucky, it won't even slow him down. Of course, she doesn't have to get lucky if he's standing still when she pulls the trigger, which is why he intends to move on her when she finally shoots the Blade.

The Blade straightens up and draws a long breath through his prow of a nose. Old school to the max, threats from a whore don't appeal to him, as Bobby knew they wouldn't. If he was armed, his piece would already be in his hand.

Angel smiles. 'Nothing to say?'

'Yeah, I got something to say. Go fuck yourself.'

The conversation having come to a dead end, Angel pulls the trigger, surprising Bobby. Nevertheless, he moves before the echo dies off, his head down, hands reaching for the gun even as the Blade falls backward. He puts everything he has into the charge, but he's not fast enough. A bullet whizzes by his ear when Angel fires a second time. Then he's on her, slapping the gun away, pulling her into a bear hug, overwhelming her with his bulk and his strength. When he hears the little automatic clatter on the sidewalk, he knows he's won. Not so the Blade. He's lying on the ground with his head propped against the Explorer's front door, one hand clutching his throat in a futile attempt to stem the blood gushing from a little hole beneath his Adam's apple. He looks at his boss and tries to speak, but there are no words left for the Blade, only a trail of bubbles that spray from the hole to hang for a moment in the darkness.

'Tell me your fuckin' name.'

Bobby's dropped into survival mode, a core space hollowed from a mountain of ice. He's thinking it's tough shit about Marco, but he can't take his eyes off the blood streaming down the side of the SUV. In the dim light, the blood appears as black and thick as motor oil.

'Louise,' Angel replies, her tone quavering just a bit.

'That's not your fucking name.'

'Sue me.'

Bobby Ditto's massive left arm tightens around Angel's chest as he draws the .40 cal with his free hand. He pushes the barrel into the back of Angel's head and pulls her in close to the Explorer. They're now standing in a little pool of the Blade's blood.

'You think I won't kill you because you're a woman?'

Angel manages a tiny laugh that's very distant from the guffaw she hoped to produce. 'Tell me something, Bobby. Are you still hoping your men in the basement are only asleep?'

'Hear this, bitch. I die, you die.'

'And vice versa.'

There's nothing to be gained by arguing and Bobby keeps his thoughts to himself as he weighs his options. He's telling himself that he should force the whore into the Explorer – the *armored* Explorer – and get the fuck out of Red Hook. The Blade's lying in his own blood, his blank eyes sightless, and the minutes are ticking away. How long before somebody comes driving down the street, somebody with a cellphone? How long before Carter shows up? One thing is certain, with the alarm still set, Carter won't be comin' out the front door, which means he might be comin' from anywhere. No, the thing to do is take the whore and bargain for the money later on. Only Bobby can't make himself believe that any sane man would pay $497,000 for a whore. Bobby Ditto wouldn't pay that much to get his mother back from heaven.

'I die, you die,' he repeats. 'But I'm not leavin' without my fuckin' money.'

Carter's greeted by the crack of a small caliber handgun when he finally hauls himself on to the roof. His first thought is of Angel, a thought he puts to one side. Both bags, the tool bag and the money bag, are attached to the other end of the rope on the floor of the warehouse. First things first. Carter slides the M89 off his shoulder, lays it on the black tar roof, then pulls up the bags, his ribs throbbing with the effort. The tool bag comes through easily, but the hard-sided suitcase wedges in the hole. Carter has to lie over the opening and yank it through with his bare hands, which does nothing to ease the pain. Still, he doesn't hesitate. Spurred by the sound of voices in the distance, one of them Angel Tamanaka's, he picks up the M89 and scans the roof in search of cover.

He notes, first, a low wall topped with red tiles at the edge of the roof. Most of the tiles are missing now, individual bricks as well. The broken pattern suits Carter, presenting an advantage compounded by the deep shadows on the roof. Forty feet away, a small air conditioning unit casts an even deeper shadow between itself and the wall. Carter's nylon ski mask is soaked with sweat. It clings to his face like a suction cup, but he's glad for it now. In the darkness, with only the top of his head exposed, he'll be a shadow within a shadow, for all intents invisible.

Carter takes the last few yards on his knees and his elbows. He's not unmindful of the need for haste. Gunshots tend to attract attention. Nevertheless, he remains calm as he lifts his head a few inches above the ledge and surveys the field of battle. At the other end of the block, Bobby Ditto's standing behind the Explorer. He's holding Angel tight against his chest and he's pointing a gun at her head. Just behind Bobby, the unmoving legs of a man Carter assumes to be the Blade project on to the sidewalk.

Carter doesn't drop the M89's folding bipod. The ledge is too irregular, and he settles for laying the rifle's stock on a patch of smooth brick. He finds himself admiring Angel, at least on one level. She definitely has pluck. But her leaving the van was a bad mistake and she's compromised the operation. Carter's able to recall a time when war was personal. He was a gung-ho soldier boy on his way to Afghanistan, prepared to do his bit, proud to serve his country. But Carter doesn't have enemies now. He has competitors. Like Roberto Benedetti, who needs to be removed, post haste, from the game.

In the military, Carter almost always operated with a spotter. The spotter calculated distance, elevation and windage, matching each to ambient temperature, barometric pressure and angle of aim, upward or downward. Carter's on his own here, but he's far from handicapped. Mounted on the M89's telescopic sight, a BORS optical ranging system does, in less than a second and with far greater accuracy, what took his spotter minutes to accomplish.

After allowing for all the variables, the effective distance between himself and the top of Bobby Ditto's skull, according to the BORS unit, is 127 yards. Carter turns the elevation dial on the scope until it reaches the 127 yard mark and that's it. The system has compensated for every other factor, including the downward angle. All he need do is train the scope on his target, squeeze the trigger and put a bullet in a two-inch circle. Without flinching, of course.

Eliminate the brain and the body stops. No message from the brain to the finger and Bobby will never pull that trigger. There's even room for error. Bobby's head is about four inches across. An inch either way won't matter, not given the energy of a 7.62 mm hollow-point round. Bobby Ditto's brain will literally explode.

Two inches off, on the other hand, and Angel Tamanaka wakes up on the wrong side of the grass.

Carter lays the butt of the rifle in the hollow of his shoulder, lays his cheek against the carbon fiber stock. He's at home now, at rest in the safest place he's ever known, his weapon cradled in his arms, his child, his baby. He dials up the magnification, peers through the sight, lays the cross-hairs dead-center on the top of Bobby's head. Then he slips his finger through the trigger guard to caress the trigger, an old habit that's become ritual. Still unhurried, he brings the trigger to the point of release and holds steady while he centers himself, breathing in, breathing out, seeking the quiet space between rest and action, between life and death. Only when he finds that emptiness inside himself does he squeeze the trigger.

THIRTY

The goodbye sex is great, but it's still goodbye. Angel's had enough. Something about watching the top and back of Bobby Ditto's skull fly off while his face remained in front of her, eyes open, mouth fixed, has taken the wind out of her adventuring sails. She's not psychologically qualified to live in Carter's outlaw world, simple as that.

Angel saw and heard nothing before the bullet found its mark. There was no jet of flame, no crack of the rifle. One minute she was standing there, waiting for . . . Angel doesn't know what she was waiting for, only that one minute she was helpless, the next she was sprayed with . . .

And that's the problem. A part of her mind shies away from the moment when Bobby's head exploded, coating her hair, her face, her shoulders with gore. Another part returns, again and again, to the instant of impact, after which she'd fallen to the sidewalk, limp as the dishrag in the bottom of her purse. If Carter hadn't dragged her to the van and shoved her inside, she might still be there.

Meanwhile, Carter was all business, and maybe that was the scariest part. He stripped her when they got back to his apartment, stripped her as you'd strip a child, and pushed her into the shower. Then he collected everything they'd worn or used and packed it into four garbage bags, the .32, all of their clothing, including their shoes, the Glock, the rope, the grappling hook and all the tools, the spent cartridge from the M89, which he crushed with a tack hammer. Everything except the M89 itself.

Finished, he returned to the bathroom, dried her off and put her to bed. 'Don't move, Angel,' he said as he drew the covers up to her neck. 'I'll be back in a couple of hours.'

Carter didn't tell her where he was going and Angel didn't ask. But later she learned that he'd carried the bags to an eighty-unit apartment building in Queens where he once lived. Using a key he'd never surrendered to get inside, he'd ridden an empty elevator to the ninth floor, then dumped the bags into a chute leading to the trash collection room in the basement.

'The room's actually a compactor,' he explained when he returned. 'On whatever day the garbage is picked up, all the trash in that room will be compacted, wrapped in heavy plastic and carried to the curb. The city will do the rest.'

Angel listened to his explanation with one ear, unmoved even by the sight of all that money, piles and piles of money, a waterfall of money dropping from the interior of the suitcase to the comforter on the bed. But then Carter slipped out of his vest and his shirt, revealing a smoky-red bruise that virtually covered his ribs on the left side.

'Close call. A few inches lower and it would have come through under my vest. In which case . . .' He winced as he probed the center of the wound.

'You want to go to the hospital?'

'The rib's not displaced. There's nothing a doctor can do. What's that they say? Grin and bear it? No harm, no foul?'

Angel shakes her head. 'Joke if you want, Carter, but you came within a few inches of dying in that basement. You're what? Twenty-nine years old?' She picks up a packet of hundred dollar bills and lays it on top of the slug in his hand. 'Was it worth it?' she demands.

A week later, Lieutenant Solly Epstein met them in Central Park. He'd come to collect his share of the loot, but his message was encouraging. The Organized Crime Control Bureau, his unit, had pronounced the incident drug related, which it definitely was, and they were looking at the usual mob suspects. Meanwhile, the media had taken OCCB's theme a step further. The Red Hook Massacre was big time news, yet at no point, in the hundreds of articles and hours of airtime, did anyone suggest that the massacre was the work of a single individual. There were, on the other hand, several pieces linking Mexican drug cartels, in style and psychology, to the carnage.

'Al Zeffri's not talkin',' Epstein explained. 'He claims he doesn't remember anything about that night, which could be true because he didn't regain consciousness until late the next day. You must have hit him pretty hard.'

'I had to make sure he didn't come up behind me.'

Epstein glanced at Angel and winked. 'I woulda thought blowin' his knee apart was enough guarantee. Anyway, you got nothin' to worry about. Not only hasn't your name been mentioned, it doesn't appear in our database. As far as the NYPD's concerned, you don't exist. You're still a ghost.'

Angel spells it out a week later, as she and Carter lie in bed. They're going at it twice a day by now, the sex hard and fast and as necessary as breathing. Angel can't get enough, and can't wait to get away. Never has she been more attracted to a man, never more repelled. Carter's death on two legs and she's drawn to him like a junkie to a fix.

'I'm leaving,' she tells him.

'When?'

'As soon as you set up my account.' The account in question will be established in a Cayman Islands bank. There's a cost, ten percent of the principal, but Angel's happy to pay. 'You were right,' she adds. 'Eventually, you'll be caught or killed. I don't think you care all that much.'

'But you do?'

'I murdered a man.' Angel hesitates before adding, 'I'm not feeling guilty, not by a long shot. The Blade deserved what he got and the world is better off without him. But I can't go back there again. Taking a life, it's too big for me.'

Her independence finally declared, Angel returns to her pursuits. She completes her Art History paper, collects her diploma, purchases a spare-no-expense, hot-weather wardrobe. The surface of their dining room table quickly disappears beneath stacks of books on Caribbean art, exhibition notices, website printouts, travel brochures, real estate listings from a dozen nations. By early June, when she books an airline ticket to Piarco International Airport in Trinidad, she has everything in place: her bank account, a small rented townhouse in a resort community, plans to open an art gallery in Tobago, appointments with a dozen artists' representatives.

If there's a fly in this ointment, it's Carter's attitude. He's not trying to dissuade her, not clinging to every moment of togetherness. No, Carter leaves the apartment shortly after breakfast and doesn't return until evening. Angel assumes he's off to one or another of his training sessions, but he doesn't tell her where he's going or where he's been. He doesn't tell and she doesn't ask.

There's a simple explanation, of course. Carter's become indifferent. Stay or go – it's all the same to him. But the evidence doesn't add up. Their nights are spent in bed, Carter a one-man gang-bang, Angel urging him on. This proves especially true on their last night together, which they spend in Vincent Graham's den on 37th Street. Carter's taken, not to mention inspired, by the mirrored ceilings and Vincent's toy collection, especially the restraints, the handcuffs and the shackles. They do argue, for just a moment, over who gets to play the prisoner and who the prison guard, but finally agree to take turns.

Long after midnight, when Angel and Carter are too sore and exhausted to do more than lie next to each other, Angel explains why she bought the two guns, the revolver she left for him to find and the little automatic, and why she'd arranged access to Graham's apartment. Carter doesn't blame Angel for not trusting him. In her position, he would certainly have done something similar and he tells her so.

A segue into their feelings for each other might easily follow this conversation, yet the hows and whys of their doomed relationship go unmentioned. They don't discuss even the possibility of meeting again. No, in the end, they turn out the lights and roll on to their sides. Carter falls asleep within a few minutes, as usual, leaving Angel to her own thoughts.

Talk it out, resolve the conflicts. That's the conventional wisdom, repeated hundreds of times each year on dozens of 'talk' shows. But that's not happening here and Angel finally realizes that Carter's reticence hasn't impaired their communication, not at all. The Tibetan who painted the *bhavacakra* would have understood perfectly. Their unfolding karmas brought them together, two infinitely small particles, in order to complete some necessary transaction. That done, those same karmas are driving them apart. Call it fate. Hell, call it serendipity. Whatever business they had with each other is finished. Time to move on.

Carter watches the cab until it reaches 14th Street and turns right, on its way via New York's system of antiquated highways to John F. Kennedy Airport. Most of what Angel Tamanaka still owns – her clothing, along with a few photographs, a knick-knack or two, a battered teddy bear named Slippy – has gone ahead of her, packed into a pair of antiqued steamer trunks. Every other possession has been sold or given away.

But not to Carter, who's retained no personal items, not even a hazy photo on his cellphone, the single exception being Angel's Ruger revolver. Its firing pin restored, the weapon now rests in a trunk in Carter's Bronx storage room, too fine an instrument of death to be summarily tossed.

With no particular destination in mind, Carter heads west along 9th Street. The moist June air is warm enough to evoke the oncoming summer, but Carter doesn't mind. He's got a couple of hours to kill before heading over to the gym and the city sidewalks have long been a place of refuge. Carter's feeling a familiar sensation, a sort of clutching around the heart, born not of love, but of the fear that seized him when the state took control of his life. At the same time, and he admits this to himself, he's relieved. Carter's had three acknowledged loves in his life, his mother and Janie, both dead, and the military, where he learned to kill without remorse. Each had abandoned him, leaving him to fight on his own. Or so he's come to believe.

And Angel? Yeah, he'll miss Angel, definitely. Even thinking her name produces a familiar warming in his crotch.

Carter laughs softly, catching the attention of a young woman coming from the other direction. The woman moves several feet to her right as they pass, an acknowledgement, Carter thinks, of just how many psychotic human beings roam through the city. Careful, careful, you never know, keep your distance.

What Carter can't escape, though, relieved or not, is emptiness. There have been times in his life when he's felt as cold and isolated as an asteroid traveling between planets, and this is one of them. What will he do? Where will he go? At present, Carter has more than seven hundred thousand dollars in three bank accounts. He can, if he chooses, live on his savings for many years. There's no compelling reason for him to resume his gangster-killing career, or any other career.

Carter pauses for the light at Second Avenue, coming up behind two women, one of them pushing a stroller. He watches the traffic flow past, the cars, the trucks and all the busses – school busses, city busses, double-decker tourist busses. In the mountains of Afghanistan or the deserts of Yemen, there was always a moment just before dawn when the world seemed to pause in its turning, the silence so deep you could hear the beating of your own heart. Not so in New York, the ultimate 24/7 city. No matter what the hour, somebody's on the way to somewhere else. But Carter doesn't have to stay in New York. He can go anywhere he wants, if he can only make himself want to go somewhere.

On the other side of the avenue, a woman sits on a square of cardboard with her back to a sunny brick wall. She's somewhere in her twenties, dressed in a black sweatshirt, black cotton pants and black sneakers. Utterly forlorn, she stares down at the gray sidewalk, her little-match-girl expression firmly in place. A black dog, gray at the muzzle, its fur dull and dusty, lies beside her with its head between its paws.

A cardboard sign, hand-lettered, explains her situation: HOMELESS/ HELPLESS/HUNGRY. Just in case you haven't gotten the point.

Carter's run into this woman and her dog many times in

the last few years. The mournful posture, the all-black costume, the wilting dog, the faded sign, the coffee container with a few pennies in the bottom – as performance art, her act is unforgettable. Carter takes a five dollar bill from his wallet and holds it over the coffee container.

'Tell me where you go in the winter.'

The woman's unhesitating response is as succinct as her sign. 'Fuck off, asshole.'

Carter drops the five into the cup and heeds her advice. He continues west, to Broadway, then heads north to the farmer's market in Union Square. Here the vendors face each other across a broad corridor on the western and northern edges of the Square, competing for the attentions of the shoppers who stroll between them. Carter passes vendors selling ostrich meat, bamboo flower honey, wheatgrass and lavender eye pillows. Two elderly women staff a long table stacked with fancy preserves. A bearded, one-eyed man pushes grass-fed Angus beef at thirty dollars a pound. The Fungus King displays thirty varieties of mushroom.

In no hurry, Carter shuffles along with the crowd. He's visited markets on three continents, and always found them enticing, an exercise in mutual self-interest, buyers and sellers equally engaged. There's a twist, though, when it comes to Union Square. The vendors post their prices and the customers don't haggle. In Sierra Leone, buyers and sellers debated the value of every bean.

As he nears the eastern end of the market, Carter stops to buy a container of wild mint tea and a cranberry scone. He carries them past buckets filled with enough lilac blossoms to perfume even New York City's carbon-soaked air, and into the park.

Union Square Park will never be confused with an English garden, but it's reasonably well-tended and there's always something in bloom, spring through fall. Just now, in early June, the tea roses have come into their own. Carter finds a bench near a blooming rose bush and takes a seat. There's an elderly woman sitting at the other end of the bench. She's cooing to a tiny chihuahua nearly hidden inside the handbag on her lap. When Carter unwraps the scone and the dog's attention wanders, the woman gathers her bag and her dog and departs.

Left to himself, Carter's own attention wanders back to Angel as he eats and drinks. He wonders where her plane is right now, but then glances at his watch. In fact, her plane's still at the gate and won't take off for another hour. How long, he wonders, before she fades? Perhaps he'll always carry her with him, as he carries the boy soldiers, but that's not what he thinks. His sister's death punched a hole in his life, a hole Angel temporarily filled. Now the hole is back. Still, it's a beautiful day and the park is crowded with workers in search of a quick lunch and a breath of fresh air.

Carter's always been a people watcher, not to mention a paranoid death merchant who habitually monitors his back, his front and both sides. Nobody sneaks up on him, especially not Merwyn Thoma with his pronounced limp, his floppy bow tie and his ivory-handled walking stick.

Carter last saw Thoma six years ago, on the Afghan-Pakistan border. A spook who worked for some unidentified agency, he'd outlined the rules of engagement for a mission into the tribal areas of Pakistan's North-west Frontier Province. Carter remembers listening with interest, but not because the rules applied to him or his comrades. It was Thoma's earnestness that intrigued him. Did he really believe they'd offer their target an opportunity to surrender? On the one hand, there was nothing in Thoma's manner that suggested otherwise. On the other, he wasn't coming along to make sure the men whose lives were at risk complied with his instructions.

Merwyn's only in his forties, but his hair is snow-white and so fine that strands float in the air even on this windless day. His face is criss-crossed with fine wrinkles, his eyelids folded at the corners, his mouth a firm, disapproving line. Though careful to maintain a respectful distance, he fixes Carter with a patented stare when he finally sits down.

Repressing a smile, Carter returns the stare for a moment, then says, 'If you don't get the fuck off this bench, I'll cut your throat from one ear to the other.'

The threat is wasted, as Carter knew it would be. The psychological training for spooks is every bit as demanding as the physical training Carter endured on his path through the ranks to Delta Force. Still, he feels a little better as he watches Thoma dismiss the bluff with a shake of his head.

'You should never have left us,' he says. 'You were among the very best of the very best.'

'Maybe I got tired of killing.'

'I doubt that very much, but I haven't come to discuss your business. No, I've come to make two things clear.' Thoma raises his walking stick and taps Carter's knee. 'Your country needs you, Carter.'

'That's one thing, Merwyn. What's the other?'

'You will answer the call of duty.'

Carter laughs as he hasn't laughed in years, startling a flock of pigeons feeding on a dropped sandwich nearby. They rise a few feet into the air, their cooing distinctly accusatory, but quickly settle down as Carter shifts the cane away from his knee. Carter's thinking that Merwyn's probably right. Whatever the spooks have on him will be enough to secure his cooperation. Which, he supposes, leaves a single issue to be discussed.

'What's in it for me?' he asks.

12 - 11
ML